T0367961

The Night
CHILD

T.M. Palecki

ARCHWAY
PUBLISHING

This is a work of fiction. All of the characters, names, incidents, organizations, and dialogue in this novel are either the products of the author's imagination or are used fictitiously.

Archway Publishing books may be ordered through booksellers or by contacting:

Archway Publishing
1663 Liberty Drive
Bloomington, IN 47403
www.archwaypublishing.com
844-669-3957

Because of the dynamic nature of the Internet, any web addresses or links contained in this book may have changed since publication and may no longer be valid. The views expressed in this work are solely those of the author and do not necessarily reflect the views of the publisher, and the publisher hereby disclaims any responsibility for them.

Any people depicted in stock imagery provided by Getty Images are models, and such images are being used for illustrative purposes only. Certain stock imagery © Getty Images.

ISBN: 978-1-6657-1165-4 (sc)
ISBN: 978-1-6657-1164-7 (hc)
ISBN: 978-1-6657-1163-0 (e)

Library of Congress Control Number: 2021918014

Print information available on the last page.

Archway Publishing rev. date: 10/19/2021

DEDICATION

For Cam: Thank you for being my support, my best friend, my warrior.

Some vocabulary you should know:

Cob – A very sturdy Welsh/Norwegian horse that is known for its sure-footedness, intelligence, and loyalty. They are small, standing at around fourteen hands, and stocky. They have very long, wavy manes and tails of a slightly lighter color than their thick long coats.
Dull – A Norse word for conceit.
Daufi – A Norse word for stupid or dim-witted.
Hus – A small farm or farm house.
Keila – A place where livestock is raised.

Some Norse/Celtic names and their meanings:

Alden – wise guardian
Carn/Carrick – rock
Clare – bright and clear
Dirk – ruler of people
Erik – honorable/powerful
Esta – cat
Guth/Garrick – spear king
Hadwin – friend in war
Ivar – archer
Kelvin – friend of the sea

Landen/Landon – owner
Lombard – long beard
Mane – moon
Roan/Rowen – red

ONE

Mane

The day was breaking, and the morning skies were painted with hues of pinks and red, casting light on the mountains and forest lands that surrounded the small, stone roundhouse. Esta sat up and stretched, looking at the beauty of the sunrise. Her vison focused on the large figure in the sky. It approached rapidly, growing larger by the second. She sprang from her bed and grabbed a leather bracer from a table. Spinning back to the window, she pulled the straps tight just as the window filled with a flurry of feathers, clicks, pops, and screeches.

An owl may seem a strange animal to have as a pet. Yet when Esta had found the young owlet on the ground near its dead mother, she'd bundled it in her shawl and carried it home. How she had come to be in that place, at that time, on that day? Well, that was why some people in the village had said she was strange, gifted, sighted—even a witch.

Esta had been born into a home where knowledge was revered. Her father, Carrick, had a *hus*, or small farm, and it did well. He had married the beautiful, mysterious midwife, Clare. Clare could read. She could also write and decode ciphers. This alone had caused much speculation when she had arrived on the island as a young woman with her father. He had come to settle on the island to save his daughter from the superstitions of those across the sea. He had taught her his craft of healing, and Clare had taken that skill and applied it to both animal and human. It was a skill she was determined to pass on to her daughter. Over the years, Clare had gained the respect of the village. The elders, more than most, had come to understand that the midwife had knowledge beyond the birthing of children. She could soothe burns and set broken bones. She could pull painful teeth. She could even slow the spread of fever and sicknesses that cut through other villages unchecked. This knowledge alone was enough to keep her in high regard, add to that her ability to ply her knowledge on the village livestock, and she became irreplaceable. All this knowledge was now being painstakingly passed on to her daughter, Esta, who already had an aptitude for her mother's trade. There was, however, one large difference.

Esta, it seemed, could understand the internal feelings of others. It was not to the point of knowing exactly what they were thinking; rather, it was an understanding of their emotions—how they were feeling—and what actions were about to come of those emotions. She could do this with both human and animal alike before words were spoken or deeds were done. This ability had not always been welcome nor understood, since at times Esta showed her understanding of emotions that were not meant to be shared.

Esta was around nine when her gift first came into the open. She had whispered into her father's ear that the man at their table meant to rob them while they slept. She'd been able to feel the man's jealousy, his desire. Her father had lain in wait, only to find the man filling a sack with their possessions in the middle of the night, not knowing that he was about to find Carrick lurking in the darkness, waiting for him. Carrick's anger had exploded on the man they had welcomed into their home. Esta had been able to feel the rage building within her father, feel the hatred swell until it spilled out in a flurry of fists. Carrick had slammed into the man, wrapping his hands around his throat. He'd wanted to kill the man but had finally found the ability to control his rage enough to turn the man out into the night without his belongings. The next morning, he'd taken the satchel to the village constable and seen to it that the elders would turn the man away from the island.

Esta had learned to whisper to her parents when she thought the information was necessary to pass on. With that knowledge, her mother could calm a worried patient, prepare a mother for her child, or calm frightened livestock. Esta's understanding of their fears and their joys gave her mother a great advantage. Esta could tell by the eighth month if a child would be born a boy or a girl. Even the mind of the unborn had become somewhat predictable to her. In one case, she'd become aware of a stillbirth. She'd placed her hand on her mother's shoulder during the long, difficult birthing and gently said, "He is gone. Let her sleep. He will come out on the morrow."

The village had come to know her from a distance. The elders kept her to themselves, unwittingly creating an air of mystery around her. They believed that it would be best for her to remain in a controlled circle of friends.

Esta had stopped many things from happening or caused many things to happen in her little village. She had laughed aloud at moments of complete silence, turning heads and receiving questioning looks. She had saved animals and humans from one another and from themselves. From the day Esta had been given the owl, she'd become the Night Child. And as we so well know, the night can be a dark and dangerous place.

The heart-shaped face of the great owl appeared on her window ledge. She woke with a start to see the owl on the sill. After a moment of intense silence, Esta swept from her room, pulling on her overdress and rabbit boots as she quickly skirted across the front of the house. It was hard to run while trying to hold her shawl about her head and shoulders and keeping her skirts high enough off the ground to avoid tripping. Esta darted across the back garden and through the small grove of apple trees and the herbs and flowers she tended. A quick cut across the corner of her father's field and the narrow expanse of trees that separated the holdings and she was there. She entered the clearing near the neighbor's large outbuilding just as a cloaked man loosed his arrow. She screamed as she watched the owl twist in the air. Then as it tumbled toward the ground trying to right itself, she saw that it had a tiny owlet in its talons.

She felt its life ebbing away as if it were she herself feeling her heart slow and then stop. She felt the pain when the owl skidded across the ground, breaking a wing when it folded back unnaturally. Esta watched the owl lift her head with her last ounce of strength to search for her owlet. When she saw it safe in the hands of a human—safe in Esta's hands—the connection was broken. Esta gasped and let out a sob of grief at nearly the same moment.

Across the clearing the cloaked archer tossed off his hood. He began walking toward her at a steady, angry pace. Still on her knees holding the downy-white owlet in her hands, Esta looked down into its small, dark eyes, feeling its fear and confusion. She carefully checked to make sure the small bird was not injured. Her gentle spirit eased the owlet's heartbeat. Esta glimpsed the man coming toward her across the field. At last, she could see his boot leather. There he stood at her side, silent, staring down at her. She looked up, tears running down her flushed cheeks. The large man took in a gasp of air and stepped back. Esta could instantly feel his shock and amazement. He held her gaze, looking deep into her eyes—her piercing gray eyes with their flecks of gold. His face flushed as his feelings about her tumbled all over the place. She flushed now with embarrassment, still not used to people's reactions to seeing her for the first time. Many in the village had kept their distance. Now she was nearly a grown woman, no longer hiding behind her mother's skirts.

Esta quickly recovered. "You killed her. Why did you do that?"

The man looked down at her now, and she could feel his sudden remorse and sorrow at hurting the owl.

"I had to, my little lamb. They were taking my young livestock. They have nearly eaten all me fowl, and just this morning the big male took me best rabbit."

Esta knew that the farmer had the right to protect what was his. Any hus-man would have done the same. Most liked to have the owls around to keep the mice and other vermin in check. This was different. This man's livestock was small enough to become prey. She could not hold his actions against him, even though she wanted to. Esta wrapped the little owl in her shawl, stood, wrapped her cloak around them both, and began to walk away.

"What do ye plan to do with that owl, child? Ye should let your da put it down. Yeh tell Carrick I am sorry to upset his poppet, yeh tell him."

His words faded as she walked back into the thick of the woods that separated her father's hus from his. Suddenly the owlet shrieked loudly. Esta looked down into the big, black eyes.

"I know, but we must get you home and warm. Then I will find you something to eat."

Once home, Esta went straight to her room. She pulled the heavy pin that held the thick hide away from the opening. The leather flap quickly fell against the stone, closing off her room from the rest of the little roundhouse. She looked around for anything she could use as nesting for the small, downy owl she held in her hands. The only thing she could find was a woven basket she used for gathering the herbs and plants her mother often needed. She took off her cloak, bunched it up on her bed, and then placed the owlet in its center. She began to gather rags and place them in the basket but stopped. The owlet was snapping and shrieking. Unhappy. It did not like the soft nest Esta had made with her cloak. She pictured in her mind's eye the few owls' nests she had seen: a hollowed-out tree, a large beam or ledge of a barn, a large rock ledge high on a cliff.

"Oh," Esta said, "you need a crate. Something flat and hard."

The next few weeks seemed to fly by. Esta named the owl, or should one say, agreed with the owl's feelings and acceptance of the name, Mane. It was amazing how fast Mane grew.

Esta teased her, "You truly are quite an ugly little thing. It is hard to believe that you will be so beautiful so soon."

It was not difficult to keep Mane satisfied. There were always mice, moles, and the occasional rat left by the family cat. The cat was a great hunter. Proud of herself as well. Esta could feel that pride, and she rewarded it with cream from the top of the milk can, knowing full well that her praise and her treats would keep the small rodents coming—the rodents that would feed Mane. Esta knew that hand feeding Mane would not only tame her but make her dependent upon Esta for her food and care. She made a promise to herself, and to Mane, that the bird would learn how to hunt. She would make sure that Mane would not be in danger of being killed by a local farmer protecting his chickens, though it would mean that Esta would be responsible for her always. Esta smiled when Mane began to test her wings; she was only four weeks old. Esta would hold Mane up on her forearm and send her off and down upon the cushioned bed for a soft landing. It did not take long before Mane was flying from one piece of furniture to another.

This, according to her father, Carrick, was testament that the owl was now ready to live out of doors. He decided that he had seen Mane "huck up" the last owl pellet he cared to witness.

Esta argued that Mane was not like other owls. "No, Da," she pleaded, "Mane cannot survive out there alone. She needs protection!"

After much debate and discussion, a plan was put forth that both Esta and her father could live with. Clare had not been happy with Carrick's decision to exile Mane from the house. Behind closed doors, she'd reminded Carrick of the life that Esta was confined to live. She had few friends, and those she had were chosen by the elders, including her future mate. If the owl made Esta happy, how could he even dream of taking that joy from their daughter? It had worked, and the two of them had put their heads together to find a way for Esta to keep Mane close without the bird leaving its mark upon the inside of the cottage. Carrick built a box on the outside of the house, taking half of Esta's window. She could open the box from the inside or the outside to get to Mane, yet the box was built so that it prevented Mane from entering the house on her own. At night, Esta could open the inner door of the nesting box and close the lid to the outside. This kept Mane safe and made them both feel better, simply due to the fact that they could see and hear one another.

Esta knew that owls were most often nighttime creatures, so Mane was often left alone to sleep during the morning chores. As for Esta, she spent her afternoons learning at her mother's side. Each evening, after the family meal, Esta would walk in the near woods with Mane, the large owl drifting on the breeze above her or resting upon her shoulder. This was her time to teach Mane how to be herself, how to hunt and eat as the other owls in the woods did. There would come a time when Mane could fly free from her box at night if she so desired. Yet Esta had a feeling that the bird was most content with her life. Having imprinted on Esta, she felt safe and loved when the two were together. Esta would toss a rodent to the ground and watch as Mane swooped down upon it. Soon, Esta knew, Mane would notice small creatures on her own and no longer need help from Esta or the family cat. Esta was quite the sight to a wandering villager—a wild-looking young woman with an owl upon her shoulder, strolling along as if it were quite normal to do so. That is how she came to be known as the "Night Child." She had heard this name echo on the lips of the villagers as she passed and felt the closed-in feelings of night, darkness, and children, of strangeness and fear. Words were whispered among the small groups that watched her from a distance. There were moments that she wished she were just like the other girls in the village. She longed for the friendships and the laughter. Those feelings of wanting always disappeared, though, when she was in the woods with Mane sharing the feelings of freedom and flight, love and contentment. The other animals, too, gave her the gift of belonging. Esta's gift allowed her to sit and wonder at all manner of creature. Deer, rabbits, and the occasional fox would sniff her skirts and allow her touch. They could feel, as she could feel, the special bond of understanding and trust.

On days that she was not needed to attend to the sick or injured with her mother, Esta often walked the trail through the near woods next to the village green. The green was the center of trade each day. All manner of goods was exchanged, brought to the green for sale and for trade—everything from tanned hides and furs to leather boots and bracers to beautiful gear for the cob horses ridden by the youth. There were many vegetables, fish, and meats, bone combs and hair pieces. Truly, anything you could want or need was available at the green.

The village of Elvoy had thrived since the first fisherman had made a home there. The three hundred full-time residents had come together over the years to create a peaceful and prosperous island home. The population was large in comparison to most villages of only one or two score, the reason being that the people of Elvoy were able to make a good living from the crops they grew, the resources the sea provided, and, thanks to the presence of few predators, the livestock they raised.

Years ago, before the village had sprung up, the rivers on the isle of Elvoy would flood the valley in times of hard rain. But when the Romans had ruled Britannia, they had cut many spillways into the land, and knowledge of this technique had found its way to Elvoy, even though the islands near Elvoy had never been invaded by the Roman Empire. When the Roman rule of Britannia had ended, two such men had come to Elvoy. It was said that these men were the reason the valley had become fertile ground, for they had gathered men and women to dig the trenches that now crossed the valley floor. This allowed overflow from the rivers to wind its way across the lowlands and removed the excess water from the river that wound its way from the peaks of the island to the sea, taking care of the crops and keeping livestock and humans alike in fresh water. The valley had not had a flood in years. Also, thanks to Roman rule, the wide range of crops being grown upon the island was remarkable. The village farmers prospered, growing everything from wheat to apples. The village *kelias,* stockmen raised animals including sheep, longhaired cattle, pigs, and all manner of fowl. It was a nice existence. Being that Elvoy was an island kept most people from wanting to live there, since they would feel trapped by the sea. This, however, did not seem to matter to those who did live on Elvoy. When the sea allowed the boats to travel, trade was good between the island and the mainland. This was true for the cluster of little islands near Elvoy as well, each island holding its own yet needing the trade that made life better for all.

Near the place where two rivers came together at the base of the valley near the sea sat a small castle. It had never been occupied in the whole of Esta's life. Once a noble had lived there, claiming the island as his own. This had not lasted long. As the mainland had witnessed kings come and go, rule over the islands had changed hands many times. Yet the size of the island and the fact that any noble would find himself cut off from society left little to be desired. The people of Elvoy seemed to keep their lives and livelihoods, despite the power struggles of the mainland. The wars and uprisings had eventually pulled the nobleman back to their king, and the little island had been once again forgotten. The peaceful people of Elvoy were simple and easy going. Since the castle had been neglected, it had become a place of mystery and decay, with arches covered in ivy and honeysuckle vines. It had been a place where the youth would climb around and dream of knights and legends. It was a hollowed-out ruin now, though, robbed of much of its stone to meet other needs; it had become a quarry, the source of the stone from which the roundhouses were built. Not a soul paid it much attention anymore.

Elvoy had little trouble with the wars. The cluster of islands looked promising to an invader, but the sea was the only approach, and there were few beaches on Elvoy. Most of the islands coast having high cliffs that fall straight down to the ice-cold waves of the ocean. So, for the most part, the people of Elvoy had been left to fend for themselves, in every way. They had endured raids and occasional runs on their food stores, yet they had learned how to defend the village and ward off most attacks by offering shelter and supplies to those passing through. The island elders had, through trial and error, discovered the best way to protect Elvoy from the outside world. They lived their lives, carrying on the traditions that made life on Elvoy both peaceful and prosperous and the people so content. The most important of those traditions was to keep the island under careful watch. They had found that knowing about and preparing for any and all visitors was a good practice, be they friend or foe.

The elders had taken great care in building this practice into a tradition. It was treated differently from the coming-of-age celebrations, for which the youth waited in anticipation. At the age of fifteen, young men were given the task of riding the perimeter of the island. They would ride through the mountains and the near woods on trails that gave them a view of the sea whenever possible. The boys who had just turned fifteen would learn their task from one who was older, one who had gone out before. They would learn about caring for their mounts and about how to navigate and survive outside the protection of their fathers' shadows. A young man's fifteenth birthdate was celebrated by the island as a whole, marking his arrival to manhood. The gift the young man would be given on this long-awaited date was relished and longed for: a strong, sturdy Welsh cob. The little horses stood between fourteen and fifteen hands tall. They were built for covering long distances at a steady trot over all manner of landscapes. The horses were coveted by their owners, who often raced across the green for weeks after getting their mounts.

Esta always enjoyed the first encounters between horse and rider. The feelings would often flood her: the pure joy and excitement of the young man, the nervous wonder of the animal at the care and love being given by the human. This match, however, did not always turn out well, though if the truth be told, the problem almost never rested with the animal. It rested with the human. Most of the young men in the village looked forward to their rides through the foothills and surrounding mountainsides, hunting, setting snares, and keeping an eye on Elvoy from the mountain passes to the valley below them. Any approach from the sea could be seen for miles. The farmers and tradesmen knew they would have to give up the daily labors of their sons for the length of their tours around the island, but the exchange was accepted, as it gave the villagers peace of mind. The village peacekeeper and the elders made sure the tours were given out fairly. The boys took it in turns to make the guard rounds, each round taking about a fortnight to complete. It was believed that these years of taking turns in the wilderness made the boys into men. It forced them to form strong bonds and learn the importance of working together for a common good. They were never sent out alone but in pairs. And during a year when there were several young males the same age, perhaps three would ride out together. Once the boys returned home, they would not be sent out again for several months. They would make one summer tour and one winter. That was the way of it.

Esta, now fifteen herself, knew several of the boys getting their mounts this year. She could not help but have feelings of jealousy. She knew how silly it was to feel such a thing. After all, she was happy. She had Mane. She walked in the near woods in the fading light and counted the stars above her. She worked hard and enjoyed her time learning her mother's trade. She was in many ways even more talented than Clare, her gift giving Clare insight she would not have had otherwise. More important was that Esta would now begin to go out on her own. Her upcoming birthday signaled her arrival as a healer in her own right. Esta would begin seeing livestock and humans without her mother's guidance. Clare worried yet knew that the village must become accustomed to having Esta fulfill their needs. She knew that her daughter would one day become the village healer. She knew that Esta had it within her to be far better at it than she was herself due to her daughter's extraordinary gift: the simple fact that she could feel when things were not working—or better yet, when they were.

TWO

The Lost Watch

sta loved her evening walks. Mane flew through the trees, and Esta could catch the glint of the slowly setting sun on her wings. Out here, on her own in the wood, Esta felt at peace. She could allow the feelings of joy that came from Mane in flight to fill her. She would smile and laugh and even run through a field or down a well-worn path without checking herself, without looking around to make sure no one else was watching. She could push back the hood of her cloak and remove the carved-bone comb that held her hair in check, letting it cascade down her back and float about in the breeze.

The young people in the village had each other. Esta could feel their bonds of friendship, which at times had given her feelings she had not experienced herself. Her childhood had been happy—she could not say that it was not—yet it was spent with her parents and those whom her parents or the elders deemed worthy. Esta felt older than the girls she met on the green. She was, as she knew, different. Being different often meant being alone, and the feelings that came at her from others pointed out that very fact.

Esta had not walked for long when Mane came back to perch upon her shoulder. The bird gave off a feeling of unease. The air around them became thick with feelings of fear. She stepped cautiously through the trees and into a meadow, where a young man sat upon his mount, his head back, eyes closed, laughing. He was laughing at his fellow traveler, who was slowly picking himself up off of the ground. She could now read another emotion. Anger. Anger and hate.

The boy came up shouting. "'Tis not funny, Erik. The stupid sod! C'mere. I will teach you to throw me off!"

Esta caught the sudden flash of concern from the mounted rider, Erik.

"Ease off, Roan. 'Tis not the animal's fault. You ask too much too soon!"

It did no good. The boy had hold of the rope and began to jerk the pony's head down. The horse's eyes were wide with fear, and its nostrils flared as it pulled back, trying to free itself from this angry, hurtful creature before it.

"Stop!"

The shout startled both boys, and they whipped around to see who was there. Instantly Esta was hit with Roan's shock and amazement, while Erik's feelings were of a joyful surprise. She quickly brushed the feelings aside and strode into the open. Mane on her shoulder, Esta marched toward the boy on the ground. Roan was full of anger and conceit. She could almost taste it. It was thick and clouded the feelings that were coming from Erik, whom Esta had known the whole of her life. She had interrupted what should have been the beginning of their guard duties. They were packed up and obviously just setting out. It was Roan who spoke, Roan who was fuming with anger and embarrassment. Esta only knew him as the son of the skinner, a boy she had often felt sorry for.

"What the hell do you want?"

It did not sound like a question or a demand, more like a signal to butt out.

"The question is not what I want, you ignorant *dul*! How dare you harm that animal! Who gives you the right to scare the poor thing to death?"

"*Daufi*!" The boy gave the horse's reins a stiff jerk. The cob's eyes rolled back in its head, and Esta could feel the anger mounting. It was going to strike out at the boy. As the cob's front feet began to dance and lift off the ground, Mane suddenly took flight. She flew straight at the boy's face, giving off a loud shriek. Both horse and rider were startled. Roan let go of the reins to throw his hands up over his head. Once free, the cob spun and bolted for the cover of the forest. Mane circled once, and Esta felt her satisfaction as she followed the cob into the tree line. Esta could not hide her smile. This boy would now have the time to cool off, if he were able.

It was dead silent for a brief moment, and then there was a great burst of laughter. Esta turned to see Erik laughing so hard that he nearly fell off his own mount. His thoughts were full of delight at the sight of Roan getting his due. Esta had to turn her gaze to the ground once again to hide her smile.

"'Tis your own trouble Roan," Erik said, laughing. "I told you to lighten up on the cob. It takes time."

Roan turned his anger on Erik, who was still mounted and still chuckling as he spoke.

"You could have helped me! You could have gotten off your stupid cob and helped me!"

Esta could feel a slight change in Erik's mood. The anger quickly vanished as he shook his head.

"Help you what, Roan? Beat your cob? Frighten it to death? What?" Erik seemed annoyed now. He knew this would slow his progress and wanted to continue on his own if need be. He seemed to want nothing more of Roan.

"I will fetch the cob; you should head back to the village. It does no good to have you fighting your mount. We'll be out there for days."

"Leave it!" Roan snapped. "I do not want it. Stupid cob has cost too much as it is."

Erik was not sure how to respond. "You cannot just leave her out here, Roan. The cob is your responsibility. She could die out here."

"Good!" Roan shouted. "I never want to see that animal again! I'll kill her myself!"

Roan bent to scoop up his hood, and he was gone, stomping through the brush back toward the village. For a moment, it was as if Esta did not exist. The arrogance and anger from Roan was all she could feel. She stood quietly, waiting for her opportunity to exit. Then Erik had her locked in his gaze. Something was wrong. She could see on his face that he was frustrated but also a little amused. But what was he feeling? What was it that she was getting from him? Love. No, more than that. Deeper.

"Since it was you and your bird that caused the beast to run, it is only fitting that you help me find it." He raised a brow at her, as if he expected her to obey.

Esta stared at him. She was puzzled. His face, his words held anger. His feelings? There again: knowing. Years of knowing her as a child. He knew her. He loved her. He would give anything.

"Did you hear me? I need your help!"

Esta shook her head to clear her thoughts. She looked up at Erik on his beautifully groomed cob and smiled.

"Mane has her."

Esta turned away. She could feel her cheeks flush, feel the heat rise to her face. She walked in the direction the horse had run, knowing Mane was keeping an eye on her. Esta could feel Mane's calm. The cob was fairly close and was no longer panicked.

Erik sat, a little bewildered by what he thought he could read on her face. She was quick to disappear into the thicket of trees. He dismounted and followed her into the semidark cover of the near woods. The trail left by Roan's cob was easy to follow. Her feet had dug into the earth as she tried to flee her master, the mistreatments making her run into the unknown. It did not take long for Erik to catch up with Esta. She was calling Mane softly, saying her name and then giving a short whistle of a tune Erik could not quite place but knew he had heard before.

"Mane. Come Mane, come." Then the whistle again. "They are close," Esta whispered.

Erik was about to ask how on earth she could know that when his own mount raised her head and switched her ears—a sure sign that something or someone was there, just beyond where the eyes could yet see.

Esta held up her hand to Erik as if to still him. Again, Erik was taken aback by the girl's outward confidence. They stood stock-still for several moments. Then, from just over Erik's left shoulder, they heard a very cautious, short whinny. Erik's cob responded. He gave her a quick rub on the top of her head between the ears. This caused another happy noise to escape her. Roan's horse, hearing the answer and feeling no danger, stepped into the clearing in front of them. Erik began to make his move to retrieve her but was stopped.

"If you wait, she will come to us. She needs to build trust. Stomping over there to gather up her reins and walk her back to town in a huff does no one any good."

Erik looked at her. That had been exactly his intent. He wanted to gather up the cob and get out of there, find Roan, and punch him in the face. How did she know that? And the question just slipped out.

"They say things about you. In the village, they say you have second sight." He paused. "Do you … do you have second sight?"

He was calm. There was no accusation in his tone, just a quiet wondering. He watched her. She kept her eyes on the cob and calmly shrugged.

"I do not have second sight." Esta looked into his eyes. She said the only thing she could think of. It was, however, more than she had ever said to any living being before him. "I do not know what to call it. It is different."

She turned back to face the cob when Erik raised his brow. Why was she telling him this? People in the village had guessed her abilities before, though it was never openly talked about. Her parents had told her to keep her knowledge to herself. They had said that others would not understand. Why, then, did she feel she could tell Erik everything now? As they stood there, Mane flew over and perched herself in a tree above Esta. The cob came slowly, step by step, with much hesitation. They did not rush her. They did not speak. They only looked at one another in a sort of tense gaze. Quiet and still, they let the cob come to them in her own good time.

When at last she was there before them, she came to Esta. Reaching out, Esta blew at the cob's nose and rubbed her head and neck. The cob seemed to find comfort and calmed quickly.

"It seems you now have another animal to add to your menagerie." Esta looked confused.

Erik shrugged. "You heard Roan. He never wants to see the animal again. And it is obvious that she has found her true master."

Esta laughed aloud, which brought a snicker from the horse.

"See what I mean," he said.

"As tempting as having a cob of my own might be, I am not sure it would be worth the public punishment on the village green for theft."

Erik snorted. "'Tis not theft."

"I am afraid," Esta said quietly, "that Roan may see it that way when I go riding through the village on his horse."

Again, Erik snorted. "Roan is a fool! But I see your point. I should speak with his father. Roan is not ready for the responsibility of guard duty, and now I am behind my tour. It will take time to decide who should go out with me. There are always those who prefer guard duty to their work in the fields."

Esta understood that. She loved wandering the near woods with Mane. She always felt at home there. She dreamed of building a stone cottage in the hidden comfort of the forest. If she were being honest, she would admit that her gift was more pleasing in the woods. Animal emotions were far less complicated. And being as she was, the animals of the woods always seemed to accept her presence. Mane's as well. Even those animals that would normally be Mane's prey would allow them near. It was a secret that Esta kept even from her parents. Foxes, rabbits, and deer would often come so close that she could reach out and touch them. Some seemed to seek out her touch, while others seemed to feel comfort from her presence.

Erik interrupted her thoughts. "There is no reason to walk all the way back to the green. She seems rather taken with you. Can you ride?"

There was no time to consider her answer. Erik had simply picked her up at the waist and placed her astride the cob. For a moment she was frightened. She feared that the horse may bolt out from under her, or worse, take her hurtling through the trees. The cob gave a loud whinny, turned its head as if to sniff her skirts, and twitched its ears. Esta reminded herself to breathe, and she instantly relaxed both herself and her mount.

Erik was there at her side. He gathered up the cob's reins and gently placed them in her hands. "She has been well trained. It was more Roan's problem, not hers. Keep a steady pressure when you want her to do something. Do not yank on her head. Just pull straight back to your belly button to stop. Keep your elbows in and your hands near her withers." His hands were on hers, and he moved them to and fro as he spoke. It was like he was talking to someone who had some idea of what they were doing, but she did not. He was not afraid. She could feel no fear. All she could read coming from Erik was a sort of content confidence. There was also a trace of joy. Given everything that had happened, Esta could not but wonder at it, although she quickly realized that the joy was due more to her presence than to the situation. So she remained silent.

For the first half an hour or so, they were still in the near woods. Erik took the lead, and Esta followed. She found that she liked it. She could feel that the cob was relaxed and content as well. The horse had only one moment of alarm, when Mane decided to sit atop of Esta's shoulder instead of flying back to the village.

Esta gently reached up to scratch between the cobs ears and whispered, "It's alright. I guess Mane wants to experience riding a horse as well. Between you and me, though, I think she's just being lazy."

Mane replied with a few clicks of her tongue on her beak, a sound that had made Esta jump back the first few times she had heard it, thinking that Mane was snapping her beak in anger. As it turned out, Esta learned that this type of owl, with its beautiful, heart-shaped face, did not make a pleasant hooting sound but a series of clicks, knocks, hisses, and high-pitched shrieks. Once the cob realized that Mane was not a threat, she settled again into her easy stride, following Erik's mount back toward the village at a slow and steady pace.

When the pair broke free of the near woods, Esta could see that they were across the little valley from the market green.

"So, how are you doing? Would you like to see what her trot feels like?" Erik said, smiling at her.

There were those emotions again. Love, wild, freedom. Why did it shock her so?

"I will follow your lead." Esta motioned toward the green with her head.

Erik took her in again—her strawberry-blonde hair thick and very loosely braided down her back, her deep-grey eyes flecked with gold, her skin like honey, and that owl, that enormous white-faced owl perched upon her shoulder looking back at him. Wild beauty. That is what she was. None of this Night Child nonsense, for she was not a child any longer.

Esta could hold his gaze no longer. She blushed and dipped her head to look at the reins in her hands.

"Well, come on then," Erik said. "If you feel in danger of falling off, just pull back like I showed you and say halt. I will stop as well."

By the time they reached the green, the easy trot had turned into a canter. Erik could not help but smile when he heard the quiet giggle from behind him. She was enjoying it. She did not fear the steady increase in speed that Erik encouraged. He waited for a fearful scream or some anger from her for the race across the green. Esta, though, was unlike other women. He liked that.

The sun had nearly set when they rode through the green. Esta did not question Erik when he turned down the path that would take her home. Within minutes, they were on the winding path that ran through the edge of the woodland. It was much faster on horseback, Esta realized as they reached the fields of her father's farm before the sun had set. Not wanting to ride through the fields, Erik nodded at her family dwelling.

"I could not have you walking after all your help."

Esta laughed. "Yes, I am sure you could not have managed without me."

With a whistle, Mane flew to the roof. Esta dismounted and handed the reins to Erik, still on his mount.

"Thank you, Erik. I never knew why the boys loved their cobs so much. I understand better now."

Erik smiled down at her. "Be well, Esta. Until we meet again."

Hit again with the strange emotions that came when he looked into her eyes, Esta returned his farewell and quickly entered the roundhouse.

Erik pondered all the way back to the green. How he would explain to Roan the need to give up his mount. This was Roan's first tour of guard duty. He had been teamed with Erik for one purpose: the hope that he would make it through his tour in one piece. Erik had made at least four tours in the two years since he had turned fifteen. He was quick, efficient, and very good at keeping himself and his tour partner well fed, warm, and dry. Erik had given the elders the idea for the small tour huts after one of the boys had died during an early frost. Not prepared for the change in the weather and not skilled at building a good shelter, the young men had been left to huddle together for warmth. One of the boys had lost a few toes, but the younger boy had died during the night. The village had begun to question the wisdom of sending the boys out. Some at fifteen were better suited than others. Erik had gone over the tour map with the elders to determine the best places for resting both the boys and their mounts. There were ways to build and conceal the small huts. Much like their own wheelhouses yet much smaller, the huts would house a fire chute, dry wood, and clay cooking pots. They would be located off the beaten path, not visible to the untrained or unknowing eye—tucked into an outcropping of rock; in the midst of some windblown, downed trees; or in a mound of earth that looked natural.

Erik and several others had volunteered to build the huts in between their regular tours. It had taken them two full summers to complete the huts in a circle around their island. The council of elders had praised the boys for their efforts before the last hut had been completed. Every young man who had been able to stay in the huts while on his guard tour had nothing but an enormous amount of gratitude and respect for those who had built the shelters. They would save time and lives. Before they'd had to look for shelter each night, stopping early to make some form of lean-to in bad weather, and then gather wood and try to build fires in the rain that fell often on Elvoy, so the huts were a welcomed sight. They had been placed very specifically, a good day's travel from one another. All of that meant more time spent on guard watch, less fear of the elements, and a nice, warm, dry place to lay your head down for the night. It helped to keep the young men on schedule as well, since they needed to make sure they reached the next hut in a timely manner. Once there, they would replace the wood stock before they left the next morning.

Roan approached the small yard in front of the skinner's barn with caution. He knew that it would be best to get any form of punishment over with as quickly as possible. He had left his cob in the woods, and he had walked away from his duty to protect the island. His father would be furious, he knew. He actually had every right to be so. However, Beor had an iron fist when it came to dealing with his son. Roan knew that he would pay for any slight, imagined or real, in the same fashion. His father would take his anger out upon Roans very flesh.

Beor stood in the yard near the large cauldron, speaking with one of the village fishmen. Roan knew this man. He needed good leather boots and jackets that would protect him from the bitter cold of the open sea. Roan also knew that his father had little desire to trade with a fishmonger for food; he had others who would bring him a wide variety of red meats, which he preferred. Instead, this man would barter with ale. He would bring his father a mead made from berries and hops. His father would trade well for a few casks of ale, and they looked as if they had just struck a deal, as they clasped hands and nodded. It was clear that the two men had already broken into one of the casks. Their tankers were full, and they laughed with an ease that Roan knew only came when his father had been drinking. It was a laughter that seemed to come from lightheartedness but masked a rage that loomed just below the surface of his smile.

"Damn," Roan muttered to himself as he stood, his back pressed up against the barn, glancing around the corner and hoping for a clear path to the house. If he could get to his mother, he could explain what had happened, and she would advise him on what was best to do. If he could just get to his mother. His father may not even know that he had returned. Roan closed his eyes and tried to breath. Perhaps, if he just walked with purpose toward the house, his father would ignore his presence. It would depend upon the amount of mead he had consumed and the mood he was currently in. If he ignored Roan, as he often did, Roan would reach his mother. If he did not, Roan knew that the result would be physical. He pulled his hood up, took two long breaths to steady his nerves, and walked around the corner toward the front of the house at a steady, rapid pace. His father's back was to him, and that meant that Roan could cover a good bit of ground before he would be noticed. That would have been the case but for the fishmonger's narrowed gaze. Roan picked up the pace, but it was in vain. The fishmonger pointed an unsteady finger in his direction and bellowed as if he were waking the dead.

"I thought you said Roan was on duty. Seems he forgot to kiss his ma farewell, maybe left his favorite pilla behind?"

The man laughed loudly, and Roan knew that would be the trigger. His father had a blind pride that had caused him more than one beating in his day.

Beor spun and looked across the yard. He narrowed his eyes and then bellowed Roan's name. Roan took a few more hesitant steps toward the house and then stopped. He turned his face toward the two men and then reached up and threw back his hood. Beor crossed the distance between them in a matter of seconds.

"What has happened? Why are you here?"

His words came at a quick clip, and Roan was not ready to answer them. His hesitation earned him a cuff along the side of his face.

"Answer me, boy!" Beor's anger was mounting.

"My cob got loose and is in the woods." Roan told the half-truth with ease. He knew that the entire story would only cause his father more anger. Beor did not care for the village peacekeeper, or his son. And he had even more scorn for Esta, the daughter of the village healer and midwife. He seemed to despise the girl. Roan knew from many remarks and comments that his father would see the child cast out or worse for her strange behaviors.

Beor looked in the direction of the woods. "Where is Erik? Why is he not here with you, boy?"

Roan was quick with his reply. "He is looking for the cob."

"He is looking for the cob?" Beor spat. "Why are you not?"

"I came to fetch a rope and perhaps a few apples." Roan tilted his head toward the apple tree growing behind their dwelling. Beor gave his son a questioning look and then shoved him toward the house as he turned his attention back to the fishmonger.

Once inside, Roan quickly found his mother. He pulled a leather bladder from a nook and began to fill it. He also grabbed a knife, a water skin, a snare, and a candle. He was packing for survival, for he knew that when his father learned the truth about the events of the day, he would need to either run or take a beating unlike any he had endured before. He remembered now the first time that Beor had hit him. He had been only around eight or nine years old. He had been so proud of himself; he had taken one of the rabbit skins from the shed and roughly sewn it into a scabbard for his father's birthday. Roan had imagined the look of surprise that would be on his father's face and the joy the gift would bring him. He had been so excited. But the gift was presented only to have Beor burst from his chair in anger. He had looked for the missing skin several days earlier and had asked Roan if he had seen it. Beor had leaned over the table and picked Roan up by the front of his tunic. He had jerked the boy across the table, spilling the contents in all directions as Roan's arms and legs swung about wildly. Wide-eyed, he had looked at his father that day in fear, and Beor had beat him for the theft of the skin. He had given the boy a black eye and bruises nearly from head to toe. Roan's mother had tried to intervene and had been sent staggering back into a wall by a slap to her face. Beor had told them on that day that they were never to question his will. He ruled the home with an iron fist.

As the years had passed and Roan had found himself bearing the brunt of his father's anger, he'd learned to keep his mother and younger siblings out of harm's way. If one of the younger children did something to anger Beor, Roan would often step in and try to salvage the situation, often becoming the one who was punished. He looked at his mother now, rushing about to gather what she thought he might need. If Beor realized that she had helped him in any way, she would pay dearly for it. He glanced into the corner where his younger sister played, so innocent and unaware of what kind of danger she may be in. He thought of Landen working in the shed, stacking the wood for the cauldron fires and gathering the tools that would be used. Landen would take Roan's place in the skinning shed. Roan now wondered if he would also take his place as his father's whipping post. Was he leaving them all to face the punishments that Beor would hand out on a regular basis? How could he leave them to that kind of fate?

Roan broke his silence, letting the story of what happened in the woods and his fear of leaving his mother spill out in a rapid tangle of words and tears. His mother pulled him into her arms and told him that his time had come, that he could become a better man.

A sudden sound of hands clapping came at them. Beor stepped into the frame of the door, his large hands clapping loudly and slowly as he brought them up in front of them.

Roan's mother spun, a look of sheer panic on her face. She placed herself between them and gave Beor a look of pleading.

"He is just a boy …" Her words trailed off. She knew, as Roan knew, that they meant nothing to him. There was only one difference between this situation and every other time that Roan had known he was about to be beaten: he was leaving. He was leaving, and he was not ever going to come back.

Roan lunged for the pack on the table and spun around, swinging the pack through the air. Beor ducked, and that was the only moment that Roan had to slide past him and run through the threshold. Beor yelled after him but was momentarily detained. He pushed his wife hard into the table, watching her tumble over it and land on the stone floor. Beor ran out only to see that Roan had disappeared around the corner of the shed. The boy was running, and Beor knew that he could not catch him. He also knew that the boy would pay, as he always had when Beor was displeased.

Erik could see the dim lights flickering through the shutters of Roan's home. His father was a skinner. A tanner, some called him. He tanned most of the hides in the village. It wasn't that the villagers could not tan their own hides, but trade was good in this area. With four nice-sized rabbits, a person could have a warm, fitted pair of fur-lined boots. Those boots could be paid for in many ways: four more rabbits for the skinner, a piglet, milk, and cheese. The list of tradable goods was endless. But Erik thought that being the skinner must be much like being the butcher. They looked at animals differently. They did not mourn them. Instead they looked upon them as goods—meat, fur, leather, sinew— not as living, breathing souls. The animals were not in any way to be connected with human feeling or emotion. So, would Roan's father be willing to let the cob go? Would he trade it back for another and hope Roan would bond with it? Erik did not care for Roan. He was cruel, and not just to his mount. He seemed to have a dislike of all animals. Perhaps that was understandable, having grown up having to put them down for their hide.

Erik could see a small glow coming from the barn. Outside hung a few stretched hides. A steaming cauldron hung over a fire on a tripod with a large wooden paddle beside it on the ground. Roan's younger brother, Landen, stepped from the barn to drop a bloody hide into the water. He looked up at Erik and then bolted back into the barn. A moment later, Roan's father was there.

"You found it, then? You should have left it for the boy. No matter."

Erik could hear the anger in his tone, not unlike Roan's anger, bubbling just under the surface.

"Sir?"

The man looked past Erik and the cob. "So, where's the girl, then? Home I suppose?"

Erik did not like the way he asked about Esta. "Yes, sir. I took Esta home to thank her for catching the cob. She rode it back to the green for Roan."

There was a flash of hate on Beor's face, and the skinner seemed even angrier. Erik had no desire to talk further.

"If I am going to make my round, I must be going. I really don't mind making the rounds alone, but the elders do not like it. If Roan is not at ease with his mount—" Erik did not get the chance to finish.

"Roan has no mount! You allowed that … that girl to ride it. It is lost! I only hope that I will be compensated for my loss! As for Roan, I have sent him ahead on foot!"

At this, the skinner turned his back on Erik and walked back into the barn, leaving Erik stunned and confused.

There was no possible way to make the shelters along the guard's route on foot. Unless Roan had acquired a large pack when he'd come back here, his cold-weather and night gear was still in his pack upon the cob. Erik was suddenly aware of why Roan always seemed so angry and harsh tempered. This man was well known in the village as unkind. That was putting it lightly; he was cruel to his family, his wife and Roan often getting the worst of it. Erik could not understand why Beor had sent him out on foot. The sun would soon be setting, and Roan had nothing to keep him warm or safe that night. The skinner was a hard and cruel man. He rarely left the skinner's shed, and when he did, he left the island.

Erik looked down into Landen's worried eyes. He knew. He knew his brother was in great danger.

"I will find him." Erik made the statement for the young man's ears only. Landen nodded and glanced back at the barn. He tilted his head toward the green and nodded again. Erik understood and trotted off, Roan's cob still in tow.

Erik first headed for his father's house. He needed help. He also wanted the council to know how Roan had ended up alone in the woods this night, so he needed to tell his father what had happened. The light was almost gone now, but the cob knew his way home. There was no time to call the council together before tomorrow. Erik worried. The nights were cold, and Roan's pack was still on his horses back. When Erik had told his father all he could, they set out together with lanterns to pick up Roan's trail.

From the skinner's house, Roan had turned into the near woods back toward where he had been thrown from the horse. This path would also take him back past Esta's home. Would he go there looking for his horse? Looking for Esta?

"We should stop at Carrick's house. Perhaps Roan believes Esta has the cob. He may go there looking for it. Landen said he'd headed for the village green."

Dirk looked at the path on the ground. There was no way of knowing. "There is no reason to take to the woods if you believe he will seek out Esta. Let us see Carrick."

Erik, in agreement, turned to take the through road to the other side of the village.

Carrick, Esta's father, grew root vegetables, mostly tubers and carrots. They grew well on that end of the valley where the sun remained upon the ground most of the day. Closer to the house, there were herbs and trees. Esta's mother cared for the herb garden, and Esta gathered what they could not grow from the near woods and the meadows. They were comfortable.

It was late for visitors. The family sat about the table. Clare, Esta's mother, had just filled their bowls with a beef-and-vegetable stew, and Erik and his father could smell the bread, fresh from the ovens in the little stone cookhouse. The glowing red embers could still be seen and the heat felt, even from their mounts. Esta looked up into her mother's face, eyes bright with the knowledge of who approached the house.

"We have visitors. Something is wrong."

Carrick stood and went to the door. He opened it and stepped outside just as Erik and his father were dismounting.

"Carrick." Erik's father held his arm out in greeting.

"Dirk, Erik, welcome. What brings you here? Are you in need of Clare?"

Dirk shook his head. "Not yet, but we may be. Roan is out in the near woods, making a start at his rounds without his mount or his gear."

Esta was confused. "Did he not make it home, Erik?"

"He did. His father sent him out again." Dirk's tone said it all. There was not a great deal of sympathy in the village for the skinner. He tended to upset people with his terse manners and sharp tongue.

Clare appeared in the doorway. "Well, do not stand about in the dark. Come in, eat, and talk. You will do Roan no good if you are weak and without a plan."

Dirk and Erik both wanted to set out after Roan. Neither of them, however, had eaten a meal since before midday, and their stomachs answered for them.

Clare had already filled bowls and sliced bread for the visitors. Erik sat on the bench seat next to Esta, and she nearly blushed at the emotions of pleasure she felt from him.

Dirk and Erik explained the anger and harsh words from Roan's father. "He blames Esta for Roan's trouble with the cob. He sent Roan out into the darkness believing it will make a man of him."

Carrick looked at his daughter. "Trouble with his cob? Esta?"

Erik did not want Carrick to believe that Esta was responsible in any way. "Nay, Carrick, Esta was only a witness to Roan being thrown from his mount. He became angry, and the cob bolted. I may not have found the animal if it had not been for her help."

Dirk was sure that Roan would not go far. Carrick agreed.

"If he were smart, he would hole up near the village and try to find help in the morning."

Carrick was only stating what he would do. His words, however, sparked a memory for Erik. He smiled at them.

"I think I know where he is." Erik stood and nodded. "Carrick is right. He knows he has nothing. He has no idea that I went back for him. But there is a shelter, the one we built for the council as an example. I don't think there is anything there. Roan will at least be out of the cold and safe. He could build a fire and hunker down for the night."

Dirk stood. "You may be right. We will check there first. Thank you, Clare, for a much-needed meal."

Clare stood and went to the hearth. "Let me place some in a jar. Roan will be hungry."

She carefully filled a clay jar with hot stew and wrapped it in a soft cloth.

"Father, I think I should go with Erik," Esta said. "He may need my help finding Roan."

As shocking as the sudden statement was, Carrick had long since realized that his daughter knew when to insert herself and when to remain silent.

Dirk, though, only knew that the "Night Child" was strange and different. He had watched her grow up. The elders had all but thrown his son Erik and Esta together at every opportunity. He had to admit, however, that she had always been a quiet, smart, and sweet child. Alden, the most honored of the elders on Elvoy, was very fond of her. Still, he knew that she seemed to have caused this situation, even though Erik had said it was not her fault. Dirk had great respect for both Carrick and Clare. He knew that Esta was special. He just did not understand how. They now wanted him to send this girl out with Erik, and it made him nervous.

Carrick could read the hesitation. He looked past Dirk to where Esta sat at the table. "Is it dangerous?"

Esta knew this question. It was all encompassing. Is it dangerous for Roan or Erik? Is it dangerous for herself? Her father wanted to know what emotions she was getting and from whom.

"I believe, father, that Roan may hold me responsible for his horse running away. Mane spooked the cob. Roan was upset and not thinking clearly. I feel this will help put things to rights."

Dirk was not so sure. He felt the need to speak with Carrick alone, question things he had never questioned before. Erik also wanted to know how Esta seemed to have an understanding of things that remained unspoken. But right now, he only wanted to find Roan and make things what he saw as right. That meant that Esta would end up with the cob.

"Esta may be right, father," said Erik. "Roan may be at the shelter, and if Esta and I show up there as if we have been looking for him since he walked away from us, he may calm down. We could be home early on the morrow. If you and I arrive with his cob in tow, he will know that we have seen his father. Knowing Roan, this will only set him off again."

This was a plan Dirk could understand.

"Go then, but it must be quick. I will expect you back no later than midday on the morrow. The council will have another ready to set out with you then. We are behind our task." Dirk stood and nodded his leave. This meant that things were settled in his mind.

Erik stood, and in moments they were on their way with soup, bread, and the packs full of what Roan would need to stay dry and warm when they found him. The shelter was not far from Esta's father's farm. The crops were near their reaping, so cutting the horses across the fields was not an option. They had to go round and then cut back into the near woods and toward the base of the mountains that ringed the little valley. It was less than a quarter day's ride. They would be there soon, but the late start meant that it would be the dark of night when they arrived at the shelter.

"He is there," Esta said in a whisper when they were still a good hundred paces away from the shelter.

"How do you know that?" Erik had stopped, and Esta could feel the confusion within him.

"Listen." Esta thought quickly. "There is no sound. No birds, nor owls, nor other animals moving about. He is making no effort to quiet his movements for them."

Erik listened hard. She was right. There was no sound—no sound at all but the little rustling of their own mounts. Yet Erik could not shake the feeling that there was something different about Esta, something to her understanding, something he had yet to learn.

Esta, on the other hand, was more concerned about the feelings of anger and hate she sensed. Those emotions were so strong that she could barely read Erik's feelings, though he sat right before her. The cob beneath her could smell it too. He knew the scent, and wanted no part of it.

"We should call his name."

Erik was puzzled by this. "Why?" He felt it was a waste of breath. They knew he was there.

"It would appear as if we had been out looking for him, that we care. His father sent him out here, Erik, with nothing. How would you feel?"

Esta was right, again. Roan was most likely feeling hurt and alone.

"You are right." He turned his mount to face the shelter and called out for Roan. Esta followed, calling his name.

"Roan! Roan!"

As they grew closer to the shelter, Erik began to wonder if they might have been wrong. Then came the answer.

"I am here. Stop yelling." Roan stepped into the moonlight. "Should you not be halfway around the valley by now?" He stood in the opening of the little hut, light from the fire inside behind him, the moonlight upon his face.

Erik dismounted and walked toward the shadow outside the roundhouse.

"I should, but my partner got angry and walked off. We can't have the council upset with us, Roan." Erik could see him now.

Roan snorted. "You mean your father, and I am afraid it is too late for that. And what is she doing here?"

Esta dismounted as Mane flew into the nearest tree.

"Esta insisted that she bring soup and bread to make up for spooking your cob." Erik raised an eyebrow at Roan as if to say, "Be nice."

This was news. Esta could feel some of Roan's anger ebb.

"Let us build up the fire and warm the shelter," Erik said. "I am afraid we are stuck here for the night. We can decide what would be best to do on the morrow."

Without a word, Roan turned and went back inside, letting the entrance hide slap against the opening. Erik looked back at Esta and brought his shoulders up in a quick shrug. Esta pulled the pack off the cob, and they ground tied the horses where they would be out of the wind. Inside the shelter, Roan tossed a few more sticks into the center fire pit and moved himself to a wall to wait.

As the fire blazed, Esta put the thick stew into a pot. The smell of the stew and the warmth of the fire had Roan relaxed, and Esta could feel his mood shift to comfort and away from fear and anger.

Erik was annoyed by the lack of manners. "Will you not thank Esta for the stew, Roan?"

Erik's voice was calm. The flare of anger from Roan was like a flash of light, quick to appear and gone just as fast.

"I would. Thank you, Esta, for both the stew and the bread." Roan was sincere, but his eyes were cast down. He would not look at her.

"You are welcome, Roan. I am sorry that Mane startled your cob. She forgets at times, I think, that she is a bird."

Erik chuckled. "A bird? A bird with the wingspan of a giant."

Even Roan laughed then, nodding in agreement.

"'Tis not her fault that she has been hand-fed. She is overlarge for her breed, like the bread maker's wife." Esta giggled.

The little roundhouse was warm, and the three sat in comfort. Esta began to yawn. Her bright eyes seemed overlarge as she tried to keep them open. She answered questions about her father's farm and her owl. She listened as Roan talked about her mother's skills as a healer when his younger brother and sister came into this world. He was willing to talk about anything to keep her awake. He knew that Erik was just waiting for the chance to scold him for his actions. He also knew he would have to tell Erik that his father had cast him out and that he could not return with the cob. He was afraid his father would kill it. Roan glanced at Esta, curled up near the hearth, leaning against the rock wall with a blanket over her lap and losing the fight to keep her eyes open. What would his father say if he knew Roan had shared a shelter with the Night Child— that wild witch of a girl who had second sight? His father was afraid of Esta, afraid of anything he did not understand. He had made his dislike of Esta clear many times, his harsh words often heard in council meetings or on the village green. Only the warnings that came from the elders and from Dirk would still his tongue, but words are difficult to take back once they pass the lips. Beor went out of his way to avoid Esta. He told anyone who questioned that fact that Esta was unnatural. Perhaps a witch, perhaps something else yet. He tried to make sure the village knew her as he did. The villagers, however, only knew that he was cruel, so most did not heed his warnings. Yet people in the village had echoed his words, said that she had second sight. They said that she knew things before they happened, that she could tell what people were thinking. Most of the village kept their distance from her, and some even made sure they never came in contact with her at all, much like Beor. Still others would pretend that it did not bother them. Perhaps it did not. For there were also those who would seek her out. The elders would often sit and visit with her. They could often be found at her dwelling, sharing a meal with her family. The circle of friends around Esta and her parents was small, to be sure, but it was powerful.

Erik reached over and tapped Esta on the shoulder.

"You should lie down, Esta. You will only wake with a sore neck if you sleep against the wall like that."

Esta said nothing but slid down and curled up to sleep. Outside an owl shrieked. Esta stirred and shushed Mane, which caused both Erik and Roan to chuckle softly.

"I have not seen you this relaxed in all the time I have known you. What has happened to you, Roan?" Erik's tone was not accusatory, yet Roan did stiffen slightly.

"I guess when there is nothing left to lose, a person can just sit back and wait for what may come." Roan was not angry. He was not being sarcastic. He sounded as if he were just stating a fact.

"If you mean the cob and the way your father feels about Esta having ridden it, I think we will be able to remedy that."

Roan looked at Erik in surprise.

"You have seen my father, then?" Roan already knew the answer.

Erik only nodded.

"Then you know that the cob was not the only thing being cast off." Roan sounded hurt.

"I do not think your father meant to cast you off." Erik said it, but he did not know if he believed it.

"Then you do not know my father."

Roan looked at Erik and smiled, but his eyes held a sadness Erik had never seen before.

"What will you do?" Erik asked, concerned.

"Do my tour; learn how to make a go of it on my own. If you will help me."

Erik brought his head up. "Me? How can I help you?" Erik was not sure how he could help Roan with anything.

"My father made life difficult for all of us. I am lucky. I have been released from his grasp"—Roan tossed a stick of wood into the fire—"but Landen, the babe, my mother … What of them?"

Erik was not sure how he could help, but he understood why Roan would fear for the rest of his family. He needed time to think about how best to help Roan or whether it was even possible.

"We need sleep. Let us talk about this in the morning."

Roan placed more wood upon the fire. The shelter was warm, dry, and snug. As Erik prepared his bedroll, he looked to the wall where Esta slept.

"Is it true what they say about her?" Roan thrust his chin toward where Esta lay, eyes closed and dreaming.

Erik looked from where Esta slept to Roan. He had been watching Roan carefully since they had arrived. "I do not yet know. There is something. It is not evil, not even a conscious thought for her. Yet it is there."

Erik was not sure how else to explain his thoughts about Esta. Nor his feelings about what she may or may not be capable of. It was hard to put into words what he thought she might be able to do and what his fears told him. He slept very little that night. He had a new respect for Roan but was not at all sure what Roan thought he could do out here. Roan couldn't believe he could live here at the shelter.

THREE

Seekers

Morning brought rain and fog. When a hot cup had been passed and cloaks were donned, the three set out for the village, roan and Esta both on foot. It seemed that Esta was not ready to except the cob, and Roan was not ready to argue over it. Erik rode ahead, stopping often to wait for them. Finally, feeling he could take it no more, Erik pulled Esta up behind him and had Roan follow on the young horse. The day was getting away from them. For some reason, the animal was willing to follow without complaint and gave Roan no problems. It did not escape Roan's notice that Esta had given the animal a little scratch between the ears and whispered softly to it before she'd handed the lead rope to him. He could not shake the feeling that she had requested that the cob behave, and it annoyed him greatly. He had no way of knowing that Esta had only tried to send the cob warm, calm feelings.

As they came upon the edge of the near woods by the village green, Esta harshly whispered for Erik to stop. She slid off to the ground, facing the green with clenched fists. She began to gasp and visibly shake. She had tears in her eyes. Roan came up beside her, alarmed at the look he saw on her face. For a moment he just looked at her.

"Erik, something is wrong with Esta!"

Suddenly Erik was there. His face before hers, his hands upon her shoulders.

"Esta. Esta, what is it?" He watched as she focused on his face. He could see how frightened she was. "Esta?"

"There … there is much pain. Much fear. Someone is holding them. There is sorrow." Esta gasped. "Sorrow for the dead."

This caught Erik and Roan off guard.

"Dead?" they said in unison. The boys turned toward the green, ready to set out quickly.

"No!" Esta reached out and took hold of Erik's arm. "Do not! It is not safe."

Erik was confused by the statement that the village was not safe. He also knew that Esta was afraid—more than afraid, she was terrified.

The boys left Esta with the horses and made their way into the tall grass on the edge of the green. They looked across the open field to where many men stood near the council house. They were warriors of some kind. Big men, with swords and shields leaned against the wall of the buildings near them.

"They do not look to be Norsemen? I cannot tell from here," Erik whispered uncertainly.

Never before had the Norsemen raided Elvoy. It would have been like taking from kin. They had always stopped for food and shelter. They certainly had never taken a life here before. There had never been the need. Elvoy was simply not a place to be conquered. It was a small farming and fishing village on a peaceful island. One of the men seemed to be wearing some strange sort of helmet. It looked as if a cob's tail were growing right out of the top of his head.

"Who are they?" Roan asked.

"I think they are English, possibly Norse from one of the other islands. Why would they do this? The island peoples have always lived in peace. I do not understand."

Roan looked to the smoke coming from behind the council house. "Why would they burn it?"

"I do not think they did. Not all of it. My guess is that they burned the homes of the council? The elders have the dwellings behind the longhouse." Erik looked toward his own home, but he could not see it, as it was hidden behind the large council house, which sat near the edge of the green and blocked their view of the main road leading into the village.

"My father?" Roan's words were the same as Erik's thoughts. Esta had said that there was much sorrow for the dead … Sorrow for who?

"We need to move. I don't know how safe we are here. I think we should go back to the shelter. I will try to get to Carrick. His home is the last house before the mountain pass." Erik gathered up the horses. "We must move, Esta. On your feet. Come, now!"

Esta stood and began walking. Erik did not like the way she looked—stark white with tears streaming down her face. She was silent, and he wished she would speak.

"I want to get you both back to the shelter," Erik said. "We need to think. We need a plan." He wanted to see if he could get close enough to gather some information. Alone he may be able to go unnoticed, but never would he try to slide through the guards with three.

Esta shook her head. "We should all go."

"No, Esta. I want you to stay hidden until I know what happened in the village." Erik was sure he knew best.

For the first time, Roan spoke up. "What is it that you know, Esta?"

Roan's voice was calm, but it was clear that he wanted answers. Erik felt an overwhelming need to defend and protect her.

"Roan, this is not the time—"

"It is the time, Erik!" Roan interrupted. "She sits shaking and tells us there is sorrow over death? What death? Whose death? How does she know that people are dead from across the green?" Roan was still looking at her.

Anger was building in both of them. Esta could feel it mounting. Roan was determined to get answers, and Erik was ready to defend her even to violence.

"Enough!"

They turned to her.

"You are both right. Erik, let us return to the shelter. Then yes,

Roan, I will tell you both all that I can." Esta turned. She gave a soft whistle, and Mane flew down to light upon her shoulder.

Erik motioned for Roan to follow, and the three walked quickly back to the shelter. Not wanting to leave the horses tied so close to where they were hidden, Erik moved the cobs further off the trail, up the side of the mountain. No one would find the horses unless they were wandering through the woods. He already knew the shelter was well hidden from the eye. They all made sure nothing but very dry wood was used to warm the small shelter. Erik took extra precautions by eliminating any trace of their movement off the trail to the little stone cottage. Mane sat above the shelter in the trees. She had been silent so far. Esta knew that she would give them their first warning should anyone approach. Roan's eyes were downcast. He shook his head at Erik in despair.

"This is all my fault."

Erik and Esta looked at each other in surprise, but Roan said it again.

"It is. It is my fault. If we had been on our rounds, we would have seen them. We would have known."

Esta shook her head. "'Tis not your fault, Roan. My father has told me of the guard duties. These men did not come overland. They had to have come by sea. Their boats must be at the lee."

Erik agreed. "That is true, Roan. They had to have come right into the bay. The question is, Why? For what purpose would they harm anyone here? The village has not seen violence in nearly seventy years. When the nobles left to fight their wars and took our men with them, not many ever returned."

"Then why?" Roan still sounded unconvinced of his innocence.

"I do not know why," Esta said. "I do know fear with much anger and sorrow is heavy upon the village."

Esta knew the time had come. She had never in the whole of her life been able to talk about her gift. Even her parents discouraged conversation about it. They worried about her and her future, so they quietly accepted her whispered warnings or matter-of-fact statements but never spoke of the origins of her knowledge.

Erik's voice was soft and low. "Esta, is my father gone?"

Roan's eyes snapped up to look first at Erik and then at Esta, waiting for the answer, wondering if this girl, this Night Child, knew his father's fate. His fate.

Esta gathered her thoughts. She had to try to block out the emotions that came at her from both of the boys. "I know not who has perished, Erik, only that there has been loss. I feel it."

"Loss. More than one then?" Roan had caught the meaning in her words.

Esta nodded. "Yes, but I do not know how many."

"Then how do you know?" Roan's voice held a note of anger.

Erik did not like to see Esta's reaction to Roan anger. He thought he was beginning to figure out her gift, if that were possible. Years of being around Esta and her family had given him a better understanding of the kinds of things she would sometimes say or do.

"Roan! That will not help."

Erik looked at Esta and shrugged his shoulders. "I am trying to understand, Esta. If you do not know who is dead or how they died, can you explain how it is that you know that someone has died? What can you see or feel that tells you what is happening there?"

Esta looked deep into Erik's eyes. Again, she needed to block his feelings out.

"It is a feeling, not like a guess. It is their feelings. I feel what they feel."

Roan was confused. "You know their thoughts?"

Esta shook her head. "No, not unless they are very strongly tied to their emotions. I feel strong emotions—sorrow, loss. I was hit by it, much of it, in different ways."

She looked at them but could feel the confusion that frustration brings. She held up her hand to still their questions. Pulling in a long steady breath, she closed her eyes for just a moment as she let it out.

"When I was young, I would suddenly feel joy or anger. As I grew, I found that anger and hate felt different. The anger of frustration, the anger of hurt feelings, the anger of jealousy—all of these feel different. Sorrows are many and come at many different levels and depths. Joy is very vast and complicated, and love is the strongest and the most fragile. Young people feel things deeply yet much more simply than adults do. They only know they hurt, that they are sad or happy or upset or frightened. Adults mix feelings together; those mixes tell me much. I have learned that hate can often mask love, jealousy, or desire. Anger can come with sorrow and loss. I can tell the difference between female and male emotions. I also can feel the emotions of other living things, mostly fear and contentment. I know when the fear will lead an animal to strike out in an effort to protect itself or its offspring. Animal emotions are also simple, very easy to read: contentment, hunger, fear, anger. Humans are much more complex."

Esta leaned back against the wall. They were looking at her, both of them, mouths hanging slack, questions whirling around them. She kept up her guard against them, not wanting to know how they felt about her now. She feared their disgust, their fear of her.

"You know everything we feel?" Erik was not sure he had her as figured out as he had thought.

"Not always. I can block it out." Esta looked at her hands.

"Good!" Roan blurted out. "Keep it that way. I don't want you in my head."

Again, Erik felt the urge to protect her rise in him, but this time, Esta stood her ground. She raised her head and looked Roan in the eye.

"I do not invade others' minds because I want to, Roan. Strong emotions come at me like waves upon the shore. I have no control over them, even when I wish not to know, when what they feel is directed at me. When what they feel is hate. When what they feel is anger over my very being. When they think me evil. When they feel nothing good within their soul. When I can only stand there and take it!" Esta stood and calmly walked out of the shelter.

Erik feared she would wander off or even go back to the village. He was about to stop her when she looked back through the door and told Erik, "Don't, I will not go far," and let the heavy-skinned flap fall over the entry.

Erik looked hard at Roan, who felt the weight of it.

"What?"

Erik shook his head. "I have had much trouble understanding you, Roan. When at first my father told me I was to take you out, I was angry. I only knew you as the ill-tempered son of the skinner."

Roan did not respond.

"After I spoke with your father, I felt sorry for you."

This brought Roan's eyes to Erik's. "Do not!" he said.

Erik shrugged. "I said I felt that way then, but when Esta and I found you here, you were different. You seemed ready to walk away from your father's house. You seemed more a man than at any time I have known you."

Roan was angry. "And because I do not want my thoughts and feelings known to anyone but myself, I am no longer a man?"

Erik sighed. "No, Roan. You are a man. The trouble I see is what kind of man you will choose to be. You carry anger like a stone around your neck. At times, when you sit and think, it weighs very little. But you keep trying to drag it up a mountain when it is at its largest, when it weighs heavy upon you. The entire world can see it. So, imagine how heavy it must weigh on her."

Roan was quiet. Erik had, whether he knew it or not, spoken the words of a mentor, as if he were someone who really cared. Roan found himself wanting to be angry even at that, angry at being talked to as if he needed help. He knew that there was nothing but truth in Erik's words.

Erik stood. "Remember how this began. Esta did not see or know what happened before she walked into the clearing. As she just told us, she feels our emotions, so she could only feel the emotions that were presented to her. She only felt your anger and your cob's fear. It was not her actions that caused you to stomp off, it was your own. You focused your anger on her to the point that she could feel your hatred. Ask yourself who it was that caused your cob to buck you off in the first place."

Erik left Roan to ponder and walked out into the woods to find Esta. Roan looked after him. He remembered well what had occurred, how he had angered Erik with his complaints that morning, how he had said that he liked a cob with a little spirit, not a docile old flea bag like Erik's. He had been full of conceit, wanting to make Erik feel as if he were less, his cob less, not worthy. Erik had pulled a switch off a tree as he'd ridden under it, and when they'd entered the clearing, he had swatted Roan's cob on its hind end, sending it bucking forward and Roan off into the dirt. Erik's laughter had rung out, and Roan had turned his embarrassment and anger onto the animal. Once he started down that road, he could never seem to bring himself back. He always went to the extreme. He knew he was often wrong. He knew his temper was much like his fathers. And he knew he hated that more than anything else, seeing his father within himself.

Erik had been right when he'd said that Roan had been different when they had found him at the shelter. When his father had turned him away, Roan had walked into the near woods blinded by hate. He'd walked into the woods fuming, plotting a way to prove himself to be a better man. When he'd gone to the shelter, he had decided that he would never return to his father's house. He'd even thought he might leave the island. He'd known in his heart that he was free from his father's rule, free from the constant feeling of disappointment. He'd begun to think of a future—a future that did not include Beor. The fear that had hit him at first had not lasted long, and a feeling of relief had washed over him. His mind began to race now. How would he survive? He thought he could start by making boots, wrapping weapons, and making leather scabbards and sheaths. He was good at that, and he enjoyed it. It was a trade. He could keep food upon his table. He began to ponder: Was he still free? Could he still leave this island if he wanted to?

Erik did not have to go far to find Esta. She sat in the clearing where he had ground tied the horses. Roan's cob had his nose in her face.

"Go on, now. You've had your pet." She gently pushed the horse away. He snickered and walked a few feet from her before putting his nose back to the ground, finding the slim remains of grass and clover.

Erik approached with caution, waiting for Esta to give him a wave or a nod of acceptance.

"There is a runoff creek close at hand," Erik said. "Would you walk with me to water the horses?"

Erik untied the cob and handed her the tether. She stood and followed without comment. As the two cobs drank and foraged on the sweet grass that grew near the stream, Erik tried to clear his mind. Esta gave a short chuckle.

"I see that is a useless task." His tone was teasing.

"You are worried. You cannot hide that. We all are. I fear for my family as much as you fear for yours." She was matter-of-fact about it.

It was true. Erik saw no reason to deny it. "Esta, how close do you need to be to ... to feel someone?"

His question puzzled her. "I don't know. I've never tracked that sort of thing." She looked at him, trying to see if he held judgment.

"But you felt the sorrow from the village all the way across the green?" Erik was trying to make her think, to put a distance to her gift.

Esta shook her head. "There were very strong emotions coming from the village, coming from many."

Erik nodded. That made sense. "What about people? Are there some people you can read better than others, like your parents?"

Esta looked up at him, eyes bright. "Yes! My parent's emotions are so familiar to me that I think I could feel them from a distance."

Erik nodded again. That was it, then. They would circle the village to Esta's home and see if she could pick anything up.

Roan sat in the clearing when they returned. Erik gave Esta a quick glance and caught the slightest movement of her head. It was alright.

"I am sorry, Esta. I took my anger out on you. I offer my apology, and I hope you will feel that it is true." Roan hung his head.

It was. She could feel it. He did mean it, even if he was still afraid of her. He also still carried much hurt and anger just below the surface, as always.

"I accept your apology, Roan. We are as one here. I am friend to you. Please believe that."

Erik wanted to ask her the full meaning of her words, but he knew they were meant only for Roan. He purposefully took the two horses to the far side of the clearing to tie them.

"I will try, Esta." Roan tried to smile at her.

"Can I tell you something? Something I fear you may not know?" She waited for his anger but found him only curious.

His eyes widened, and he nodded.

"You are not your father."

Roan's eyes snapped to hers. Esta held his gaze.

"You are much stronger than you think. Many people love you, even though you at times make it hard for them. Landen most of all. Your younger brother looks to you with admiration and looks to you for strength."

Roan's eyes had grown wide as Esta spoke to him, but it was the mention of his younger brother and sister that caused them to fill with tears. Hadwig was so young. She would not understand why he was gone. He suddenly realized that he had left them behind and what that would mean for them. They would be the focus of his father's anger now.

Esta felt his sudden fear and knew who it was for. "He will be alright. He has learned much by watching you. He knows how to handle your father."

She knew. She knew all about his hurt, his anger, his pain. Again, Roan had to push down the anger. Control it. "I hate him!"

She knew this was not entirely true yet understood. "Do not be angry, Roan. It is not your feelings that caused so much understanding. Your father's emotions are hard to block out. I have often had much admiration for how you and your family have … coped."

Roan laughed. "Coped. That was never how it felt. I know not what to say. Thank you, Esta." He paused in thought. "Thank you."

This time it was there, a true and honest emotion from Roan without fear or anger lurking behind it.

They waited for sunset. Knowing their island so well and having Mane to scout ahead helped. Once between the shelter and Esta's home, Mane gave a long warning screech. The three of them tucked themselves away in the dark and waited. Esta was held tight between them, Erik on one side, Roan on the other. Esta could feel their fear that they would not be able to protect her. It was strange to feel the need to protect her coming from Roan and Erik both. She was overwhelmed by it. The men who moved through the near woods on the well-worn path walked past them without so much as a glance in their direction.

Once they had passed and moved well out of earshot, Esta whispered, "It is me. They are looking for me." Her eyes were wide with fear.

"Why?" Erik asked. He tried to find her eyes in the dark, to turn her face toward the moon so that he could see her.

"I do not understand," she whispered.

Roan looked at the both of them. "We should move off the path. They are using it. We should go back."

"No." Esta was adamant. "I just need to get close enough. Then we may be able to learn something."

"Esta is right," Erik agreed. "Come, we need to keep moving."

"This way." Esta turned them off the path. "We will go to the back of the garden. The trees there are thick and the near woods close."

Erik nodded and let her lead the way. Roan kept a lookout behind them. Esta moved quickly though the near woods, Mane flying ahead, her white wings aglow in the moonlight. She was their guide.

Erik kept his eyes on Esta, the dark frame ahead of him. The moon came and went as they made their way through the trees. At last, Esta stopped. She turned her gaze through the trees, and Erik could just make out the large, dark shadow of the wheelhouse. There was a slight light coming from between the shutters.

"Esta?" Erik could not see her face.

"Shh." Esta held her hand up to silence him. "Stay … right … here." She pointed at his feet with each word. Erik knew he must obey.

She moved through the brush and into the garden. Erik felt his heartbeat quicken with fear for her. Suddenly she turned back toward him and waved him off, shaking her head. He got it. His strong feelings were not the ones they were looking for. He tried to breath, to calm his heart rate. She moved to a large tree and sank down out of sight. She sat at the base of the tree and closed her eyes. They could no longer see her.

"What is she doing?" Roan was at his side, staring hard at the tree. They both waited for movement.

The sliver of light from the crack between the shutters widened, and both Erik and Roan could clearly see the man in the window. He was angry, and his face showed it. He looked like one of the northern men that had started using their ships to take from others what their cold earth would not give them. Erik knew these men would not hesitate to kill. They were on a quest. What was it? Why Esta? The only violence Erik had ever seen had not happened on his island. Once, when traveling with his father, he had seen men like those here. They had been on the shore of Teris, and they had left little behind. They had taken free men as slaves and killed many without cause. But they had never come to Elvoy before. Not like this. Their peoples were much the same—farmers and tradesmen each just trying to live a free man's life. Elvoy had nothing that they could not find elsewhere. It also lacked much of what they were really after.

After only moments, the shutters were pulled shut. The warrior was gone. Erik's gaze was still fixated on the light when Roan stirred.

"She comes." He pointed.

Esta moved silently through the dark, back to where Roan and Erik stood waiting.

"Let us go. They are circling the house, waiting for me to come back. We need to move away."

Erik nodded and once again let Esta and Mane lead the three companions into the near woods and away from the house. He was surprised when a short time later they walked into the clearing where the horses were tied. Esta did not pause but walked past the cobs nibbling on grass and down the hillside to the shelter.

"Is it safe to light a fire?" Erik asked quietly.

"I think so. Mane will let us know if someone gets too close." Esta sent the owl to the trees above the shelter.

Roan was impatient as always. "What happened? Who was that?"

Erik heaved a sigh and turned on him. "Roan, the fire. Let us have light and warmth."

Roan was about to give Erik a piece of his mind, but Esta wanted no harsh words.

"It is alright. I'm trying to piece together my mother's feelings to form the story she was trying to tell me. Please, give me just a moment to think. Here"—Esta pulled several apples from the hood of her cloak—"eat."

Both boys grabbed for an apple; they were all hungry. Erik realized they had gone the day without eating.

Esta closed her eyes and pictured the feelings her mother had sent out to her. They were a message, of that there was no doubt. They were purposefully placed in order, some strong, some soft. Then the pattern would repeat. Again and again, Esta went through the pattern her mother had given her.

Love, new love, fresh like spring, new.

Sorrow, loss. Deep sorrow.

Love, binding love, loss.

Love, possessive love, control.

Love, freedom, soaring, love.

Erik and Roan watched closely. It was not until the overwhelming feelings of concern coming from the boys could not be ignored that she knew she had to stop. Erik had been fine with her concentration and silence until the tears began to stain her cheeks. He and Roan exchanged concerned glances but remained quiet. But the tears continued to come and with them, looks of pain. This, coupled with the fact that Esta had begun to tremble, and Erik had had enough. He was about to spring forward when Esta opened her eyes.

On her face was a look of sadness that only those who have experienced it can see. Erik was scared. He knew that look. He had seen it in his father's eyes, felt it within his own heart when his mother had died. Esta looked at him. She shook her head and tried to open her mouth so that the words would come, but all she managed was a sob.

Erik sprang across the center of the little hut and folded her into his arms. She wept, and Erik knew her pain.

It was his eyes she stared into when she tried to speak, not Roan's. Erik feared bad news, knowing that it was his father's job to protect the village. He had no doubt that Dirk would fight.

Roan felt fear as well, for Esta would not meet his eye. He sat awkwardly with his eyes cast down and his hands in his lap. He was grateful for an excuse to heap more wood upon the fire when it ebbed. It allowed him to turn his back on both the sorrow and the closeness he saw in the two of them.

Esta tried more than once to calm her breathing, gather herself together. Both times she tried to put words together and immediately fell into another set of sobbing tears.

Erik tried to ease her pain. "Who, Esta? Can you tell me who?"

Esta sobbed again at the knowledge that Erik could tell she had suffered a loss based on her reaction. She pulled in a deep, steady breath. Then another, and another. The trembling eased, and her breathing slowed. No more short gasps of air. Erik sat back, pulling himself away from her. She sat with her eyes cast down, and her hands pulled at her apron to wipe her face.

"My father is gone. They have my mother …" She could not finish.

"Do you know who they are?"

Esta shook her head. "No, only that my mother wants me to flee."

"Flee where?" Roan asked, still there though they had both all but forgotten his presence.

"My mother's thoughts were very clear, very purposeful. She knew I would come. She kept the pattern simple, and she kept repeating it over and over and over again." Esta began to tear up once more.

"What was the message, Esta? What did she want you to understand?"

Esta was so overwhelmed by her own grief she could feel nothing else.

Roan handed her a cup of steaming tea. "Here, drink this. Then tell us everything, Esta. How you know that your mother's message was to flee."

Erik again wanted to verbally punish Roan for his lack of couth. He also wanted to understand how Esta had found meaning from random emotions.

Esta swallowed hard, the tea was so hot that it burned her all the way down on the first sip. She tried to hold on to that feeling. It was better than where her true emotions were taking her.

"You have to understand that I know my mother well, how she talks, how she puts her emotions in order. We have communicated like this before."

Erik and Roan sat back, waiting for her to gather herself.

"First there was love and the newness of spring. This is Erik. Then there was loss and sorrow. Since Erik only has his father ..."

Erik nodded. The only person he had left to feel loss or sorrow for would be his father. "Go on."

"Then love, a blinding love. That kind of love means husband or wife. And since it was my mother's feelings of great sorrow, it would mean my father." Esta closed her eyes and pushed through the urge to sob once more. "Things changed then, she wanted me to feel the next emotions more urgently, she pushed them. Again there was the feeling of love, but not the good kind. Possessive and controlling. A desire to have. This was focused hard at me. Then I felt freedom, flight, soaring freedom like what a bird would feel, like what I have told her Mane feels when she flies above the trees."

Erik was beginning to make sense of it. "Someone seeks you out to have you, control you. They must know of your gift. So, she wants us to seek freedom."

Esta only nodded.

Roan was confused. "Why?"

Erik was suddenly frightened for her. His sudden shift of emotion hit her, and she looked up at him, eyes red and swollen with tears. He tried to pull back his feelings, but he knew this could be very serious for the entire village.

"Whoever they are, they know somehow of Esta's gift for knowing what people are feeling. They seek you out, Esta, for their own gain. They are here to take you away. They mean to control you."

Esta was also beginning to understand the meaning behind her mother's warning. "Those people, our fathers, they have died because of me." As she said it, the full weight of its truth hit her. Her breathing began to speed up, and new tears began to spill.

Roan knew as well that this was strange. "How would anyone know of her when even the village had no idea, only wild guesses made with no real knowledge? They just think of her as odd."

Again, a statement from Roan that Erik found offensive. "Roan!"

Esta shook her head. "'Tis true, Erik. What is there to know, and of what value could it be?" Roan's statement had not offended her; he only spoke as he felt.

"Esta, even you are not so naive that you cannot see the value of your gift?' Erik said, looking at her. He could see she was puzzled. She truly did not understand. "Esta, people are ruled by their emotions. A warlord would have a great advantage with you by his side."

And there it was—more truth than either Erik or Esta was prepared for. Erik suddenly realized why the council had pushed him to seek Esta as his bride, why his father and Esta's father would spend long hours talking while forcing the children to see each other frequently. Erik had watched Esta grow up, listening to his father often praise her for what a remarkable and beautiful young woman she was becoming. They had been groomed to be together. A town's peacekeeper would also do very well with someone like Esta by his side. Had he been manipulated into wanting her? Manipulated into loving her? Did it matter?

Erik had to admit that he had begun to have feelings for Esta even before she began to resemble a woman. He loved her honesty and her wild spirit. He loved her because of who she was, not because his father pointed out what the whole world could already see. The fact, however, was there: in the eyes of the council, Esta was an asset to be placed where they felt she would benefit them most, where they felt her gift would be best used. Used—that was exactly what was to happen to her. She would be used. If Erik could not find a way to stop it, he would lose her.

"We have to find out what is happening in the village, find a way to get Esta out of here."

Roan cut Erik off. "We cannot go into the village. They will cut you down, Erik, just as I am sure they did your father. You know that!"

The words cut deep. There was no time, no room for sorrow, not when they were all in such danger. Erik knew it was true, yet he was at a loss to know what to do. They could try to stay hidden, but really it was only a matter of time before someone found the shelter.

Roan's mind was reeling. "I think I know a way."

Esta could feel his emotions hitting her. It was not the anger or the fear that she expected. It was freedom. She was confused by it. A longing for freedom while gathering respect.

"My father's boat. It is empty and at the end of the lee."

Erik shook his head. "I am sure they are guarding the lee. We would never make it to the boat."

Roan nodded. "Not on land. I may not be a good horseman, Erik, but I can swim."

Esta looked up frightened. "No! I cannot swim, Erik. I fear the water."

Roan held up his hand to calm her. "Not you, Esta. Just me. I could slip out to the boat and then make sure that I am seen getting away. They will think you are making a run for it."

"You cannot outrun them, Roan. Their boats are swift; they have many men at the oar. They would overtake you."

Roan shook his head. "No, they would not, because their ships are heavy, and they rely on the men to row. I would go with the wind. They have been outrun many times before."

Both Esta and Erik were confused.

"My father's boat is small and light. The sails move the boat very quickly through the water. It was built for speed. I can move to the island passages. They cannot follow me through the gap. Their boats are too big, too long to shoot the gaps like I can. They will need more than one boat to go around and try to cut me off."

Esta looked at Roan. "You think they will leave the island to chase the boat because they will think I am on it?" She did not like the idea of putting Roan in danger.

"How do we make them believe Esta is on the boat?" Erik looked to Roan. "And what happens to you when they catch up with you?"

Roan smiled. "They will not catch me. The question is, How much time do you need to prepare for them? How long do I keep them moving before I bring them back?"

"Bring them back?" Esta was shocked.

Erik, however, understood. "Even if I could manage to free our people, and even if I could gather some sort of defense of the island, again Roan, how do we make them believe that Esta is on the boat?" Erik was still not sure what Roan had in mind.

"Mane." Esta looked up with conviction. "They know about her. If Mane follows the boat out to sea, they will believe I am aboard. That is how I know they were looking for me before. Every time they caught a glimpse of Mane, I could feel their desire to find her take over. They became excited."

Erik believed this as well. "Will she do it?"

"I don't know. I think I can convey the need to stay with Roan. Once she realizes that she is out over the water, I do not know how far she will go. She may turn back. I do not know."

"We have to try. There is no other way to get them off the island." Roan was sure it would work.

"I am not half as worried about how to get them off as I am about what to do when they come back!" Erik said seriously.

"You keep saying that. Back?" Esta said. She did not understand.

"I can keep them out for a while. If I can make it to the mainland, I can hide out, blend in. They have no knowledge of me, and they will only look for so long. To be honest, I do not think I could stay ahead of them in open water." Roan knew the risk he was taking. He also knew the speed and strength of his father's boat. It was built for fast, covert travel between the islands.

"Somehow we must overpower those that are left behind. We can then gather and prepare for those who follow Roan out to sea." Erik pondered.

Roan looked sideways at Esta. "It will not be easy. We have no way of knowing how many men they will leave here."

"If they feel there is a chance at all that Esta is not upon the boat, they may not send their full complement." Erik said, wanting a solid plan.

Esta smiled. "Then we will have to make sure they believe I am aboard, and I think I have a way to help with that."

Erik looked at her. Her eyes were still glistening with tears, her face full of grief. Yet now, her jaw was set with determination. The planning took hours. Once Esta explained her idea, things moved along quickly. Roan and Erik stuffed one of Erik's shirts with grass and leaves and then found a long stick to ram down through the neck hole. The stick, which had taken several hours to find, had a round burl at the top to which Esta began to attach the hair. Erik had cringed as he'd watched Esta cut the tail from his cob. The color was a creamy gold, and once brushed out, it looked to be a woman's head as seen from behind. Esta's own hair was much more of a golden red than the creamy blond, but there were only a few who would be able to see the difference. These men had never laid eyes on her. Once on board the little ship, Roan would prop the dummy up and make a run for it. It would appear as if a girl with long, golden hair sat at the prow looking out to sea.

The three of them had sat up late making their plans. Twice Mane had let out warning cries and flown off low over the trees to lead whoever sought them away. Esta knew it was only a matter of time before they found the little hut, well hidden though it was. When Erik finally suggested that they get a few hours of sleep before they set their plans in motion, Esta was so exhausted she did not even have the strength to cry herself to sleep. Only a few tears escaped before she was out. When Erik gently woke her in the predawn hours, she could only remember the image of her parents in her dreams. Her heart was heavy, yet she was determined to save her mother. For the moment, that was outweighing her grief.

Roan was waiting, his cob loaded with the dummy and some food Esta had been able to gather for him in the near woods—a few roots and berries that they all knew would not last long. Mane had returned from an early morning flight with a rabbit, and Esta happily roasted the meat over a small fire. They ate thankfully. This would be the last cooked meal Roan would eat until he returned. He suddenly found himself feeling ashamed of his fear of the animal.

Making their way down to the sea was tricky. There seemed to be more men wandering the near woods. Mane flew off several times and then returned low through the trees, only to again fly off high above the treetops in plain sight. Erik knew that Esta was somehow communicating with her, keeping the way clear. At the edge of the near woods, they stopped to examine the boats moored at the long poles. The morning mist lay thick on the water. The poles stood dark against the white drifts, the masts and hulls of the cogs rising and falling with the current. The water would be frigid. Yet Esta could feel no fear from Roan.

There were two men on the rocky shore sitting near a small fire. They would need to move these men quickly into the near woods to give Roan his chance to slip into the water. They had planned for this. Erik pulled his large bladder bag off the back of his shorn cob. Esta caught the flash of regret he felt for his cob's beautiful tail. It was short lived and passed quickly to worry for Roan. Inside the bladder was the stuffed shirt. Now Roan would strip down and place his clothing in the bladder as well. He would ease down the bank when the men were distracted and would swim out to the moored boat, pulling with him the knotted burl with the long, golden hair. Once aboard, Roan would dress and cut the tether. He could then set up the dummy and head out to sea. It would look as if he and Esta were aboard. The warriors upon the beach would sound the alarm to let those in the village know of Esta's escape. If everything went their way, the men would then load their boats and give chase.

FOUR

Break Away

sta rode into the near woods upon Erik's cob. She would wait for his signal as he passed, hopefully being chased by the two guardsmen from the beach. As soon as Erik passed, Esta would then send Mane to Roan. Mane would fly right over their heads and out to sea. The men would then see the boat, Roan, and the dummy, and if Mane did well, they would have little doubt that Esta was onboard the ship and getting away.

This would be the tricky part. The day before and well into the night, Esta had worked on sending Mane to Roan, as well as working with Roan on how to receive her so that she would stay. She had given Roan her leather shoulder strap. This was where they hoped Mane would land. Roan could give her a treat and get ahold of the tether to hold Mane with him long enough to fool the warriors but not so long that Mane could not make it back to the island.

Esta waited now in a thick stand of trees in the near woods with a view of the path. She watched the little piece of dirt she could see closely for the hooves of Roan's cob. Erik would ride past quickly, and Esta would have little time to react. Mane had to pull the attention off of Erik and onto the boat leaving the lee, both for Erik to escape and for their plan to work.

The water was freezing. Roan had made the swim out to the little ship before. He had hidden there many times from his father's anger.

Now as he climbed over the bow, he had a different feeling. It was not fear; it was freedom. He was free, for the first time. Free of his father's rule, his father's fists, and his father's words.

He lay shivering and began to pull his dry clothes from the bladder. He wrapped himself in his cloak and pulled his leggings on. He heard a rustling behind him in the prow and spun round, ready to fight. There, crawling out from the shadow of the prow, was Landen.

"Roan!" Landen launched himself into Roan's arms.

"Landen? How did you get here?" Roan pulled the boy back to look at him. His clothes were damp and his skin pale. "You swam out here? What were you thinking?" Roan pulled the cloak from his shoulders and wrapped it around Landen. He quickly pulled the rest of his clothes on and leaned over the prow to cut the lines. The boat began to drift toward the mouth of the eddy, toward the sea. He pulled the shirt and cobs tail from the bladder and looked toward the shore over the wall of the boat. He looked for the owl, for Mane.

"What is that?" Landen picked up the hair of the horse's tail, all brushed out and braided.

"Landen, stay down! It is to fool them so they follow me. Listen, do you think you can make the shore if I glide the boat close at the eddy?"

Landen looked angry. "I am not going back!" Landen's eyes began to fill with tears. He could barely get the words out. "He told them how they could find her. He pointed Carrick out to them. They tried to make him talk, tell them where they could find her. He would not do it. Father killed him. I saw it! He is evil, Roan. He is helping them!"

"Mama?" Roan questioned.

"She is locked away with the others and little Hadwin." Landen looked down.

Now Roan's anger began to mount. He had to fight the urge to swim ashore and hunt down his own flesh and blood. For the first time in his life, Roan was not afraid of his father. He actually wanted a confrontation, a fight. Just then, a loud screech echoed above his head, and Landen nearly jumped out of his skin. Mane landed on the edge of the prow.

"Here, put this on your head and stand at the prow! Quick!"

Landen looked at the large bird in fear.

"Landen! Now!"

Within moments, the sail was up, and the warriors watched as a girl with long, golden hair, her owl on her shoulder, slipped away out to sea.

From her hiding place on shore, Esta could feel Roan's anger. She also knew that he was not alone, for Landen's fear of Mane was strong and clear as the bird clutched onto his shoulder a bit more tightly than was necessary. A noise behind her caused her heart to skip a beat as Erik appeared with Roan's cob in tow.

"I knew I would find you here," Erik scolded.

"I had to make sure Mane stayed put."

Esta pointed, and Erik gazed out across the bay.

"It looks human. It's working!" he said, pointing toward the ships. "They are already loading to go after them. And Look! They are coming down to the bay." Erik pointed toward the village and then smiled at her.

"It is human!" Esta said. "It is Landen. He is wearing the cob's tail. Roan is not alone." She was worried.

"How?"

"I'm not sure, but Roan is very angry."

Erik huffed. "What's new?"

Esta turned on him. "No, Erik, I mean very angry. He wants to kill his father!"

Erik was taken back. "You can tell that? Why?"

"I do not know. I feel it. And it is my fault." Esta shook her head and stilled Erik's response. "This time it is true, Erik. I feel it!"

"Come, we need to be out of sight. We will wait till dark and then see what can be done."

Erik turned and walked into the near woods. Esta took one last look at the bay. The warriors were indeed setting out upon their longboats in pursuit. Roans little sail was barely visible now. She turned to follow Erik back to the little hut.

Erik put the horses near the creek, built a small fire, and placed a kettle over the flames all without a word. Esta broke the long silence.

"I wonder how Landen came to be upon the boat."

"My guess is that he was hiding there. Perhaps from the warriors"—he paused—"or his father." He'd placed too much emphasis on that last word. Even Erik felt its sting.

"Erik, I—"

"No, stop, Esta. I am sorry. I am. We have much to do, and there is no room for foolishness. Nor for grief."

Esta did not like the feelings of guilt coming from him. "You are not foolish. There is no way of knowing who has been lost, Erik. Roan's father will do whatever he can to survive. He is not a good man. His thoughts have always been dark! It was my fault. I should have said something long before." She began to tear up.

"I had no right to get angry over it. I am sorry Esta. We all knew what he was. What he is."

He held out his hand to her, and she took it. Erik's feelings were so deep and strong that Esta had to block the intensity in order to think.

"We are alone, Erik, and I am frightened." She looked at him. He was also afraid, yet his fear was for Esta, not for himself.

"We are never alone as long as we have each other. I will not let them hurt you, Esta. I swear it!"

Erik leaned forward and kissed her forehead. Esta had to fight the urge to lift her chin and meet his lips with her own. Blushing, she turned her attention to filling their mugs with the tea. Warm and soothing as it was, it did little to assuage their hunger. As the sun went down, Esta began to worry about Mane. As it turned out, though, she had little time to worry overmuch, as she felt Mane's arrival even before they heard her announce herself. Esta stepped outside as Mane landed on the roof peak above the door. Dangling from her talons was a small leather satchel. Erik quickly cut the cord, and the bag fell into his hands. Mane flew down to Esta's shoulder, and she untied the cord as they stepped back into the warmth of the shelter.

The leather bag held two fish. Erik laughed aloud when he upended the satchel and spilled them out onto the floor. They had been cleaned and were ready to be cooked. Esta could read the feelings of pride in

Mane. She knew the food was needed, and she had allowed Roan to tether her to the bag.

"Thank you, Mane." Esta stroked the bird's head, and it clicked and snapped its proud response.

"I think I have underestimated Roan. How do you find time to fish when you are running for your life?" Erik smiled.

"They must be safe if they have time for this. I mean, they must be out of danger." Esta wanted to believe it.

As much as Erik wanted to say yes, he knew his feelings would belie his words.

"Roan was positive he could out run the longboats. He has a much better understanding of the wind and the waves than I do. We can only hope that he was right." Erik put the fish on the skewer and hung them over the flames. The smell of the cooking fish was too much for Mane, and she made it known to Esta she wanted out of the hut. Esta and Erik ate the fish in grateful silence. Then Esta took the heads, bones, and skin and boiled them in water. She then strained the contents out so that they could drink the broth. They would need every bit of the nutrition and energy the fish could give.

In the predawn hours, Erik tapped Esta on the shoulder. "We should go. It is early. We have time to reach your home before daylight. If need be, we also have enough time to return."

Esta nodded. If her home was still under guard, how many would there be? Erik was certain they would leave enough men behind to hold the village but hoped he could overpower them, one guard at a time.

Esta stepped into the apple grove and listened. The house was dark, and there was no smoke coming from the chimney. Fear began to mount in her, as she could not find her mother's emotions, her mother's presence, in the house. Erik came up behind her and placed his hand upon her shoulder.

"Nothing. I feel nothing. It is empty." She began to walk forward, but Erik stopped her.

"Let me. I will sweep the house and make sure it is safe for you to enter."

Esta knew what he meant. She could feel his fear that he would find her mother within the house. Her heart began to speed up as she tried to keep a read on Erik's emotions. With careful, quiet footsteps, he made his way through her home. There was nothing.

Esta looked in her parents' room. She hoped to see some sign left by her mother, but everything sat just as it was before. She went to her own room and pulled a leather satchel from under the bed. She placed her warm wool cloak, heavy woolen stockings, and other extra clothing inside it. In the kitchen, she found Erik eating a chunk of dry bread while putting other food supplies in his pack. Esta picked up a small barrel and walked out to the garden. She filled it with tubers, carrots, onions, and apples, trying hard to fight the feelings of anger and confusion. It was as if they were taking from her family, as if she were stealing from her own home. She did not like it, quietly moving about like a thief.

They began to slowly walk back to the hut, crisscrossing the path so that they could not be tracked. Once back at the shelter, Erik tried to comfort her.

"There was no sign of a struggle, Esta. No trace of blood or a sign that would tell me that Clare had come to any harm there."

Esta smiled at him. "I do not feel her loss. I think I would feel it. I believe she is alive."

Erik nodded. "We will wait the day out and then go to the edge of the near woods by the village green."

Esta nodded. She feared the green. She had been slammed by the grief and loss of so many there, and it had nearly knocked her off her feet. She had no desire to feel that again. But she also knew they must visit the green to get a good look at the village. They needed a plan. The only way to get one was to go take a look at what they were facing.

The day passed all too quickly for Esta. As soon as the sun began to sink behind the trees of the near woods, they set off for the green, snaking their way through the sheltered light of the trees to the edge of the village.

Erik peered through the brush. The green was empty, as was every roundhouse he could see. No light came from the shuttered windows, no smoke from the chimneys. Esta walked up to his side, eyes wide trying to see any sign of life.

"Are they there?" Erik said softly.

"Yes," Esta whispered. "It is strange. There is fear, worry. But something else is there now—anger and bravery. I think the men are planning something. There are not many guards, but the council doors are barred, and they are frightened." Esta drew in a gasp of fear. "Fire! Erik, if they anger their captors, they mean to set the council house on fire!" She looked worried. "My mother is in there."

"How many, Esta?" Erik looked at the council house.

"Four, maybe five? Other's sleep, I think. Three. They are angry, annoyed at being left behind. They wonder when their people will return for them. One is not stable. He wishes to burn them. He would like to do it." Esta shivered at the thought.

Erik looked at the green. The council house sat near the last cottage before the green. It was large and set deep into the earth. This massive roundhouse was only used when the entire village came together. The village council would be seated at the long table in the center of the floor. The rest of the village would sit on the tiered slabs of earth that encircled the council below. Here was their most sacred place. Marriages, mournings, and council meetings took place here, as well as celebrations for the harvest. It was also where punishment was dealt out to those who needed it. The council's rulings were final and had always seemed to Esta to be just.

"We need to get close enough to see." Erik looked to Esta for guidance.

"If we circle the edge of the green, we can get closer without being seen."

Esta followed Erik as they began to skirt the green. She could feel the nerves of the men inside the council house growing tense. They seemed to be anticipating something.

"They are getting restless," Esta whispered. "I feel their unease, a feeling of growing tension."

Erik pointed at the guard in front of the council house. There were several men that could be seen there near the large wooden doors. In front of the doors, wood had been stacked, and oil bladders sat near torches on the ground. A fire burned near the green, and the remaining guard slept there on the ground.

"If the villagers try to bust their way through those doors, they will be burned alive." Esta's breath came in short gasps of fear.

"Esta, if you are seen, they will give chase. If you lead them away, I can clear the door and let our men out." Erik could see the fear in her eyes. "They are on foot. Get back to the near woods. You can circle around the green; we will be ready for them. Use Mane to gain ground when you need it. She can pull them off or confuse them about your direction. You are fast, Esta. I have seen it."

Esta knew she was fast. She also knew that Erik would have to fight his way to the council-house doors and that she would not know if he was alright until she returned, whether that would be on her own or as their prisoner she did not know.

Esta circled back toward where the two of them had entered the green. She left Mane on a low branch of a tree and got down on all fours to crawl out onto the open field. She moved slowly, lying flat on the ground waiting. She was still as she could be when a guard scanned the green. She judged her distance from the guard as well as the distance back to the near woods. She knew the near woods better than most, having spent so much time there with Mane. It was darkening, but that mattered little, as Esta knew that Mane could lead her through the woods easily. She whistled and stood. Mane let out an extremely loud screech and flew the distance between them to land upon her shoulder.

Erik was right! The men shouted, pointing at her with shock and fright. That did not stop them. The men surrounding the council chambers ran. Pointing to the edge of the green. Esta stood stock-still, staring at them, daring them to come for her. She could hear them yelling orders at one another and looked around for others to appear. Suddenly, four of the men began to walk forward. Too few.

Esta laughed aloud and yelled, "You had better do better than that!"

The men stopped and looked back. They were quickly joined by another and began to trot toward her. She turned with another loud laugh that sounded strange and foreign, as if pulled from her by force, and ran for the woods. They were slow to enter the near woods after her, thinking it could be a trap. Once they believed that she was alone, though, they gave chase. She could hear the men behind her and allowed them to catch a glimpse of her now and then, keeping them just close enough to give them confidence and far enough back for her to be safe from their grasp. Each time she felt they were about to give up, she would show herself and give them hope. She even pretended to fall down at one point. It was a foolish idea that nearly caused her to be caught, but Mane flew at the nearest man's face with a loud shriek, and Esta scrambled back onto her feet and disappeared once more.

Erik had filled a large bucket with water. Once the guard had disappeared into the woods, he ran the distance from the well to the council house and threw the water over the torches that burned near the doors. He yelled for the men inside to bust out and began to defend himself against the two guards that remained. With their attention turned to the green, they had not realized Erik was behind them until he had put out the flames and shouted to those inside. A third man came toward them from the far side of the wheelhouse, and Erik knew he could not hold his own against three. He was already losing ground against two. The third man, however, went straight for the doors, trying to hold them closed against the weight of those inside. When he shoved his blade through the small opening, Erik heard a cry of both pain and anger. The doors burst open, and the village men spilled forward and into the fight. Erik suddenly had help.

Two of the villagers were cut down before the guard holding the door was tackled to the ground and disarmed. One of the villagers quickly tossed the guards sword to a man named Hondeer, who had much skill with a blade. He quickly joined Erik, managing to pull the two invaders who had been attacking Erik apart, and give both Erik and Hondeer a better shot at taking them down. Seeing the numbers grow, the men coming toward them, the invader fighting Hondeer turned on his heels and began to run. The other guard, a massive man with a topknot of thick black hair and a scared face was not so willing to give up. He was armed and well skilled. The massive invader fought with Erik as though his life depended upon killing him, for he indeed thought that it did. The men from the village had formed a circle around Eric as he fought, not wanting to get too close to the swinging blades that clashed and rang with every blow. The circle of villagers began to tighten, inch by inch, step by step. Intending to overpower the hulking invader with numbers alone. Taking a step back from Erik, the topknotted invader wheeled around and made one sweeping cut at the men who approached. Erik cried out, warning them to stay back as he lunged forward to engage once again. Erik's two-handed sword was nearly forty inches in length, handed down for generations and strong as its wielder. Erik's overhead blow came down upon the man with such force that he staggered backward and into the hands of the waiting villagers. Though the men were unarmed, they were strong and brave from years of hard island life. The sheer number of village men was enough to overwhelm the guard that had been left behind.

Erik threw his blade into the hands of one of the village elders. He yelled that Esta would return at any moment with the other warriors hot on her heels. The village men began to arm themselves with whatever they could find—rakes, hoes, sticks, and the knives and swords taken from the three guards who sat tied to one another on the ground—all, that is, but one, who lay motionless.

One of the younger boys yelled that he knew where the weapons had been tossed. He led several men around the council house to the smithy, where the village weapons had been stacked neatly in a pile.

The door of the council house stood wide open, and there was not a soul in sight apart from Erik when Esta ran across the green toward him. He stood alone, his sword in his hand, still gleaming with the blood of the fallen man. When the men chasing Esta reached the center of the green, they realized what they were looking at. Their compatriots were tied up or dead, the doors were open, and their prisoners were gone. The female that their lord and master had come for was standing beside the one responsible. Blind furry seemed to drive them forward.

Erik had been clear with his orders. These men were skilled killers, and the villagers needed to be prepared to take them quickly. Erik wanted at least five village men to every one of theirs.

"Kill quickly," he'd told them. "No mercy, or we will bury more of our own, do you hear me! They will not stop! They will not surrender. You must end them as quickly as you can!"

The men in the village had had little need to carry their weapons on a daily basis. Most of them had been unarmed when the raiders came; the weapons had been found in their homes.

The actual battle was very short, yet three of the villagers were killed. Esta and her mother clung to each other. Many in the village were confused as to how and why there was only a small number of warriors left of the island. Four of the ten council members were dead, as well as Erik's father, the blacksmith, and the blacksmith's oldest son, who had used weapons that hung on the wall of their forge to fight off the attack. A couple farmers who were caught off guard while working in their fields had been injured, and one of the dead was a woman. Surprised by the death of a woman, Erik had asked why she'd been killed. It was the skinners wife. She had refused to yield to the order for all to gather in the council house and slapped and spit upon her husband, who then stabbed her. This was unfathomable to Erik. This woman had once confided in his father that Beor was manageable as long as things were going well. Erik remembered how his father had asked her if she wanted Beor banished from the island. He had left her with a black eye and what Dirk had suspected to be broken or bruised ribs, yet the woman had shaken her head. He was not someone to be banished, she had said. She'd felt that it would only invite more trouble. He would calm, and then he would set out to sea in his boat for a few days. When he returned things would be normal again, until the next time he became angry. Dirk had tried to tell her that nothing about her situation was "normal." But she was a proud woman, and she did not want to think about what would become of her and her children if they lost their home. Erik found himself looking around for Roan and Landen's sister. He spotted her sitting huddled in the arms of Clare at the feet of her mother's body. The woman was covered with a dark cloak, yet Erik could see her. A vision of the woman's face, of Roan's face, flashed in his mind. This would be Roan's undoing, for Erik knew that Roan would now very purposefully try to kill his father. He was already so angry and had such a hard time keeping that anger in control. How would he deal with the loss of his mother at his father's hands?

Esta could not contain the tears. She felt she was responsible for this. It was her fault that all these people had died, and she did not understand why.

The dead were gathered into one house to be honored later. There was not a soul who wanted to return to the council house, but a meeting was needed to put all the pieces together and to make a plan. The remaining council members were visibly shaken. It was Erik who pulled the group together. He quieted the crowd and stepped before the council. Erik stressed the importance of readying the bay for some sort of defense. He explained how Roan and Landen had led the others away, how they would at some point return. Members of the council talked about how the boats had come into the bay at daybreak and how they had been met with supplies and an offer of safe harbor. Everything had seemed fine until they'd reached the heart of the village and begun to ask questions about Esta. The council had tried to protect both Esta and Clare— they were valued members of the community—but the leader had been determined to find the "witch child" he had been told about. They had heard of a girl who could read men's minds, even cause men to do her bidding. They'd heard that this witch could also speak to animals, and they would obey her commands. The council had tried to dismiss the stories as silly misunderstandings; a young woman with a pet owl was far from a witch. That was when the skinner had gotten involved. He'd shouted that the council should not protect Esta. He'd backed up the claim that Esta was a witch and had spoken to the leader as if he knew him. Beor had called the leader by name, even though he had not arrived at the green until after the man had introduced himself as Lord Guth from Land's End. Beor had offered to take them to her. It had been at that point that Erik's father had gotten involved and a fight had broken out. Angry at Beor's readiness to hand over a child and accuse that child of being something dark and evil, he had tried to use his position against Beor. Erik's father and an elder had been killed in the fray, and everyone had then been herded into the council house. Some had tried to run, but in the end, everyone had been rounded up and placed inside. At that point, a small group of men had headed out for Esta's farm.

It was too much. Esta could no longer stand it. So many feelings were directed at her and her alone: fear, anger, hate. Some villagers were worried for both their own safety and hers. Others hated her for bringing this upon them. Others blamed her for their losses and feared that they would never be allowed to live again on Elvoy in peace. The weight of the blame and hatred began to pull her under. There were just as many who feared for her, but it was lost in the blame.

She whispered into her mother's ear, "I should go with them. This is my fault."

Erik spun around to face her. She had thought that only her mother could hear her. He was angry. She caught the emotion strongly; it was mixed with his consistent love and worry for her.

"Do not say that!" Erik did not whisper. In fact, he held his arms up for silence and turned slowly until a hush had fallen over the villagers.

"You all, every one of you, owe your life to Esta in some way. She has saved this village from plague, and saved you from each other! She has lost as you have lost. Carrick was an important member of the council. My father would be ashamed of you all for letting your fear turn into a selfish wish for someone else to suffer in your place! This village has never needed someone to tell us to look out for one another before. Now you would turn your backs on Esta to save yourselves?" Erik turned to the remaining council now. "And I tell you this, they have found a village to pick clean, and pick it they will! They will not stop at Esta! Your daughters will never be safe. They will return to this village whether Esta is still here or not!"

The oldest member of the council stood. Erik saw all eyes shift to the man behind him. He turned, ready to fight even the council if necessary. It was Alden. His eyes were bright as if they held the secrets of the ages.

He'd come to Elvoy as a child slave to a Viking warrior. When the warriors had left, they'd left without their little slave, who had hidden away in the near woods. He'd never asked anyone for help, never made himself a burden upon anyone in the village, and had quickly become a man who was both respected and honored. Now in his old age, he spoke quietly but with much conviction.

"Esta is a gift to this village, as was her mother before her. They both still remain the healers of our sick, the givers of our young. Esta did not ask for our island to be set upon. She has never left this island. It is her birthplace, as it was many of yours. Someone—I believe we can all guess who it was—has told others about her. They have told others a tale of what they may believe, but they have no true understanding. There are not many among you who have not needed one of these women at some time. I am willing to fight these men not only for Esta. I fight them for all of us." Alden looked down the line of the council table at the empty seats and at those who remained. "Erik is right. Giving these men anything they seek will only guaranty their return. We need to become a bigger problem than we are worth."

Erik breathed; his shoulders seemed to lower as he let the air out. The councilors looked at each other. With Dirk gone, they were not sure of who to place in charge of their defense. But Dirk had been training Erik to take his place for years. They knew he would do what Dirk would have done. They would place their faith in that.

"It is up to you Erik. What would you have us do?" Kelvin, the youngest of the elders motioned for Erik to continue.

Erik nodded. He turned his back to the council. "I need the women to go and gather all the weapons from your homes and anything that could be used as a weapon as well. Bring it all back here. Men, gather your cobs and your carts. We will meet at the beach. We must make it difficult for them. They need to see that they will meet resistance. We want them to feel fear upon coming into the harbor. Get to the beach as soon as possible."

FIVE

Shooting the Gap

As much as Roan was worried about Landen, he was glad he was there. They had remained just out of reach of the longships, but try as they might, they could not shake them. Roan knew it was only a matter of time before they would be overtaken. He was ready to try something different. If he could slide between two of the islands at just the right time, he could shake the boats, and they would have to go around the island to catch them again. He could skirt the heavy currents and get back to Elvoy a good half a day ahead of the longships. Erik and Esta had packed some supplies for Roan's run, but the rations had been enough for Roan alone. With Landen aboard, they had been shared and were nearly spent. It was dangerous to shoot the gap. His father had only done it once to escape a Viking slave ship. Those days were gone, now that the settlements of Viking warriors had spread out into other communities. These warriors who followed them were not Vikings, but who they were and where they came from was a mystery. Their boats were something Roan had never seen before—part Viking longboat, part sailing ship. They were fast and agile.

Roan would shoot the gap at dawn. If his calculations were correct, he could ride the incoming tide right between the small islands and come out the other side with a straight shot at Elvoy and the wind at his back. When dawn broke, Roan was greeted with an unwelcome sight. The longships had closed in during the night. They were so close that both boys could hear the call of the oarsman. Both Landen and Roan put out oars to help keep a distance between the head boat and themselves. The waters became choppy, and the wind picked up, filling the sail and pushing the small boat toward the white, churning water of the gap. Suddenly, a flaming arrow streaked past Landen's head.

"They aim for our sail!" Roan bellowed.

The white water of the gap began to pull and push at the boat. Roan pulled his oars in to man the rudder and screamed rowing instructions to Landen trying to keep the boat in the middle of the gap. The rocky shores closed in on them as the gap became narrow. With the gap narrowing, the current increased, and Roan looked back to see all the longships pulling back to avoid the pull. All, that is, but one. They were sending a ship on. *Crazy,* Roan thought. It was a risk just taking the small sailboat through the gap. The longboat was too heavy; it would sit low in the water and would surely hit the rocks if it turned sidelong in the current. Roan could only keep his eyes forward and throw his body weight into the rudder. He strained against the current to keep the small sailboat between the jagged cliffs.

Landen followed the bellowed directions as best he could. "Left, left!" Roan would scream out, and Landen would dig the right oar into the rough water. Roan let out a cry as he saw Landen's right oar come into contact with the cliff. It snapped, and Landen screamed as the paddle end came back at them. But they were through, riding the waves out of the gap and into the open water. Landen fell back breathing deep as if he had been holding his breath. Roan, however, had turned and stood. He stared back at the gap and the longship. The oars on the longboat jutted in and out, trying to avoid the rocks. Roan could not believe it, but he started to think that they just might make it. Then it happened. In nearly the same place that Landen had hit the wall with his own oar, the back of the longboat jerked sharply to the right, and its oars snapped as they made contact with the solid rock wall. The back of the ship hit and bounced off so violently the boat slammed against the opposite wall of the gap, snapping that side's oars as well. The front of the longboat caught the cliff just as they emerged from the gap and spun the boat round, sending at least two men over the side.

Landen turned his attention to getting the sail ready and heading in the right direction before he looked back again. With the wind at their backs, they had made it several hundred yards away from the longboat by the time it righted itself. It was still taking on water and had more broken oars than whole, they were forced to turn up the coastline to make landfall at the nearest possible spot. Roan and Landen were now free to cross the inlet to their own island.

Erik had learned from the remaining elders that a man by the name of Lord Guth was the reason these men had come to Elvoy. It seemed that he was determined to find Esta and take her by force if need be. The big question was, Why? Since sending Roan out in the boat, Erik had been busy preparing the island for the return of Guth's men. They knew exactly what those men were doing; they were looking for "the gifted one," the Night Child. He shook his head as he heard the things that Guth believed Esta could do: control men, control animals, even read the minds of any living thing.

"But that is not true! I cannot read minds, nor can I control animals," Esta said, looking at Erik.

"This leader must believe the stories. He also believes you can keep him out of harm's way and tell him what others are planning."

Esta was angry. "Even if it were true, even if I could do these things, I would never."

Erik held his hand up to calm her. "Esta, you are not to blame for another's greed."

She was. It was her gift—or at least what this man believed her gift was—that brought this destruction upon their village. Erik could see the hurt and the anger in Esta's face. He needed no gift for that.

"It is not your fault. There is no time to argue it. We need you now.

We must be ready when they return, and I need you by my side to help me. Esta! I need you!"

So, there it was. Her gift would be used for the destruction of others.

The boys scrambled to set the small sail and head straight for Elvoy. As Landen turned, Roan saw the wound. A splinter from the shattered oar had embedded itself into Landen's shoulder. Blood oozed from its edges, staining both the wood and Landen's shirt. Roan wanted to tend it, but Landen only wanted one thing: land. He wanted to feel earth beneath his feet. The small boat was spotted coming into the lee waters. Men lined the rocks and could be seen on shore as well. Large fires burned on the beach. At first Roan thought that their plan had failed, but soon men were waving their arms, letting them know that it was safe to make landfall.

Erik met Roan on the pebbled beach. His eyes flashed as he watched Landen come up behind Roan holding a bloody shoulder. Roan could read the question forming in Erik's mind before he asked it.

"He was hiding from father aboard the boat. Good that he was! I would not be here if not for his help."

Landen beamed with pride as he allowed himself to be spirited away by Clare, who would tend his wound.

Erik looked at Roan and waited for the information he needed.

"They are but hours out. There will be one less longboat. They tried to follow us through the gap. We were lucky; they were not!"

Erik grinned at Roan's new confidence. "That should help. Come, we were just to meet with the elders. I will fill you in on the way."

Roan fell into step with Erik, his stockier frame contrasting with Erik's lean height.

Esta sat quietly. She could still hear the words, but somehow, they seemed distant and hollow. The men would encircle the beach. The enemy would be allowed to make landfall, and fires would be set that would trap the men between the sea and the waiting armed men of the village. On each side of the lee, they would be able to see a line of archers with arrows ready to be set ablaze. If they chose to fight, some would die, and their boats would be set on fire so that none would leave the island whether or not they perished in battle. It was the hope of the council, though, that the warriors would choose to leave the island instead of taking the chance of losing their coveted boats. Here is where Esta came in. She would tell the council if they were going to attack, flea, or leave and then return.

Esta was suddenly aware of Erik's presence. Again, she was hit by his feelings for her, now mixed with concern and a trace of fear. The fear was different this time. It was more fear that she would not do what she was asked, that she would not help him when the time came.

The men walked away from the council house to make ready for the possible battle. Erik could see that Esta was not happy with what she had heard.

"I will not allow anyone to harm you, Esta, and they will not take you."

She shook her head as if annoyed by his comment. "I do not want anyone else to perish because of me. I want no more loss of life. No more!"

Esta sounded determined. Erik wondered what she was determined about, what she was planning to do.

"Esta, they believe you are gifted. They have been told you are able to read minds, so allow them to believe it!" Erik had a slight smile on his face.

"I cannot!" Esta was confused.

"You read emotions. Those emotions can tell you what someone will do. So, let us use it Esta! They will believe what you tell them. Some will be frightened of you; others will not. But I believe we may be able to convince them to leave without bloodshed, especially if they believe they will lose the battle."

"You want me to tell them not to fight?" Esta was frightened. She could not see these men, theses warriors listening to her.

Roan approached. "They will be frightened of the very sight of you, especially if you plant that giant owl upon your shoulder."

Esta turned to find that Roan was smiling. "This is not a game, Roan. If I fail this task you all expect of me, people will die!"

Erik took her chin and turned her gaze back to his. Again, Esta felt the emotion pour from him. She realized that Erik was beginning to block his feelings at times. Now he released them, and they enveloped her like a tidal wave.

"I will never allow you to come to harm." He did not sound stern; he did not raise his voice. It was a statement, calmly made and full of conviction. "Esta, please listen to me. You cannot fail this task. We ask only that you stand by my side as you are."

"Esta," said another voice. It was Landen. He had been bandaged and had come up to stand next to Roan with sadness in his heart. "I am sorry, Esta. I did not know father would ..." His sadness was so pure.

"It is not your fault, Landen. I know what thanks I owe you."

Landen looked up at Roan. Esta could read anger flash, but it was not directed at her.

"That is not our way, Esta," Landen said. He paused as Esta turned her gaze toward the lee. Mane was flying toward them. "It was our father who caused your loss. It is we who owe you!"

Mane came in quickly, pulled up, and landed on Esta's shoulder with many clicks and pops. Then all at once, she let out a long, high-pitched shriek.

"They are coming," Esta said, looking to Erik. It was funny; she felt less frightened because of Landen's strength. If one so young could stand so strong, she could as well.

Erik turned to Roan. "Tell the others."

Roan gave a swift nod and ran in the direction of the largest fire on the beach. There stood the remaining village elders and council members. A group of young men with bows and arrows split off from the fire to run in different directions the moment Roan arrived. They were headed for the rock outcroppings that formed the lee. The elders, too, began to move away from the fire. Erik turned to Esta.

"It will work, Esta. Trust in me."

"I do trust you, Erik. I will try." She reached for his arm and turned him back to face her. "I know that you believe this will work, Erik. Please know that I will not allow another soul to perish for my protection. I will end it. I will go with them if I must." Esta dropped her hold on Erik's tunic and turned her gaze back to the lee. She could feel his resolve. His determination.

The villagers took their places along the tree line of the beach and the rock walls of the lee. As the longships came into the bay, they would only see the few people who stood near the fire on the beach—Erik, Esta, Roan, and the elders. In the tree line, Landen stood with Mane. He would release her to fly to Esta when the warriors made landfall and were walking toward her. Erik wanted them to see the large owl swoop down the beach and land on Esta's shoulder. He wanted them to know who she was, who they were looking at. They had dressed Esta for the part as well. The elders had asked for and received the items of clothing Erik felt would strengthen Esta's image as a person with otherworldly powers. She wore a stark-white fitted gown with red trim. It had been meant to be a marriage gift for an elder's daughter, but she had handed the gown to Esta and smiled.

"Do not fret, Esta. It is a good you do here. I cannot marry if our island is taken. I would not wish for my Kelvin to fight these men." She placed her hands over Esta's. "I know you have a good heart."

Her name was Greta. Esta had always known her to be kind and generous. Today was no different. She could feel Greta's fear for the one she loved. She could also feel the love, much the same as what came at her from Erik. There was no anger or hurt over the gown as Esta had expected. Esta had given her a weak smile and a nod. She'd held Greta's hand in hers for a moment longer than was needed, giving it a slight squeeze and mouthing a heartfelt thank you before releasing her. It was the closest thing to a real friendship that Esta had ever felt, a true feeling of caring between two girls who wanted nothing but the best for one another.

The second item Esta wore was a bright-red cape. This had come from the elder's ceremonial trunk. It had had to be quickly altered to fit her. The result was shocking. Esta's hair had been combed and a crown braided to pull it away from her face. The white gown now looked like it was ablaze against the black rocks of the beach, and its red trim was a near perfect match to the red of the cloak. Even some of the villagers had stepped back as she'd emerged from the council house. She'd been able to feel their fear; they'd been frightened of what she may do.

Roan smiled at her now, a rare smile that went beyond his lips. "If the desired effect is to make them think you have powers beyond us mortal men, then they have truly succeeded. You look as if you could will the sky to rain or the moon to fall from the heavens," Roan said, raising an eyebrow and cocking his head to one side. He smiled again and headed for his post.

Esta was not sure, but he seemed to believe his own words more than he was willing to admit. She now stood next to Erik, who held his sword at the ready. She turned to face the men walking toward her and slid her hood back just as Mane landed upon her shoulder. It was all Esta could do not to smile. Their fear of her flooded her senses. Most of the men who stood before them on the beach were frightened—of her.

The plan was that Erik would speak for her if needed. She turned to Erik and whispered, "They are frightened, but their leader is angry. He does not fear me."

Erik nodded. "Hold your ground!"

He raised his arms, and the villagers moved into the open. The young men stood along the rocks with their bows in hand and arrows ready to be set ablaze. Behind them along the tree line, men and women with all manner of weapons in hand stepped out of the trees and into the light.

The leader of the raiders was a large, dark figure. He looked about at the men and women who stood ready to fight. He weighed the odds of a favorable outcome, and Esta could feel his anger mount.

"You have nothing to gain here except the destruction of your ships and the loss of many men," Erik said, sounding strong and confident.

"We only seek the girl. Give her over, and you'll not see us again." Guth pointed at Esta with his blade.

Erik stiffened. "Leave now, or fight." He leaned in as if Esta had said something in his ear. "You cannot win, and though many will perish, it seems that both you and I will be among the dead this day." Erik paused. "I may die this day, but my father's murderer will also die!"

Esta was taken aback by the tack Erik was taking. She watched as Guth stiffened, but the feelings she got from him were confusing. He stood firm and felt conflict. He wanted her, but he was also not sure of the meaning behind Erik's words. He had not killed anyone. Esta could feel him trying to work out weather Erik's words were true or not when all plans changed.

A cry of pain rang out over the silence, and all eyes turned to the rock jetty on the left side of the lee. Esta reached out and grabbed Erik's arm. The young men and women on the rocks had been taken by surprise from the near woods behind them. They had been so focused upon what was happening on the beach that they had not seen Roan's father or those with him approach. The scream that had broken the silence came from a young woman standing next to Roan on the jetty. The villagers there had had their arrows nocked and were ready to draw, their eyes intent on the longboats in the lee. A knife had suddenly slashed across her left forearm, and her bow and arrow had clattered to the rocks. As they did, everyone on the jetty had been taken from behind. Strong arms had grabbed them around their upper bodies, and they could now feel cold steel under their chins. Those that had managed not to be overpowered had no choice but to drop their weapons and place their hands above their heads in surrender. Now that several of the young villagers on the jetty had knives to their throats, Landen and Roan among them, they were all being pushed forward toward the beach. Behind them was Beor. Guth's head bent low, and Esta saw him shake it, as if this were not what he had planned. She also sensed from him a feeling of anger that was directed at Beor and not at the villagers.

Esta's grip on Erik's arm was fierce. Two young men were wounded badly, and the warriors had disarmed the rest. Pushing the village archers toward the beach where Guth took in the condition of the young female. The knife had cut deep into her forearm in a long, jagged slash.

Erik raised his hand, and the men at the tree line came forward, while those on the other side of the lee set their arrows ablaze. Both leaders knew there was about to be bloodshed. Erik was furious with himself for not having been ready for this. Esta was in tears, the fear and anger thick in the air around her. It was time. She would surrender now. She began to take a step forward, but Erik's arm shot out in front of her. It looked to those watching as if he were holding her back. Esta felt the fear increase in a few but not in their leader. His eyes had narrowed toward Beor. He barred his teeth as if to make it clear to Beor that he was not happy with him.

"If those men are harmed, your ships will burn!" Erik shouted in anger.

Guth looked to the men behind him. Weighing the chances of saving the boats if a real fight broke out.

"You would sacrifice your people?" Guth asked. He seemed satisfied to wait Erik out. "I have no interest in harming anyone. I seek only the enlightened one."

Erik stiffened. "Well, you may not have her! You will never leave this island."

Esta reached out and touched Erik on the arm. "Erik, stop. We have no right to place others in danger," she whispered. "The others are angry. They do not want to see the ones they love die, not for me. Even the elders falter in their resolve."

Erik shook his head. "I will not let them have you!"

Guth watched the exchange. Esta's wide eyes told him she was afraid, but of what?

"Bring them!" Guth motioned for his men to bring their prisoners down onto the beach. He waved for the females to be released. They rushed across the beach, and their families let forth cries of relief. Now there were only the young men Erik had placed on the lee's left—six in total, eight with Landen and Roan. There seemed to be some kind of silent bargaining going on, for not a word was spoken.

Erik knew that Guth had released the women to soften the hearts of the villagers, but the six young men were in danger. He knew that Roan's father would do anything to get off the island at this point, for he would die at the hands of his own people if he did not. He needed to make sure Guth knew that Beor was not a good example of the men upon this island.

"You barter with confidence, my friend. It will not do. Your ships will burn if anyone else is harmed!" Erik shouted this so that those on the rocks knew their duty. "And although you may or may not win your prize, you will have no ships to get off this island and fewer men to protect it!"

It was a standoff. Esta could feel the fear from the men on the beach; fear on both sides was thick in the air. The warriors, however, feared losing their ships more than the loss of life. The boats meant everything to them. They were the way home.

She leaned into Erik and whispered, "They fear the loss of their ships."

Guth took a step forward as if wishing to hear her words.

Erik nodded. "We have nothing else to say! Release our young or fight!"

Erik turned to face the villagers on the beach behind him. He raised his sword over his head and smiled at them. It was a huge, victorious grin. He pumped his sword in the air and let out a warrior's cry. The villagers, men and women alike, followed suit, all raising their weapons overhead and letting fierce cries escape them.

Erik turned back to face Guth. "Choose!" he said as he pointed with his sword to the archers who aimed the burning arrows at the ships.

Guth turned in fury and waved an arm. His men scrambled back toward their longboats. As they piled into the boats, they raised their shields against the archers.

Landen screamed as his father pushed him toward one of the ships. Roan and the others were also being tossed onto one of the longboats.

"He's taking them!" Esta screamed.

Erik ran forward toward them, as did many others, but the ships were quickly out into the water, and Erik stood on the edge of the surf, unsure of what to do. One of the archers let an arrow fly, and it landed with a thud upon the hull of the lead ship. The flames were quickly doused by the waves, and the arrow was pulled free and tossed into the water. The six captives were spread out aboard the ships. Erik searched the longboats, looking for Roan. He only glimpsed his angry expression as Guth stepped into his view. He said nothing as he held up his hand as if to wave and pointed at Esta.

Esta was so filled with her own grief and fear that it took her several moments to realize that she was surrounded by it. Fear and anger slammed into her as she turned to Erik with tears in her eyes.

"Why?"

Erik was beside himself. He wanted to give chase, he wanted to scream, and he wanted revenge. How could the skinner be so cruel? He could see the man wanting to take his own children—Roan and Landen were like slaves to him—but why the others? He knew these people. He knew their parents. They could only mean to bargain for Esta with the lives of those they had taken. If that were true, Erik knew Esta would be lost, for she would never allow others to suffer in her place. She had already wanted to give herself over, even before this. Now others had been injured and several young men taken.

The elders were there now. The entire village seemed to be there now, lined up on the beach watching the longboats fade into the distance.

A small sob escaped Esta, and a hand came to rest upon her shoulder. It was not Erik's but Clare's.

"Come, Esta. Come away."

Esta could feel her mother's fear. She knew Esta would give herself over to save the others. She wanted to get her daughter away. She wanted to flee the island.

"We cannot leave them. I will not let this happen."

Erik was there, waiting. "We go to the council house. We will get them back, Esta. Without your sacrifice."

The words were there, but Esta did not believe them. It was not because Erik did not believe them, though, for he was determined to save them all. It was as Esta feared. He would sacrifice all in his love for her. She knew she could not allow it.

SIX

The Sacrifice

On the longboat, Guth and Beor were deep in hushed conversation. Roan stared hard at the man he felt was to blame for everything—for the attack on the village, for the death of his mother, and now for this. Did his father mean to place him and Landen into the hands of these raiders? They would become slaves to these men. Their lives would mean nothing. What of their younger sister, now alone on Elvoy without a soul to care for her? Roan continued to glare at his father. He stared at the leader, Guth. He wanted answers. He watched as Guth pointed at him, and in a flash, he was being pushed forward toward the man. His father, standing near, only returned Roan's hard stare.

"You are Roan?" Guth did not sound angry or as if he were demanding anything.

"I am." Roan turned his hard glare to the man. "Know this: I will not help you in your quest, for I am no traitor to my people."

Roan's statement was aimed at his father, and his words hit their mark. The skinner stood and swung the back of his hand across Roan's face. Roans head snapped back, his lip split, but Roan remained calm. For the first time, he was not afraid of his father. In fact, he welcomed Beor's fist, for it only fueled his rage. Roan reached up and wiped the blood from his chin. He looked his father in the eye and spit blood at his father's feet.

"Enough!" Guth stepped forward. "You will restrain yourself or swim!"

It was Beor who was the target of his anger, not Roan. Guth looked at the skinner in disgust. Roan could not help but wonder at the way they spoke to one another. It was clear that this man, Guth, did not hold his father in esteem; it was there upon his face. Roan found himself wishing that Esta were there to read what emotions were coming from this man. Beor was moved to the other end of the ship by two men, who also treated him as if they cared little about the man, and Beor was treated no better or worse than Roan and Landen had been. They were not bound, and not a soul seemed to acknowledge their presence. The other warriors on the ship simply manned their oars and carried out the slow and steady motions that moved the longship through the waters off of Elvoy. Guth spoke to the men on one of the other ships, and it made a slow turn, then sat in the water as if anchored. Roan knew that the boat had been left to watch the island. Guth took his time before he spoke again, after Landen had also been brought to the prow.

"I do not wish to harm you or those in your village," Guth began slowly. "I was told of the seer, and I am in need of her."

Roan laughed. "Need? And for what purpose is this… need?"

There was a long pause. Guth was weighing his options—to tell this boy of his plight or to keep his secret. Guth shook his head.

"It matters little to you, I am sure. I do need her, and I do intend to have her. I do not intend to harm her. I swear to release her as soon as is possible."

Roan laughed. "You expect me to believe that you will let us go? Let her go? After what you have done in our village?" This made no sense to Roan on many levels. This man was a leader who had brought his men across the sea to capture a girl he "needed." For what, he knew not. Men, many good men, had been killed and many hurt by these warriors who "meant to cause no harm."

"What is it that you feel Esta could do for you? She is no seer." Roan tried to sound conversational as if he could not understand why they wanted Esta.

Guth raised a brow. "Your father seems to think she is that, and more."

Roan chuckled. "Let me guess. She is a witch? She is this because she has a healer's touch and an owl she found on the ground as a pet?"

Landen looked up at his brother with wide eyes. "Esta's owl is big, but it is not heavy, and it did not hurt me."

Roan smiled at his brother. "She. Mane is a female."

Guth looked at Roan. "Mane? She has named that beast for the moon?"

"Beast?" Roan chuckled. "Esta found that bird as an owlet. It is no beast. She raised it. It is as simple as that. She is the daughter of our village midwife and healer. She is learning her mother's trade, and that is all. Now you have taken her father from her. Do you believe she would help you now in any way, even if she were this … seer?"

Roan looked out to sea. Elvoy was a distant shadow on the horizon now.

Guth felt nothing but rage at the fact that he had allowed Beor to harm so many on the island. This boy was right. Why would this girl help him now, even if the stories were true?

"So, the stories are false? She has not saved your village from sickness? She did not stop a killing or tell a woman that her babe was dead inside her?"

Guth had no need to wait for an answer. Landen's head snapped around to stare wide eyed at his brother.

"Ah, then there may be more than healer in her." Guth gave the top of Landen's head a rub. The boy pulled back, ducked away from Guth's touch, and hung his head in shame.

"I am sorry, Roan." Landen was ashamed.

Roan shook his head. "You did not tell him anything he did not already know. He is determined. Let us hope we can find a way to help her when the time comes." Roan looked to the back of the boat to where his father sat alone. He sat down next to Landen and whispered, "Stay away from father. You steer clear of him, you hear? I do not think this man will tolerate him for long, and I want you nowhere near Beor when his patience finally gives out."

Landen looked down the center of the boat and nodded. "That is not a problem. I hate him!"

Roan nodded. It had never been spoken aloud between them before, those words they both held on to when it came to the skinner. Now they were said, and now it was real.

"I know." Roan leaned back against the hull of the ship and pulled his knees up close. "Believe me, Landen. I know. And if this raider does not kill him …" Roan paused to look at the man who had caused so much pain. "If he does not, then I will. I will if it is the last thing I do."

It took time to gather the village into the council house. The wounded from the short skirmish on the rocks needed tending, and Clare and Esta took extra care to make sure they would heal well—all but one. Although only four young men had been wounded, one young woman now lay dead. Somehow during the short tussle on the jetty, her wrist had been cut—a long slash that had gone unnoticed when the women were sent scrambling back across the beach to their families. Her father had bound the wound and sat her near a tree, where she had bled out when no one was looking. If Clare or Esta had seen the wound, they would have known how serious it was. Her father had gone back to her when the boats had left the lee. He'd shaken her before realizing that she had slipped away. He'd screamed, and others had come forward to help, but it was too late. She had died alone and afraid. Her parents had wailed, her father blaming himself for not looking closer at the wound. Now, as the family mourned her passing, Esta sank deep within herself. She refused to enter the council house and instead stayed with her mother and the families of the wounded.

She bandaged and stitched wounds and applied healing herbs to relieve pain and stop any infection. She gave food and water and every ounce of comfort she could, her heart sinking ever lower when one family refused to allow her near. Clare snapped at the women who stood in Esta's way. She asked if she would rather tend to her son's wounds herself. Esta quickly apologized and told her mother to help the boy, that she would tend the others. Although Esta felt only gratitude from the other wounded, she could not feel comfort for herself. She knew there was only one answer.

Inside the council house, Erik tried to rally the men for an attack. The truth was that they knew not who had attacked them, where they had come from, or where they had gone since they'd left the island. It did no good to plan for an offensive. The council had no doubt that the raiders would return for Esta at some point and would continue to do so until they had her in their grasp. Perhaps with many more men. What to do when they arrived was more the issue.

Erik was willing to fight, but as much as the council wanted to hang onto Esta, they knew that the village as a whole was not. They were not like Erik. Most were simple people, farmers and those who made their way upon the sea. Those who did not farm or fish made things that would be used by those who did. They were not warriors. They had not been a fighting people for as long as most of them could remember. Most simply lived a quiet life on the island, knowing they had made a choice to live in this out-of-the-way place, away from the troubles of the world. The council feared much more loss of life and perhaps the loss of many of their young if the warriors decided to take slaves. It had been known to happen before. They had no way of knowing what the men who wanted Esta would do or how far they would go to have her.

When Erik found Esta several hours later, she stood alone on the pebbled beach looking out to sea. Her red cloak was tossed over a large boulder, and her white gown was now stained with blood. She had tied her hair back with a leather strap, and Mane seemed to be toying with it. Esta pushed Mane off her shoulder, and she flew to a low branch on the edge of the tree line.

"How do I find them?" Her question was soft. She did not turn to face him.

"I do not think we will need to find them, Esta. They will be back."

Erik was sad. She could feel his defeat. She knew it was hard for him to try to mask it. He was also angry; she could feel that as well. But it was not the kind of anger she expected. It was as if he felt disappointment in the elders.

"They plan to build a sea wall, with towers across the beach so that this will never happen again," Erik hissed. "They talk of stone walls and weapons for the future while we face the enemy at our door right now."

Esta turned to face him. The full weight of her bloody gown, wet bracers, and washed face and hands hit him hard. He was shocked by her appearance.

"They are frightened, Erik! And they have every right to be so. Do not scoff at their fear. They do not deserve that." She looked back at the sea.

Erik was not so sure she understood the villagers. "They want to pretend to stand firm only as long as they feel they will win." He shook his head. "They know not what they do."

She tried to smile at him. "They are right in what they do. My parents have always taught me that the needs of the many should outweigh the needs or wants of the one. They fear for their children, for their homes and loved ones."

"They are weak!" Erik spat the words.

"No, Erik, and you do not really believe that yourself. They are frightened; there is a big difference, as you well know."

Erik did know. He understood their fear. He just could not bring himself to let Esta go. His desperation made her laugh.

"I do not believe that I will be harmed. He wants me, yes, but I could not sense that he wished me harm."

Erik looked at her hard. "You know that? For certain?"

Esta smiled. "Nothing in this life is certain. I do think that I would have felt it if he were wanting to hurt me. It is different, stronger in a way that it crosses over other feelings of desire and love. I only felt a need from him. He needs me."

Erik shook his head. He could not escape the thought of how much he needed her. "It matters little to me. I am not ready to give up."

"Erik, people we care about are in danger. People we loved are dead and need to be laid to rest. The villagers need to feel as if they are safe in their own homes. So, let us give them what they need. It is the right thing to do."

She turned from him and walked to scoop up the cloak. Mane flew low toward her home, and Erik knew where she was going: to help her mother prepare Carrick for his journey to the other side.

Erik knew there was no getting away from it. The village elders had asked him if he thought Esta's life was in danger, if he thought she would someday try to come back to them. They had made the choice to let her go. What hurt him more was that Esta had already made that choice for them. He allowed himself the slight comfort that he had told them before he'd left the hall that she was already preparing to go and that she had more courage than all of them put together.

It would normally take more time to lay a loved one to rest. There were customs that needed to be followed, traditions that both Erik and Esta needed for their own reasons. Neither one of them could leave the island without seeing it through.

The circle of stones was complete. Esta had gathered the rocks from the river's edge. They had to be right. Her father deserved only the best. She had searched out stones with just the right shape—rounded stones with flattened tops. They needed the white spider veins running through them to create the look she wanted when placed together on the ground. She had made her father's circle larger than needed. She felt it only right that her father's marker befit his worth to those left behind here on earth.

He was dressed in his best clothing, his hair combed and trimmed. His ornate carved-bone comb was placed under his folded hands. His handmade leather halter lay along his side with hair cut from his cob's tail. The hair had been braided and adorned with flowers and herbs from the garden. They dug a deep pit into the ground and prepared it to receive its passenger. A thick bed of soft grass, herbs, and flowers lay at the bottom. Erik and another elder carefully lowered Carrick into his grave upon his plank. He was surrounded with gifts and other items he had made or that had been important to him.

Carrick was covered with a deep-green cloth to symbolize his love of the earth. Words were spoken about his love for his wife and daughter and his island home. Clare wept, and Esta allowed herself to feel the full weight of her grief. As she pulled Clare away, Erik returned Carrick to the earth he loved.

The following morning, Esta attended the burial of Erik's father, Dirk. Many more from the village were in attendance than were present for Carrick's crossing. Esta could not help but feel a pang of anger. Carrick had also been a man of importance and honor. He had deserved their homage. She tried to stand in the back of the crowd. She wanted to pay her respects and slip away. Erik, however, pulled her forward and placed her at his side. His feeling of grief was strong, so Esta focused on that and not on the many feelings of fear, anger, and confusion she sensed in those around her.

Early the following morning, Esta, Erik, and Clare loaded food and water onto a boat—Roan's father's boat. Esta tossed large satchels to Erik full of her mother's belongings, as well as a large bladder full of Esta's clothing and a small satchel that held her leather bracers and supplies for Mane. When Esta handed Erik a carving of the tree of life that her father had made and that had hung in their home for as long as Erik could remember, he knew they did not intend to return to Elvoy. His heart sank, for he knew if Esta did not return, he would not return.

Alden and Kelvin came to the beach to wish them well. Erik clasped the man's arm and nodded his farewell. Esta and Clare sat in the boat with their eyes to the sea, refusing to look back at Elvoy and the memory of their lives there. Again the elder asked that Erik and Clare return, and again Erik told him he would not return without Esta. Clare had vowed never to set foot upon Elvoy again. She could not bear to live in the home Carrick had built for them without him by her side. This saddened the elders, who knew they were losing the only healers they had. The island would surely suffer for it.

Once out of the bay, Esta allowed herself one last look back at the only home she had ever known. Erik's feelings were mixed. He was still filled with grief over the loss of his father, but he was also angry. Esta feared for his safety when he finally confronted the men responsible for his father's death. Clare sat quietly and watched the distant horizon.

Her feelings of grief had overwhelmed her, and she had shut down, just breathing in and out the crisp sea air and trying hard to mask her hurt for her daughter's sake. Even though Esta could feel the fear and anger in them, her own fear was almost palpable to her. What would happen to them when they found the warriors? What would Esta be able to do about those they had taken from the island? What would she be able to do about keeping Erik and her mother safe, keeping Erik alive?

As the boat began to rock on the open sea, Esta was hit by the urge to run. There was no visible sign of another boat. They could raise the small sail and set the oars to water. If they could make it to the mainland, they could disappear, travel to a city far away. None of them had ever traveled deep into the mainland or to the great cities that were said to be there. They had heard stories of the many people and wondrous buildings that could be found there. Every moment the boat drifted without encounter caused Erik to become more and more anxious.

Esta turned her attention to the left. "They are close."

For the first time Clare spoke. "There!" She pointed to the horizon.

The longboat had its oars in the water and advanced quickly. The men aboard were angry but relieved, for they would not have to spend another night upon the waves. As they came closer, Esta could feel their wonderment as to why their small boat sat anchored as if waiting.

"They fear you," Esta told Erik. "They think you may harm them." Esta was worried.

Erik felt a surge of pride at the fact that the warriors feared his presence.

"No, Erik. I fear they will kill you. Give them no reason to see danger."

Erik turned to her and raised his hands. "I should be the one fearing them, don't you think?"

Esta stood. She faced the longboat as it came alongside the small sailing craft.

"Keep your weapons stowed! You have nothing to fear here." She looked into the eyes of the men aboard. "You must listen to me."

Erik had never heard Esta's voice so harsh. It was deep and commanded respect and attention.

"You need not fear me. No harm shall come to you. You must stow your weapons and give your word that no harm shall come to my companions."

The men aboard the ship were afraid to anger her. Some felt her to be akin to the devil. Others wondered if she could curse them or do them harm. They wanted to bring Esta aboard their ship, but she refused. Erik settled the problem by giving the men his weapons and allowing them to be towed.

Esta was a little annoyed by Erik's feeling of satisfaction over not having to do any of the work to get them to their destination. They could simply sit back and wait to see where they would end up. His smug satisfaction turned to fear, as did everyone else's, when the boat lost sight of all land and continued to move through the water. Esta knew that the men seemed pleased to be headed home, that they had no fear themselves about the boat being in the middle of the ocean at night.

As darkness enveloped them and they could not even see the other ship but only hear the sounds of the oars in the water, Erik found himself huddled with the women. Just as frightened as they were. He woke the next morning still cradling the girls. Clare sat up and gently touched his cheek in thanks. She leaned over and brushed Esta's hair from her face. Esta woke to the same sight she'd had when the light had faded the day before: nothing but sea. Erik was worried, and he made no effort to mask his feelings. He looked down at Esta as if pleading for her to comfort him for a change.

"They are not lost. They have no fear at all, Erik," she whispered, not wanting to be overheard by anyone aboard the ship.

Erik nodded. "Whoever these people are, they have traveled a great distance to find you, Esta. How is it that they could learn of you from so far?"

Esta was still confused as to what there was about her that was of any interest at all. Her small world on Elvoy was nothing special. She was not at all well liked in her own mind, although her mother was. Esta, even after all these years, still felt fear in some of the villagers, respect from others, and indifference from many.

"I still do not understand, Erik. I have not the ability to win wars or do the things this man believes I can. I truly do not understand what he is hoping to gain with me." She shook her head and looked to the sea.

"Nor do I, but we will find out soon enough." He nodded toward the longship where a man was bringing them a water skin and what looked to be a piece of dried meat.

Esta shared her portion with Mane. This upset Erik, as he felt the bird could go longer without nourishment than she could. Esta just smiled and said they had always taken care of one another and that Mane was just as frightened about being out in the middle of the sea as they were.

The light was fading by the time Esta realized they were headed toward land. In the distance, there were fires burning along a shoreline, there to guide the longship home. Esta could feel the relief wash over a few of the men aboard—relief that they would soon be home and away from her, not that they would be safe from the vastness of the sea. Esta found it strange. One of the men was worried about punishment for bringing more people back than he should have. Esta knew this meant Erik and Clare. For the most part, once land was sighted, little thought was given to the small boat or those within it. They had brought the prize back; the others mattered very little.

Their callous disregard for her mother angered her. Erik felt her back stiffen and looked up to see the set of her jaw. Instantly she was hit by his concern for her well-being. She pulled in a breath and tried to relax.

"I believe we have arrived." She nodded toward the dark mass that loomed on the horizon.

Erik nodded back but said nothing. His fear over how he was to protect them without weapons, without knowledge of where they were or who he was protecting her from, was building within him.

Esta worried about what might happen to Erik once they made landfall. She knew his presence had not been welcomed by the boatmen when they had seen him. He was a warrior, someone they had watched on the beach as a leader. They worried about Erik's presence on the boat when they reached home and what their own leader would do. Now here they were, nearing the firelit shoreline. Many who were rowing now only thought of their own homes and those within them, yet a few on board the longboat wondered if they had made a mistake allowing the young man to remain on board.

Esta stood, rocking the small boat with the force of her action and alarming the man set to stand watch over them.

"Sit down, milady. You may tip the boat." The man looked at her in annoyance.

Esta took hold of the small mast for the sail and held her ground. "I may tip the boat! I may drown us all or just myself! I want your word that no one will be harmed. No one! Or you will never reach that shore." She pointed.

The way she had made that last statement even made Erik's hair stand on end. She spoke as if she could somehow lift and toss them all into the sea right here. It worked.

One of the men aboard stood. "You have it." He gave a short nod to Erik as if to say it again, this time man to man.

He quickly moved about the longship and then appeared at the edge of the sailboat to hand Erik his weapons, his short sword in its sheath and his bow and quiver as well. This Esta had not expected. Nor had the others in the longboat. Esta could feel their surprise. Yet the man who had spoken was respected, and Esta felt that he was willing to take the chance that Erik would not try to fight his way out of a situation where he was so overwhelmingly outnumbered.

As they came in close, all eyes were taking in the sight of the lee. The fires burned at the end of long wooden docks that jutted out into the water. Many other boats were moored there, some even larger than the one in front of them. There were dark figures moving about everywhere—people, many people. The longship came alongside the wooden dock, and two of the men jumped out. There was a bustle of activity. People were everywhere, and the little ship was unloaded onto the dock without incident. The three captives could have been invisible for all the notice they received. Only a few of the men from the longboat seemed to pay them any mind.

SEVEN

Ivar

rik's mouth hung slack just as Esta was sure her own did. They stared in amazed silence at the city before them. The buildings were nothing like their own partially sunken roundhouses or even the large wooden council house. These buildings were made completely of stone, cut perfectly to make shapes and arches, towers and walkways. It was like nothing they had ever dreamed.

"Where are we?" Esta whispered.

Erik just shook his head.

"Does the mainland look like this?" Esta wondered aloud.

"No, I've not seen this like before. I have only seen the mainland from the docks. The streets were dirty, and the smell of fish and fowl was overmuch. No. It was nothing like this." Erik was in awe.

"It is beautiful." Esta stared, taking in every detail.

The white sand sloped away from the sea, gradually at first. Then a sharp cliff jutted up. It was nothing like the dark pebbles on their own beach or the dark rock that formed their island. Sitting on the rise was a village out of a dream. The white stone walls rose up out of the ground, taller even than Erik. That same stone wove through the village as a path, clean and almost looking as if it had been swept. Circular walls enclosed many roundhouses, which were much larger and much nicer than those on Elvoy. As they passed the enclosed courtyards, Esta looked through the gates in amazement. The homes that were enclosed by the rock wall had two levels. Inside the walls were also outbuildings and gardens, some with trees bearing fruit and others with chicken and pig pens. There were weaving looms and dying tubs. They passed between ten and fifteen houses all the same and all different, all in their own little protected circle. As they came closer to their destination, Erik could catch glimpses of a very large building against another stone cliff. The building seemed to grow out of it. Giant archways suddenly loomed in front of them. They were bigger than any home Esta had ever seen. The archways were carved with the most beautiful designs. Some Esta understood; others were foreign to her. She shivered at the thought of entering, fearing what could be inside. At the last possible moment, the men turned them to walk along the front of the arches. Once they reached the side of the stone structure, they turned again down a narrow path that ended at a large wooden door. Esta again could not believe her eyes, as the door was huge, highly polished, and carved with ornate flowers and symbols. They were led through the door to a room with smooth, white stone walls. There were two wooden benches and a rug of deep blue upon the floor.

"Wait here," one of the men said. He gave a slight nod to the other, who went through another large door and disappeared.

Esta turned slowly in a circle to take in the room. She bent down and placed a cautious hand on the rug beneath her. It was nearly the color of the sky on a clear and warm spring day. She could feel her own fear mounting, along with her mother's. Erik, however, was confused, a feeling she did not at the moment understand. When the door opened again, Erik stiffened, for there stood Guth, although dressed much differently than he had been before. Instead of animal skins and armor, he wore a patterned cloak of deep blues and a pair of leather breeches with soft leather boots that came to his knees. He did not look the part of the murderous warrior. His emotions also threw Esta off balance, as he almost seemed relieved to see her. He needed her. Very badly.

"You have come far. You must be both tired and hungry. Please, this way." He motioned toward the door he had just come through.

"Who are you? And where are our people?" Erik stood firm and stared hard at Guth, who had not taken his eyes off of Esta.

"Your people are safe." Guth did not like Erik's tone but understood his anger.

Esta stepped forward bravely. "We wish to see our people. Until I know that they are well, I will go nowhere and do nothing you would ask of me."

Her voice was level and calm, even to the edge of uncaring, yet Erik knew she was terrified.

Guth looked now at Clare and Erik. He recognized Clare as the wife of the man that had been killed while they'd looked for Esta's home. It was not what Guth had wanted, but it had happened nonetheless. He had believed they had done well to get onto the island and find Esta with little bloodshed. That, he knew, was only his view, for he had not lost a loved one. These people had.

"Please wait here." Guth nodded at his guards, and they followed him from the room, leaving Esta, Clare, and Erik completely alone. Clare let out a heavy breath that sounded somewhere between a sob of grief and a sigh of relief. Esta went to her and placed her hand upon her cheek.

"I do not feel anger or hate. I do not think he means to harm us."

Clare gave a slight nod and sat down upon a bench near the center of the room. Esta turned to find Erik near the door.

"Erik, no! Do not provoke them." She walked to his side.

Erik smiled down at her. "I only wanted to see if I could hear anything." He was annoyed. "That is all." He turned from the door and gazed at the walls. "How do they do this?" He ran his hand upon the wall to feel the stone. "Where are we?"

At that moment, the door opened, and a very old, very clean man stepped to the side of the door. At first Esta thought he must be some sort of priest. His cream-colored clothes were spotless—a thick woven shirt and matching knee breeches. Although he wore no shoes of any kind, his feet were somehow as clean as if he had just stepped from the sea.

"Follow me, please. Right this way." He gestured that they should all follow him through the door. When they all hesitated, he leaned back into the room as if annoyed. "Come, come, see your friends." He nodded and smiled.

At that, Erik stepped forward, and they all followed the man through the door. Esta's eyes filled with tears as she saw the small group of islanders waiting around a loaded table. Landen saw them first. He jumped up from his seat and ran toward them.

"Esta, you are here!" There was something odd about the way he smiled at her, as if he were happy, glad to see her, but not because he needed to be rescued. Roan stepped up to Erik, and they clasped their forearms in greeting.

"What is this?" Erik asked in wonder.

"I wish I could tell you. We have been treated more like honored guests than hostages." Roan pointed at the table. "Sit down. I know you all must be famished. Eat, and I will tell you what I know." He walked back to the enormous wooden table, which was ornately carved on the sides and legs. The food was piled high on platters and in bowls. Never, not even on a feast day, had Esta seen so much food in one place. There was bread and cheese enough to feed her entire village, fruit and cooked vegetables of all sizes and colors, and meat—roasted pig and fowl and leg of lamb. The smell was overwhelming. Esta's mouth watered, and tears came to her eyes as she saw the young men from her village seated about such a huge bounty, full and well rested. She looked about the room, waiting for fear or anger to hit her, but there was not a young man here who seemed to fear for his life, nor was there any anger toward her for where they now found themselves. Not quite the picture of tortured captives that she thought they would find.

Roan chuckled at the pair of them staring at the table as if it were some sort of an illusion. "Sit. You both look the fool with your mouths agape like that." Roan pushed two boys off a small bench, and they sat. Esta suddenly looked around for her mother and found Clare making her way around the table, checking on the health and well-being of each one of them. Only then would she sit down herself.

"What is this place?" Erik asked as he sat. He was not ready to accept that this was not some sort of trap.

Roan took a seat across from them. "I know more than I wish I did at this point." He looked at them. "It seems that we are in the home of my father's brother, Guth. This man is kin to me, and I had no idea he even existed."

"What!" Esta was shocked.

Erik, on the other hand, was suddenly filled with anger. Esta could feel his emotions shift from confusion to a knowing hatred of the skinner.

"I should have known that Beor would be connected in some way," Erik fumed.

"Yes, my father's brother is Guth. He is lord here, and it was he who told me that my father had been sent from this place, never to return—that is, until he found you, Esta, and brought word of your existence back to his brother. He carries no favor with my uncle. I have not seen Beor since we arrived here, so I have had no chance to …" Roan trailed off. "I believe he may be locked away somewhere."

"He does not. Hold favor, that is."

The voice behind them made them all jump. Erik stood and placed himself between Guth and Esta.

"Landen has told me of your life on Elvoy. I can only tell you, that I am sorry." Guth looked to the boys that so much resembled his own son.

Roan stood. "I do not need your pity, my lord. Landen is young. He should keep his tongue from wagging."

Roan did not sound angry. He was in complete control, but Esta could not help but feel that Roan would speak harshly to Landen when he had the chance to do so.

Erik was not ready to accept this man as anything other than a murderer. He stepped forward and looked hard at both Roan and Guth.

"Kin or no to Roan, you have murdered our people, taken our people, and forced us here. Why? You have no need of the likes of us." Erik said, gesturing at the grandness of the hall. "Why are we here?" His words were harsh and clipped. There was no doubt of his anger toward this man.

"I did not kill your people. It was not I who led the team of warriors to Esta's home. I was in the village with the council. It was, once again, my brother showing the side of him that caused his removal from this place long ago, his use of violence as a first response." Guth looked repulsed by the memory.

Roan knew his father had betrayed Esta. He knew his father was to blame for these men coming to their island in the first place. He had not known, however, that it had been his father who had been the direct cause of Carrick's and Dirk's deaths. The hate that began to build up in both Roan and Erik was palpable. Esta could feel it running deep within them.

"Then it was not you who killed our parents?" She looked across the table to Clare, who sat staring up at them.

"No, it was not, although I should have known better than to place my brother in a position to exact his revenge or his twisted judgment upon others. He is not right." Guth's feelings were mixed. Part of him had a great deal of pity for his brother, while the other part of him hated the man. "Beor had a knowledge of the island. I placed my trust in a man I knew I should not. I was wrong."

"Where is he?" Roan's tone was steel. Both Esta and Erik knew why he had asked. He wanted nothing more than to get his hands on him.

Guth turned his gaze toward his nephew. He raised one brow as if in contemplation. "I have watched you and your brother closely since you arrived here. I did not know your mother, but I thought that there must have been some strength in her to raise you without your father's evil coming to the surface." Guth looked about the room at the frightened faces of the worried young that looked up at them. "This is not the place to talk of these things. I can see that you will not rest until all matters are on the table, so if you would follow me, we can talk in a more comfortable setting." Guth turned and began to walk toward a door.

Erik, Esta, and Roan looked quickly at each other. Esta nodded, and they began to follow. Landen and Clare both got to their feet to join them. Not knowing yet what was truly at stake, Erik shook his head to still them.

"No, Clare, we need you here with the others. Landen as well. Stay here. Let us speak with him a while." Erik did not want either one of them to hear things that would hurt them further.

"He is my father as well," Landen protested.

"Yes, but you are not yet his equal. Let me do this, Landen. Stay here. I will tell you everything. On that you have my word." Roan gave Landen's shoulder a squeeze and walked toward the door, where Guth waited.

The three of them followed Guth down a long hallway of polished stone. Esta could not get over the beauty of the place. Everywhere she looked there were carvings and symbols, ornaments hanging on the walls, rich woven rugs both upon the walls and upon the floor. The wooden furniture they passed was ornate and carved with such precision that it made their table and chairs at home look silly in comparison. Esta had not known that these things could be possible. She wanted to see more. She wanted to look into every house in the village to see if this was a dream. Surely they could not all live like this.

Guth opened a door to a smaller room with a huge fire along one wall. The warmth was instant and inviting. There was a small table near the hearth; it appeared to be made of stone as well. It was round, and the benches that sat around it were also curved to conform to the table. There were white, soft skins upon the seats. Esta ran her hand along the fur and looked up in wonder at the room. There were soft cushioned seats in clusters of two and three at different corners. Near one set of seats, there was a large weaver's loom. It too was carved and polished. Another set of chairs had a small table in the center with a game board and carved dice upon it, and yet another pair of chairs nearest the hearth had deep, cushioned seats, a soft-looking blanket draped across one seat and a lute leaning against the back of the other. Guth had remained at the door to speak to the little old barefooted man. When he turned, he motioned for them to be seated at the table.

"Lombard will bring us refreshments." He removed his outer cloak and tossed it over the back of a chair. "This is my private sitting room.

Where my wife and I—" He stopped short before continuing, "Where I spend my free hours. I am most at ease here."

And there she was, in a painting above the hearth, a dark-haired woman with a slight smile and soft, brown eyes looking out from behind a narrow face with high cheek bones. Esta could not decide if she looked kind or thoughtful. She could however easily understand why the room was loved. It was the warmest, most comforting place she had ever been.

Roan was still on edge, filled with hatred toward his father and a fear of losing Erik's and Esta's friendship because of his father's actions.

"It is not your fault, Roan," Esta assured him. "You could not have known he would harm his own people."

Roan snapped his gaze to hers, knowing she could feel his anger. He tried to soften it.

Esta tried to sound reassuring. She gave Roan and Erik a slight nod and continued, "I want to know what happened. All of it. I think we deserve that much at the least."

Roan looked to Guth and then to Erik. To his surprise, Erik was nodding in agreement.

A knock on the door caused the boys to look at each other, prepared for a trap. Both had their hands upon their swords. Guth opened the door, and Lombard shuffled in with a tray laden with bread, cheese, and meat. Behind him, another young man, also barefoot, carried a tray with four goblets and what appeared to be a hot, steaming liquid. After Lombard set the tray on the table, he poured four mugs of the steaming spiced cider and turned to leave.

"Will that be all, Master?"

Guth nodded. "Yes, thank you, Lombard."

Erik whispered in Esta's ear, "Master?"

"Lombard is old. He is stuck in his past as a slave. He is a servant and a trusted friend"—Guth sat—"but he is not a slave."

"Friends do not call one another *master*." Erik pulled a bench out for Esta.

Guth nodded as both Erik and Roan sat.

"As I said, he is unable to let go of the past."

Guth said no more of the man. He was, however, on Esta's mind. She was as confused by Lombard's words as the others were, for she felt nothing but respect between them. His words did not match his feelings for Guth, and Guth did not feel himself above his servant. Esta was also still getting feelings of need from Guth that made her uncomfortable. Those feelings mixed with the feelings of anger and hatred coming from the boys toward both Guth and Roan's father, Beor, Esta had to fight hard to find some focus.

Roan broke the silence. "I would ask again, Uncle. Where is my father?"

He watched as Guth picked up his goblet and took a deep drink of the hot cider.

"Your father has asked to return to live here at Land's End. I have denied that request. I have no doubt that he would seek you out to use you and your youngers to plea a stay."

Esta's head came up. "Land's End?" she asked.

Guth looked at her. "We are as far as one can go overland before you reach the sea. In this direction, that is."

Roan's temper was building, although he was masking it well. Esta had the feeling he did not want his uncle to think of him as being anything like his father.

Erik too was becoming impatient. It seemed neither one of them wanted to tip some invisible scale. Esta, on the other hand, was more than ready for some answers, and once the first question poured from her, the flow seemed to have no end.

"You seem to have what you wanted. I am here. Our people seem unharmed. I confess I did not expect to be treated as anything other than your prisoner. So tell me, why am I here? Where is Beor, and what is to become of him? What is it that you need from me? Again, why am I here?"

Erik and Roan looked wide eyed from Esta to Guth, who seemed to have a slight smile on his lips. This only spurred Esta's temper.

"Well?"

Guth seemed so calm. Esta knew he was worried, but his fear was not for himself. She decided to hit him with what she knew he really wanted to know. She would show him that his feelings would betray his words, if nothing else.

"Who is it?" She looked around the room for a clue. She looked at the painting. "Who is it that you are so worried about?" she demanded.

Guth's head snapped up. Knowing she had hit a nerve, Esta plowed on.

"It is not Beor. You dislike him to the point of indifference. He has lost all claim he could make on you as his brother. You want nothing more of him, yet you do pity him. You worry for another. Your wife?" Esta paused. She was hit by feelings of sadness and loss. "No, you have lost her." She watched as his eyes flashed at the painting. "You grieve. I am sorry for you."

Guth's eyes grew wider.

Erik leaned in to her and whispered in her ear, "Esta, stop this." He worried that she was going too far, for even he did not realize the depth that she could go in understanding.

"No." She gently pushed Erik away. "No, he has brought us here. We all have lost people we love because of it. Now he sits us down like honored guests and expects us to be grateful."

"Esta," Roan whispered. He feared his uncle's anger.

"I am not grateful! I am angry. My father is dead! Erik's father is dead! Roan has lost his mother; his little sister is alone on Elvoy. And you sit here and smile?"

Esta stood. "Tell me what you want of me! Tell me why I am here! I will walk out of here, and you shall have nothing. I will not help you! I will not speak. I will do nothing, nothing but sit and wait for what fate may befall me. Tell me!"

Behind them, the door flew open. Lombard and two guardsmen were there. Guth stood and held up his hand.

"It is alright."

Esta caught the fear coming at them. Lombard's fear. She was ashamed that she had caused it.

"No, Master, you must come!"

Guth did not hesitate. He flew around the table and out the door. Erik, Roan, and Esta only managed a quick glance at each other before they found themselves rushing out behind him. Guth traversed down the hall at a sprint. He disappeared around a corner and then through a door. Esta could hear the screaming before they finished rounding the corner. Guth's fear was mounting with every step—his fear for one he loved very much. His son. It was his son screaming in that room. The three of them stood in the doorway and looked inside. A child, crying loudly, ran to cling to Guth's leg.

"What happened?" Guth demanded. A woman stood at the side of a small table where wooden toys lay scattered, some broken.

"He wanted to go to the family chamber, my lord. I knew you were there with the girl, so I refused to allow him to leave."

The woman was smug. Her answer came in clipped tones as if she were annoyed by the question. Esta could feel her displeasure. She was not fond of the child or her master, and Esta had instant feelings about her. She did not like the woman.

The boy's fear began to lessen as his father held him close. Guth walked to a chair and sat with the boy in his lap. It was at that moment he realized Esta, Erik, and Roan were there staring wide eyed from the open door.

"Well, now you know," he said flatly.

Esta looked at the boy, who was calming. He peeked through a thick curtain of black curls and looked at her.

The woman spoke again. "He is getting worse. He nearly broke my fingers trying to leave."

The boy tensed and trembled. He feared her. She caused pain. Esta stepped forward.

"What did you do to him?"

Guth's head snapped up. "What do you mean?"

"He is not right!" the woman barked.

The boy again tensed. Esta could not help but feel sorry for him. She wanted to help him. As if she had said it aloud, he looked up at her in surprise. His feeling of hope slammed into her. His feelings came at her differently. The feelings had a voice. *How?* she thought. *Can you hear my thoughts?* He nodded ever so slightly. Esta's eyes flashed from the boy to Guth and the woman and back again.

"What? What is it?" Guth was watching the silent conversation between his son and Esta. He stood. "Out! Everyone out!"

He placed his son on the chair as he waved everyone out of the room. The woman made some sort of distasteful noise as she went through the door. Roan stepped into the hall and waited for Erik, who was not so eager to leave Esta's side.

"Esta?" He motioned with his head to the hall.

"Go, Erik. I will join you later. Find my mother and ask her to please wait for me in the hall."

She led Erik to the door and left him in the hall as she closed it between them. When she turned, the boy was looking at her wide eyed. She smiled at him and came to the chair.

"My name is Esta. What is your name?" Esta kneeled down to face him.

"I'm not sure if he can hear you. He does not speak," Guth said sadly while he smiled at the boy. "His name is Ivar."

Esta looked up at Guth, confused. "I don't understand."

There was a mixture of fear and anticipation coming from both of them. Guth took a breath and sat down near the table of toys.

"Who is the woman?" Esta asked quietly.

Immediately Ivar turned to look at her. Guth saw the exchange and looked at Esta in confusion. She could feel again the fear the boy had of the woman who was charged with his care.

Guth could stand it no longer. "Why does he look at you when you speak?" He almost sounded angry.

"I am not quite sure." She was telling the truth. She did not understand how Ivar could understand her, why his emotions came to her so clearly.

"What happened to his mother?" she asked.

"She is dead. The fever that took her is the same thing that made him this way. His world is silent now" Guth again smiled at the boy.

Again, Esta could feel the boy relax. Guth's smile meant calm. It meant safety. It meant love. Ivar needed to see his father smile to know his world was under control. His world was not so silent as Guth thought, for Esta knew he could hear and understand them both. She was beginning to put the pieces together. For the first time, she believed she knew why she was here. It did not make what happened on Elvoy right, but then again, there was much more to that than she knew. The time had come for answers.

"I want you to tell me what happened on Elvoy. Everything. How you found out about me, and why I am here."

Her words were soft, calm. Yet Ivar looked from Esta to his father. Guth looked at his son. He stood and tossed a handful of broken carvings into the fire at the hearth as he weighed his options.

"You are hoping I will tell you about your father's death." Guth turned to face her.

"I am not hoping. I am insisting. If you want my help, which you do, you will tell me everything that happened on Elvoy." She looked up into his eyes.

Guth looked at her, eyes narrowed. "People do not usually make demands of me."

"Asking," she replied, "has not seemed to get us an answer." Esta knew he was about to tell her. She felt his surrender.

"It is not that simple. Even I cannot tell you everything. I can only tell you what I know, what I saw for myself. I fear you may not like what you hear."

He gestured for her to have a seat.

"You fear I will not help you or Ivar. You think I will turn my back on him out of anger?" Esta felt his fear. Ivar's as well.

"Yes."

Guth sat across the table from her, and Ivar found his way onto his father's knee, where he sat looking hard at Esta's face. She smiled at him.

"I do not know what will happen. I do not want to turn my father's death into a war between us. Yet here I am. I have been taken from my home and brought to a place that I do not know. My mother is heartbroken; she has lost the man she loved. I am sure that you can understand the devastation of her loss, as I know you feel much the same. I fear for her soul. She seems hollow in a way. And yes, my father is dead. Taken from me."

Ivar's eyebrows came together, and he glanced up at his father. Esta could tell that this was new information to him.

"I will tell you of Elvoy, and you will tell me of yourself," Guth said, nodding, and Esta agreed. "Beor did not want us to land on Elvoy until Erik was away from the village. He insisted on Erik being the one to take Roan on his first tour."

Esta looked up, knowing now that her encounter with Erik and Roan in the near woods had spoiled that for Beor. He had wanted his oldest son and Erik well out of the way when Guth and his men arrived, knowing both that Erik would defend Esta right along with his father and that Roan was coming of age and would possibly also get in his way.

Guth went on. "We landed on the beach with little trouble. We asked to do some trade and to speak with the elders. You see, it was never my intention to lay siege to your village. I came to make a good trade for your services. All of that said, Beor met us in front of your council house—he and Erik's father. I could tell that Beor was angry, yet I did not know why. He did not waste time. Beor informed the elders and Dirk that I had come to your island for the witch." Guth paused as Esta raised her brow. "His words, not mine."

"You can imagine their reaction," Guth continued, "which I believe Beor had anticipated. He pushed Dirk to the breaking point, telling him that the village would be sacked. Dirk and Beor had a rather loud exchange of words, and I was unable to stop the verbal escalation. Then all hell broke loose when the peacekeeper went to make a move toward his weapon. Beor drew his sword and killed him. The villagers that were nearby began to scream, and the small crowd that had gathered when the two men had started yelling at each other grew. The shock of the killing set the men off, and a short fight broke out with those villagers and council members who had witnessed Dirk's death. The exchange of words and threats happened so quickly. I should have been ready for

•

whatever my brother may have been up to. I was not. We rounded up the remaining villagers to keep some control, but even so, two managed to break away and head out. Beor was sure they were heading to warn you and your father and had them brought down with arrows." Guth stopped.

"Why?" Esta felt the weight of guilt again.

"It was not what I wanted. I wanted to ask for your help, as I said. I tried to calm the elders and speak with them separately, but then the two men were killed, and I lost all form of credibility. Beor said you would never give in, that Dirk would fight. He was right about that."

Esta shook her head. "No, it was not like that. We— You murdered our people!"

Guth nodded. "Yes, once Beor had killed Dirk, he became eager to take his revenge on others. I knew he was unstable. I knew he was much too eager to lead the way to your home. It was not until after that I learned who Beor was to your people. When we reached your father's farm, Beor was all too ready to take your father's life. I knew he was dangerous, so I had my men keep him back. Carrick was not happy to see us, even more so because Beor was with us."

Esta shook her head. "He was worried about me. Beor had cast Roan out into the night with nothing. Erik and I had set out with the cobs to find him ..." She trailed off. "We could have kept this all from happening."

Esta knew her father had had little tolerance for Beor—they'd clearly and openly disliked each other—so it was not hard to imagine that he would have demanded that Beor, Guth, and Guth's men remove themselves from his land. Add to that the fact that Beor had cast out his own son and caused Esta to go after him, and Carrick must have been furious.

"I tried to speak with your father, but Beor made sure that your father knew why we were there, stating that we had come for the witch."

Esta's eyes snapped to his. She knew that Carrick would have been enraged by Beor's words. She also knew that he would have had a very strong reaction.

"Your father, as Beor knew he would, jumped to your defense ..."

Guth was not sure he wanted to continue. He looked at Esta closely and could see that her eyes were beginning to water. He knew this was hurting her, and he feared that the grief would turn to anger.

"When your father went at Beor, he was between two of my men. They pulled their weapons to defend themselves. He took down one of my men before I was able to stop them. I was able to pull your father back, while my men had ahold of Beor. It was tense, but I was able to tell him that Beor did not speak for me, that I wished to speak with him alone." He paused to take a breath. His face showed the anger that began to well up inside him as he looked at Esta again. "He would not stop. I signaled my men to return to the village with Beor in tow. I don't know how or why they let him loose, but that was all it took. He came charging at Carrick and calling for some sort of justice. He shouted that the witch had caused the loss of his dignity, or I don't know, something like that. Carrick drew his weapon and began to fight. My men simply defended themselves. They had no choice."

Esta could feel his remorse, his anger at Beor, his hatred of how things had happened on the island. It was hard to separate his feelings of hate from her own. Tears began to well up in her eyes, and a lump formed in her throat. She wanted to scream. She wanted to avenge her father's death. She wanted to run away from this place and never come back. She began to shake. It was too much, and she was about to break down. She would not be able to stop it.

As if from nowhere, Ivar was there. He stood right in front of her, looking sad and concerned. He reached out a small hand and placed it on her cheek. Esta looked into his eyes and, as if he spoke the words aloud, she heard him.

Please don't leave me.

It was too much. The look in his eyes was full of concerned panic. He was afraid—afraid she would leave. Esta tried to gather herself. She looked deep into his eyes and thought hard of what she wanted to convey.

Ivar dropped his hand and gave the slightest of nods. He walked to

Guth's side and took hold of his hand. Guth stood and allowed Ivar to lead him from the room, glancing over his shoulder at the girl he knew he had wounded and then at his son, who seemed to have an instant affection for her. Ivar was acting as if he knew her, as if he knew that the situation was about to become very uncomfortable and they should remove themselves. He wasn't sure if he was excited about what this could mean for Ivar or frightened.

Esta broke down at once. She cried for the loss of her father. She cried for the ones who had died because she lived. She cried for Erik and for Roan and Landen. She even cried for Guth and his son, the boy who brought her to this place—this beautiful place that she wanted to hate. She wanted to despise everything and everyone here. She already knew that her heart would not allow it, would not allow her to despise any … save one. Beor. She could hate Beor. She could despise the one responsible for so much loss. Unnecessary loss. His soul was black; Esta knew that from past encounters. What was hard to understand was how anyone could be so very evil as this man was.

She remembered now the first time that she had been confronted with Beor's emotions. She had been just a young girl. Her father had carried her into town with him on his cob to visit and barter upon the green. They would perhaps get her a new pair of rabbit-fur-lined boots before the winter set in. They'd been walking toward the skinner's when Esta had stopped and pulled her father's hand back. He'd looked down at her in surprise and asked her what was the matter. Esta had looked up at her father with tears filling her eyes just as Dirk had appeared with young Erik by his side. They had just come from their home to the green, where they'd meant to find a few things to place around Erik's mother as she crossed over. She had passed in the night of a sickness that had haunted her for years. Their grief, their sorrow had hit Esta hard. It was not that grief, though, that had caused her to cry that day. Suddenly, Esta remembered her absolute fear at entering the skinner's shed. How her heart had sped up, and her breath had caught in her throat. Evil had been near, and it had been hurting another human being for the pure joy of it.

Her head snapped up and she looked into the flames of the hearth.

Roan. Roan was being beaten that day. His father's anger and hate had focused on a boy who could not understand what he had done wrong. She'd never said a word. She'd never spoken of it. She was not even sure that she had remembered it until just now. Erik and his father had been in such pain. Had she confused it? Had she set it aside and forgotten it? No. She had set it aside out of fear. She had been so young and afraid that the harm could be passed onto her loved ones. Now she knew; now she remembered it so vividly. The skinner had always brought feelings of hurt, feelings of fear. She remembered them well.

It was hard to keep the anger at bay. Esta knew all too well where anger took people. It was an ugly emotion, no matter who wore it. It was a temporary emotion in most people, but not within Beor. And now for the first time in her life, Esta could see herself wanting revenge, wanting punishment—a punishment that would fit the crime. For the first time in her life, she wanted another human being to suffer a painful end.

She needed air. She felt the need to gather herself together and calm the fire that burned within her heart. This was an emotion she had rarely felt before. She had only felt this kind of blackness of soul a few times in her life. Never had it crossed her mind that she would feel it within herself.

Esta stood and looked about the room, hoping for another way out. Guth, or perhaps one of his servants, would most likely be in the hallway. She wanted no emotions, no other human being around her. Mane. Mane would be outside and nearby. Behind a long table that sat against the wall, there was another door. The table held mugs and plates full of fruit and bread. The door was closed, but it was not locked. Esta pulled it open and peered into a hall. A servant girl in an apron appeared and asked if she needed anything. The smell of a cooking fire and voices of cheerful chatter reached her ears. She knew she was near the kitchens.

"I'm fine. I am a little turned around. Can I get outside through here?"

The girl looked confused. "No, Miss, only through the kitchens. The outer hall is behind you." She pointed for Esta to go back the way she had come.

"Thank you." Esta closed the door. What if someone was waiting in the hall? What if they would not let her leave? The air became heavy, and Esta felt an overwhelming urge to run. She opened the door and stepped into the hall as if she intended to leave the room. Lombard was there, sitting on a small bench waiting. He stood and smiled weakly at her.

"Do you wish to join your mother, my lady?"

Esta shook her head. "No. I wish to see the sky. I need air. Please take me out!"

Lombard nodded and turned down the hall. She walked behind him, the tension building with every step. When they reached a set of double doors, Lombard pulled one of them open.

"The gardens, Miss." He stood aside and allowed her to exit and then closed the door softly behind her.

Esta stepped out until the light hit her face. She took a deep breath and closed her eyes, opening them after several steady, deep breaths. She found herself in a courtyard. There were fruit trees and a small pond. There were flowers of bright colors that Esta had never seen before. She could smell them, even at a distance. She closed her eyes once again and tried to find Mane. She let out a soft whistle, waited, and then whistled again. Mane flew over the wall and to her shoulder. Her clicks and pops were excited, and she nestled in Esta's hair.

"I know. I was worried about you as well." Esta stroked her chest feathers, and soon Mane calmed and trilled. She walked the perimeter of the garden next to the wall. A path wound through the large courtyard and its flowering trees and shrubs. Benches sat here and there offering different views and perspectives of the huge gardens. The garden wall was high and thick, and Esta could not imagine building something so strong and beautiful. There were apple and pear trees that hung heavy with their harvest. Root vegetables and flowers grew in patches as well. The place was a wonder.

The sun was beginning to set. Shadows grew across the yard, and Esta knew she would not be allowed to stay much longer. She sat on a bench near the doors and waited. She expected Guth or Lombard, perhaps her mother. She did not expect Landen. He walked out onto the grass at the edge of the garden and turned in a slow, directed circle.

"Amazing, is it not?" Esta smiled at him.

"I cannot help but wonder what it must be like to live here," he said.

Esta nodded. "Do you plan to stay here? You and Roan?"

Landen looked at her and shrugged his shoulders. He tried to see if Esta could tell he wanted to ask a question, if she could read his mind before he asked. She just smiled at him.

"What is wrong with Ivar?" he asked.

Esta could read his concern, not just for Ivar but for the entire company.

"I'm not sure. He does not speak—not aloud, anyway—even though I have no doubt that he is able."

Landen knew what she meant.

"You can hear him, though. You know what he is saying?"

Esta shook her head. "It's not that simple, Landen. You know I cannot read minds. I have told you that."

Landen tilted his head to one side, and Esta felt a little flash of distrust from him. Esta gave the seat next to her a pat.

"Come. Tell me what troubles you Landen?"

He sat and held his hand up for Mane, who chortled and nuzzled as he gave her a chin scratch. Mane was very peculiar about who she allowed to touch her. Landen seemed to understand that it needed to be her choice. Mane liked him, a good sign as to what kind of young man he was. Esta focused on Landen's feelings and felt that he was afraid. He felt a good deal of fear over something. Fear and hesitation. So, he was afraid to tell her something. She waited, feeling she needed to give him the opportunity to trust her.

"I heard him," Landen whispered. "He told me to come find you. He said that you were upset and he is afraid you will go away."

Esta was shocked. "He spoke to you?"

"No, not out loud. It was in my head. But I did hear him. So did you." Landen looked at her.

"I wasn't sure. I didn't know if it was real or if something strange was happening with me because of all the emotion I was feeling." Esta looked at Landen. "Have you ever heard or felt anyone before?"

"No, but he told me not to be afraid." Landen smiled at her. "He doesn't like to do it. He said it frightens people."

Esta raised a brow. "He can do this at will?" If so, why did he not speak with his father?

Landen seemed eager to share. "No, not everyone can hear him, only those whose minds are open."

Landen smiled again. He liked the idea of being special. He was proud that he was able to communicate with Ivar. Proud that Ivar had chosen him. Esta smiled back at him. It hit her then that this young man came from Beor. How did something so good come from something so evil? How did Roan, Landen, and little Hadwin survive without being tainted?

Roan had much anger, though when removed from Beor, he showed himself a good soul. Esta knew now that much of Roan's temper was a survival tactic. Landen had always been the quiet one. He made himself invisible to stay out of his father's way. Little Hadwin was still very attached to her mother's skirts, far too young to understand the hate her father dealt out with both words and his iron fists.

They had sat a long time. The sun had dipped below the stone wall, and servants had emerged to light a few torches near the doors. Esta released Mane to the coming darkness, and the owl circled the garden before flying inland. She would hunt and find a place to wait out the night. Esta tried to convey how important it was that she stay close yet out of sight.

"It's alright, you know. That my father must die. I understand, and I do not blame you," Landen stared at his feet.

This was new information. "Your father is to be put to death?" How and when had that decision been made?

"Yes." Landen looked up at her.

She wanted to tell him that it would be alright. She wanted to tell him she would not allow it, that she would speak with Guth and stop it. Still, there was a part of her that felt justice was needed, even deserved.

"I do not know what to say, Landen," she said softly. "I thought that was what I wanted, but I am no longer sure of that."

As the silence grew, it seemed to take on a life of its own. She knew this was not what she wanted. She was about to make her offer of help when their attention swung to the door that opened behind them. Roan stood in the opening, looking annoyed.

"Where on earth have you been? We have been worried sick. What happened in there?"

He seemed worried and angry. Esta was not ready to share anything at this point. There were still far too many questions that needed answers. First and foremost, she needed to make sure everyone was alright.

"Time slipped away from us. Where are the others? My mother?" Esta asked.

"They are in the hall. Waiting," Roan answered.

"They come then?" Landen asked enthusiastically.

Esta was lost. "Who comes? What are you talking about?" She looked from Roan to Landen and back again and then realized who was missing. "Where is Erik?"

Roan smiled at her, and she could tell that he had mixed feelings about what was happening.

"Erik has gone back to Elvoy. Guth has invited the elders and any others who wish to come here, even if only to see what is possible for Elvoy. He means to make amends for what happened on the island. He has promised Erik that he will help the island recover."

Esta raised her brow. "You cannot recover that which the earth has received."

Roan looked down. His remorse weighed heavy upon him, more so now that he felt responsible for his brother and sister. Landen looked up into her eyes, and she could feel his eagerness. He had feelings of anticipation, which led Esta to believe that he knew who was coming.

"Hadwin will be happy to see you. Happy to see both of you," she said looking at them.

Landen smiled, but Roan seemed nervous, weighed down with the new responsibilities.

"We should join the others. I'm sure you two stargazers are quite hungry."

He turned back to open the doors, and the small group made their way to the hall where food and drink waited. They ate and were shown to quarters where they could get some much-needed sleep. Clare tried to comfort Esta just as Esta tried to comfort Clare. They lay next to each other in the dark, trying hard to conceal tears and grief until they both gave way. They fell asleep exhausted and emotionally spent.

EIGHT

Beor's Fate

sta woke to find her mother had already gone. She sat and looked at the little table, where a pitcher of water and a loaf of warm bread waited. There was a small fire in the hearth, and when Esta's feet touched the floor, she found it soft and warm, a woven rung upon it. As she tore off a piece of the steaming loaf, she noticed a woolen gown and leggings draped over a chair. Her mother's clothes were there upon the floor, and as she bent to pick them up, the door opened. Clare came in with a small basket.

"You are awake." She smiled at Esta through red-rimmed eyes.

Esta looked at her mother. She wore a cream-colored gown and leggings with a green overdress. She looked clean and dressed in a way that seemed foreign to her. Even her hair was braided anew. Yet her eyes were swollen, and her smile did not extend beyond her lips. She was putting on a brave face. Yet Esta could feel her fear; she could feel her sorrow.

"Is it late?" Esta asked softly.

"A boat arrived early this morning. The elders and a few of the families of those who were taken are here. Guth wanted everyone to look well when they arrived, I guess, so he made a gift of some new clothing." Clare put her dirty clothes into the basket and nodded at Esta. "You should change as well. There is fresh water for the basin just outside. Let me get it."

Her mother vanished as Esta approached the new clothing. The soft woolen gown was of a deep tan, like that of a deer in the spring. Her overdress was much like her mother's but blue. She picked up the overdress in her hands and pulled the dark blue fabric through her fingers. It was so fine and tight. The color and the weave were beyond anything she had seen, and Esta marveled at the quality of the seams.

"They have things we can only dream of," Clare said as she poured the water from the pitcher into the basin.

"Why? Why does he give these things? Why does he bring the elders here?" Esta turned to face her mother. "He has decided to put Beor to death."

Clare's head snapped up, her eyes wide. She looked at Esta as she took a deep breath.

"Landen told me," Esta said, looking again at her mother.

Clare said nothing, only looked at Esta with wide eyes full of sorrow. Esta could feel the same conflicts within Clare that she was feeling herself. She wanted justice as a woman and a wife, but she could not reconcile that with her feelings as a healer. Healers should covet life, and in this case, she could see no value in keeping Beor alive. And she felt shame at the thought that she would feel some satisfaction upon his death. Feeling that this topic would only bring her mother more pain, Esta let it go.

When Esta emerged from her chamber, it was well past midday. She wore the new clothes, and Clare had braided her hair into one long plait in the back. She went now in search of Roan and then to find Guth. It did not take long. Esta found Lombard in the great hall, who told her that Roan and Landen were at the moment introducing Hadwin to Ivar and Lombard's master in the family chambers. He turned and nodded for her to follow.

As the door opened, all eyes turned to her. Esta could not get the picture out of her mind of a family enjoying each other. She should not be here. Hadwin sat nervously on Roan's lap and allowed Landen and Ivar to entertain her. Guth was happy to see her and came to welcome her at once. Ivar also left his company to welcome her. Esta was given a seat across the table from Roan. At last, Hadwin felt comfortable enough to join Ivar at his little table full of toys. Almost as soon as she had walked away, Esta spoke.

"I need to speak to you alone, Roan. You and your uncle."

Roan knew Esta well enough to hear the seriousness of her tone. "What is it? Has something happened?" He threw a worried glance at his uncle.

"No, no, nothing like that." She paused, not sure of how to bring up Beor in such a way as not to hurt Roan. "It is your father," she whispered.

Ivar turned to look at them as if he had heard every word. Esta had the strangest feeling that he could eavesdrop from across the room.

"Can we talk somewhere else?" she asked.

Roan's face became stoic. He glanced at his uncle again and shook his head.

"There is nothing more to be said," Roan said, nearly hissing as he spoke.

Esta was hit by the flood of emotion from him—anger, regret, hatred, and grief. The wave shifted and changed as he tried to grapple with the tumult of feelings inside. There was a part of Roan that wished that things were different.

"Roan, please. This is not what I wanted."

Esta reached for his arm, and he recoiled. Roan stood and moved to the hearth. He turned his back to the others and sat where Ivar and Hadwin were playing with wooden horses. He was finished with it. Esta could tell that he had made up his mind, and there was no changing it.

Guth moved to the door and gave her a slight nod. Breathing a heavy sigh, Esta quietly moved to the door, and Roan turned to glance at them as they stepped out. Once outside, Esta did not waste a moment.

"You cannot put Beor to death. I cannot be responsible for yet another life lost!"

Guth held up a hand to quiet her. "It is not your fault that Beor is who he is. He has made his own choices. You must understand that this is not the first time that he should have faced—"

"Then banish him again," Esta interrupted, shaking her head. "Send him away."

"I cannot. I know now what he did to his family. Would you have me send him out to harm others as he has already done?"

Guth held anger and guilt about Beor's time on Elvoy. Esta knew that Beor's family had suffered under his rule, both physically and emotionally. She also knew she did not want anyone else to suffer that fate. Her mind searched for a way to both allow Beor to live and keep him away from others that might come to harm.

"Could he not be banished to someplace where he could do no harm?" Even as she voiced it, she knew that there may be no such place.

"I could lock him away, give him a life in a small cell without the light of day, without the sound or touch of another human being. Is that what you would have me do?"

Guth was amazed at the concern being shown his brother. The girl should wish justice, should want revenge. Yet here she seemed eager to save Beor.

"Why do you wish to spare the one responsible for your father's death?"

His words were sharp. They slapped her as if they had been an actual blow. She did want revenge. She did want justice.

"I do not ask this for myself." Her voice took on an edge that Guth had not heard before. "Roan, Landen, and Hadwin, they did nothing, and yet they will suffer another loss and the stigma of having a father who is a murderer."

Esta nearly spit that last word at him. Guth knew that no matter what Beor may have done, Esta still felt that Guth was also to blame. It had been his decision to come to Elvoy after her in the first place. For a brief moment, he considered her request. Then the door swung open, and both Roan and Landen stood there. Esta could feel their conflicting emotions—Roan's anger and Landen's pride. She wanted to make things right without yet another death. A death sentence on Elvoy was extreme and rare. Esta could only remember one such sentence being carried out in the whole of her life. She knew there had been others before that, but it was not a topic of conversation. Esta suddenly realized that she did not even know what kind of sentence Beor faced. The old ways would require the removal of his head, but Esta knew other places had their own ways of dealing with people who had been found unfit to live. Stories had reached Elvoy of the punishments faced: people being stoned, hanged, hung upon a pole, or placed in an iron cage suspended from a tree. Even being burned alive was not unheard of.

Landen stepped forward and took her hand. "Let it go, Esta. Come, let Ivar and Hadwin meet Mane. Let us go to the garden."

Ivar appeared in the door with Hadwin in tow. He gave a slight nod as he led the toddler down the corridor toward the gardens. For a moment, she thought to protest. She felt she needed to state again her reasons for allowing Beor his life, but then she allowed Landen to pull her away and followed the youngsters to the sunlight of the courtyard.

Once the rest were out of earshot, Roan turned to his uncle. "Perhaps this should be done quickly and quietly. It may be better if she discovers it has happened after the fact."

Guth was still puzzled by Roan. His courage and strength were great, yet he still carried much anger—a reminder to Guth of where he had come from. A slight mistrust of Roan was hard to shake, knowing his brother's past and finding that he had not changed his treatment of others while on Elvoy. Guth hoped to find more of the young man's mother within him than his father. If not, there may not be room on Land's End for the boy.

Erik had arrived with the elders from Elvoy, and together they had headed for the front doors of Guth's fortress. They wanted to know and understand how Guth had managed to build such a beautiful city. Beautiful and defendable. Each courtyard housed a family unit. The solid rock walls of the courtyard offered protection from the elements as well as making an attack on the city futile. The views from the bluff gave hours of warning should any strange ships approach the bay, time which would allow the villagers to move into the stronghold of Guth's fortress. The walls there were four to five times as tall as any man. The buildings inside were not just made of stone but also had some sort of slate roof. Claylike tiles of different shades of white and grey made the buildings glow in the sunlight. Only the roofs of the village houses where thatched. Guth had begun to rethink this as well, and the dwelling houses in the village were about to undergo the same transformation, which would make lighting them on fire from the outside nearly impossible.

If an enemy managed to land in the narrow harbor, there was only one way up the beach to the village. Steep, rocky bluffs on either side kept most from trying. The odds were not in favor of a sea attack. Behind the village was a forest of several thousand acres. This woodland was strictly managed. Past the woods, there was nothing but sea grass and rolling moors as far as the eye could see.

There had been a time during the early years, when raids and attacks on the village had come often. Guth's father had learned through trial and error what kind of defense was needed here. Now, a king ruled far to the north who enjoyed knowing that his kingdom could not be entered at Land's End. Guth enjoyed being left alone to rule as lord baron for King Henry II and his queen, Eleanor of Aquitaine. The wars over who would rule Britannia seemed at last at an end. The lawless raiding and land wars had been quieted by the king's swift, ruthless punishments for overstepping one's station.

The elders marveled at the stonework. The walls of each courtyard gleamed in the sun. This along with the white stone walls of Guth's stronghold gave the village a sort of shimmering glow. The village was somewhat small in population; it was the size and splendor of each of the courtyard dwellings that took one's breath away. Each courtyard contained a small stable and washhouse, and earthen ovens gave off the aroma of fresh-baked bread and smoked fish. Some yards held chickens, others goats and pigs. Others had larger inner areas where the people were growing root vegetables, and still others just seemed to be there to look beautiful, covered in vines and flowers with colorful blossoms.

Guth enjoyed taking the elders about the village and teaching them the new and improved ways of making the stonework. He explained how providing each family with space to grow their own crops, raise animals, and make their goods was a way to keep everyone invested in the village. The community crops were worked by everyone who wished to be given a fair share of what was harvested—after Guth took his share, of course. The same was true of the fishing boats. The villagers traded with each other for all other goods, and traveling tradesmen came through both to take goods to other places and to leave goods behind. Guth was proud, and if truth be told, he should have been. Land's End was a beautiful, peaceful place.

Beor had been taken to a stone room at the back of the fortress with only one door and no windows. He had been sealed inside without so much as a word from his brother, not that he needed to hear from Guth. He knew his brother had little love for him. He only needed one chance. The plan had gone accordingly so far; he was back at Land's End and was in his brother's keep. However, he had not planned on being locked up. This and this alone was the only reason he was still there, sitting in a corner, staring at the wooden knots in the door and the iron hinges and rivets that made escape impossible. Why had Guth not placed him in the cells? His mind began to race. He had been here before, and his thoughts drifted back in time, reliving the events that had led him to his current situation.

Beor had always been at odds with his brother. Even as children they'd seemed to find disagreement at nearly every turn. They had grown up learning to read and write, learning the sword, the skills of combat, strategy, and how to govern their people. Beor had felt his studies a waste of his time, all those except the ones related to combat. His studies with the sword were the most important, his desire and drive being to best his slightly older brother. Yet Guth continued to be his better. No matter how much time he had spent upon the training fields with the master swordsmen in his father's guard, Beor could not seem to surpass the skill Guth would pick up in far fewer trainings. This point had been driven home by the comments made by the blade masters both behind his back and to his face. As he'd grown older, his loathing for

Guth had mounted. Beor remembered the day that the Lady Roisin had been brought to the village to meet Guth. She had come from a noble family in the far reaches of the north. The match had been put together with the support of the crown to give the people a sense of togetherness. Seeing the couple wed, it had been hoped, would help create stability. Beor had scoffed at the match, thinking that a woman coming from the Celtic hills would bring little but a rough, foreign tongue, a disagreeable temper, and an ill-favored face. He could not have been more mistaken. The woman had had long hair of the darkest auburn. Her complexion had been fair and her eyes a striking color of green. She'd been tall and slender with an ample chest and rounded hips. And Beor had hated Guth all the more for it.

That revulsion toward his brother had begun to show upon his face. It had begun to show in his deeds. When their mother had lain ill in her chambers for several months, Beor could not be bothered to visit with her, nor would he consent to hear that he should. She'd been old, she'd been dying, and she had never in Beor's estimation given him much to sit and visit about. Guth had been taken aback by his brother's indifference to their mother, so much so that he had tried and failed on several occasions to demand that Beor attend her. The same set of circumstances had occurred when their father passed away, although his passing had not been as drawn out as their mother's had.

Beor had found himself a bride upon one of his many travels away from Land's End. She'd been a beautiful woman, yet Beor knew that Guth had seen through her attempts at appearing to be well bred. She had been a woman from the docks, and Beor had dressed her up and coached her for one purpose: he had thought to make Guth jealous. Upon his return with the woman, he'd found that Guth and his wife had born a son. The birth had been too much for Roisin, and she had passed away within days of a fever. Beor had found his brother in a state of profound sadness and grief. He'd reveled in it.

As the time passed, Guth had become a doting father, keeping the toddler close and spending more time with the boy than was necessary. Beor had come to regret his choice of wife, and the result had been visible. When Guth had seen the woman with a blackened eye, Beor had told him to mind his own business. But the fights between Beor and his wife could often be heard in the corridors of the castle, and they'd been escalating. Beor's face soured at the memory. The first time he had been placed in a cell by his perfect older brother, the first time that Guth had looked at him with the dislike that had burned within Beor for years, had been on the night that he had killed her. Not that he had told his brother that. No, he had said they had fought, that he had pushed her back when she had come at him with a broken shard of pottery. The truth was that he had grabbed her by the hair and slammed her head into the stone table. He had then placed his hands around her throat while she'd lain on the floor moaning to make sure that she never again gained her feet. After that, he had sat in a cell much like this one for two days. Two days of growing resentment and anger toward a brother he could not bear.

When Guth had finally come to speak with him, Beor had made his feelings clear. Seeing the hurt and anger on Guth's face had given him a slight bit of satisfaction, as he was sure that Guth had meant to punish him for the woman's death. Yet Beor had found himself at a loss for words when Guth had simply told him that he was to leave Land's End. Leave it, and never return. Guth had left him then, left him again in that cell for another day until satchels of his personal belongings were brought to him. He had then been led out the back doors of the outer wall, where a mount was waiting. The guard had handed him the reins and turned his back upon him to close the doors. And Beor had ridden away. As he'd looked back at the castle he had once called home, Guth had been on the wall walk, watching his brother disappear into the woods. At that moment, Beor had promised himself one thing: that he would someday watch his brother's downfall. That he would rule Land's End, even if he had to take it by force.

Guth had taken Roan's words into advisement. He was not sure how to go about things with Beor. Only those who had gone to Elvoy knew that Beor had made a mess of things. Word was spreading fast about the island raid, however, for several men did not come back. Five men in all had lost their lives because of Beor's actions on Elvoy. Their families too were calling for justice. Beor's execution should be public. It should take place on the bluff as every other sentence like this had for the last hundred years.

Not a soul was aware that everything was about to change. Beor was beginning to feel a sense of dread. He had always been turned loose by his brother in the past. Guth would rant and rave about his latest transgression and then send him away. Something was different this time. After spending so much time alone in the little room, Beor now realized that his brother had finally run out of mercy. He believed he was about to be banished again until he heard the guard talking through the door about the need for a death shroud. The words had spun him around to face the door, and he could not paste his ear close enough to the gaps in the wood to listen. He was not able to gather anything more, so now he thought endlessly of a much-needed plan.

It was customary for a person sentenced to death to wear a white shroud. This was a symbol of a new birth to help the condemned into the afterworld. A fresh, clean start could be made in the next life. It would be brought to him on the morning of his execution. Although Beor had not spoken so much as one word to his brother or even seen him since being placed in his cell, he knew what awaited him, so when the door opened, Beor was ready.

Only one guard had been placed at the holding cell. Guth had not thought there would be a problem, since he intended to escort Beor to the bluff himself. Lombard, knowing that Guth was busy with the elders from Elvoy, had asked about the shroud. Guth had simply requested that one be made available. He had not given much thought to the fact that the shroud would be given to Beor before the sunset walk to the bluff. Lombard sent a young servant out into the village to collect a few shrouds for Beor to choose from. She returned with only two and brought them to Lombard for his approval. Looking at the shrouds, Lombard asked the young girl to deliver the garments to Beor's guard. She did, and the guard, not knowing any different, opened the door to deliver the garments to Beor. Beor came at the guard full force, knocking him back into the wall. The girl let out a short, horrified shriek as Beor snapped the young man's neck and pulled the guard's short sword free of its sheath as he fell to the floor. He then turned to the girl and placed the blade's point at her chin.

"Shut your mouth!" he hissed through his teeth at her.

Terrified, the girl clamped her own hand over her mouth, eyes filling with tears. Beor stepped past her to take a quick look around the corner and down the long corridor to freedom. He could not simply walk out the front doors unnoticed. There was only one other choice. He needed to get to the family courtyard gardens. There he could use the secret door and escape very quickly into the forest.

𝔑𝔦𝔫𝔢

Hostages

In the gardens, Mane had allowed both Landen and Hadwin to pet her. Ivar, it seemed, was special, for Mane not only allowed him to fondly stroke her feathers but gently stepped off of Esta's shoulder and onto his waiting forearm. Esta could feel his joy and excitement. She also caught his thoughts.

"She is so light. I thought she would weigh so much more."

It seemed that both Landen and Hadwin were privy to this information as well, for they both looked up at Esta at the same moment. It was as if Ivar's form of communication was not a surprise to them. Esta smiled at them and nodded.

"Owls have hollow bones. Most people do not know that they are all fluff and little substance."

Mane clicked and chortled a protest.

"Yet their very dangerous talons can crush their prey," Esta added quickly, "and they are the only bird with silent flight. Of course, they are the most beautiful."

They all chuckled, as this praise seemed to give Mane a reason to puff up. Esta looked at them with the knowing look of a teacher, or perhaps a mother.

"You should not keep secrets, you know. They always have a way of escaping when you would least like them to." Esta said, as she tilted her head and gave both children a nod and a wink.

Ivar looked up at her with a rather wicked grin.

The doors swung open, and Lombard appeared with several servants in tow. He carried warm cloaks of wool and fur; others carried pitchers of steaming mead and mugs of warmed milk for the children. The look upon Lombard's face when he saw Mane proudly perched upon Ivar's arm was comical. The children laughed, and Esta chuckled as she sent Mane to a nearby tree to perch.

Hadwin stared wide eyed at the coat being wrapped around her. Never had she seen anything so beautiful. The cloak handed to Esta was also gorgeous, the deepest of greens with bone-and-leather closures; soft, beautiful rabbit fur lined the hood and the inside. Never had Esta felt such sudden warmth or seen such beauty. She was wrapped in a blanket of soft fur, and she understood that the green wool would also be quite water resistant. As if Lombard had some magical connection to the elements, light snowflakes began to fall. She turned to question the man, who was herding the servants back inside, but could have sworn she saw a slight smile upon his face as he closed the doors.

Snow had always meant cold, wet, miserable conditions for the children of Elvoy. Chores doubled, as collecting wood and peat to keep warm became a high priority. Elvoy had warm wheelhouses, but once outside, they had no fur-lined cloaks or beautiful coats to keep them warm. Clothing was practical, sturdy.

Esta watched as the children tried to catch the falling snow upon their tongues. She held the warm mug in her hands and sipped the sweet mulled cider, feeling the heat all the way to her stomach. For a moment she was content … for a moment.

The door behind her swung open so harshly it made everyone jump. As Esta turned, her eyes grew wide at the sight of Beor pushing a frightened girl forward. He pushed her to one side as he took in the frightened faces before him. Her heart began to beat quickly, and her hands to lost their grip on the cup. The pewter mug clattered across the stone. It seemed to take Beor a moment to fully take in the scene before him. He gave the girl another quick shove that had her grasping at the wind to keep her feet. Landen rushed forward to help her keep her balance when he saw the smile on his father's face and the sword tip swing toward Esta. He changed course in mid stride, placing himself between his father and Esta.

"Move out of the way boy!" Beor seemed to be looking right through Landen to where Esta stood, shocked.

"No! If you harm her, Guth will hunt you down himself!" Landen hissed at his father, who was angered at the steady bravery in his son's voice.

Suddenly, Ivar was next to Landen. He stared hard at Beor and shook his head as if to tell Beor, "No."

Beor looked at Ivar in disgust, feeling hatred for the boy. Then Esta felt his hatred take a drastic and dangerous turn, and Esta's fear exploded.

"Leave whilst you can, Beor, for no amount of pleading can save you now," Esta called out, trying hard to hold her voice steady. She refused to appear weak in front of this man who had taken so much from her.

She stepped past Ivar and placed her hand on Landen's shoulder to calm him. Beor seemed to consider his options as he looked at those around him. He zeroed in on Ivar, and Esta was confused by the thrill he was getting. His emotions bounced back and forth between jelousy and hate. There also was some sort of greed that she could not decipher. He seemed to settle on the latter.

"Your father would do just about anything for you, wouldn't he?" Beor said. "Let us see just how far he will go." Beor reached out and took Ivar by the collar. He nearly picked him up off the ground as he turned on Esta. "You as well. Let's go!" He nodded toward the wall, advancing on her and allowing the tip of his blade to brush the fabric of her cloak.

Landen screamed, "You can't!" but before he had time to finish, Beor struck him full force with the back of his sword hand. Landen flew back and hit the cobblestone with a resounding thud, his head smacking the stone. He was knocked out, and Hadwin ran to his side, crying loudly.

Beor looked at the servant girl and shouted, "Shut her up!"

Frightened, the girl rushed at Hadwin, which only seemed to make her screams of protest louder. Beor knew his window of opportunity for escape was closing fast. He needed to be well into the woods before anyone started looking for them. Beor pushed Esta forward toward the back wall of the garden. This part of the wall gave way into the forest, its trees looming over the top of the wall. Beor then looked into the sky and smiled at the falling snow that would cover their tracks.

"Move, now!" He nodded for Esta to move faster, pushing her roughly forward.

"I will not! I will not go anywhere with you!" She stood her ground, fear gripping her as she tried to show strength.

Beor gave her an evil grin as if he knew she would do as he asked even before he asked it. He turned the blade upside down in his hand and pointed at the place where Hadwin lay weeping on Landen's unconscious body.

"It means nothing to me at this point, and I will do it!"

Esta looked into his emotions. She knew he would do it. He had wanted to kill her in that moment before Landen had stepped forward. Ivar's thoughts slammed into her head, almost as if he were shouting at her. The young servant girl threw her hands up to her ears and gave yet another horrified shriek.

Go! Go with him, Esta! My father will come!

Esta looked back at Hadwin and Landen as they walked toward the far wall of the courtyard. An audible sigh escaped her as she saw Landen stir, reaching up a hand to touch his sister and quiet her.

It took only a moment for Beor to find the exit well hidden in the vines that grew up and over the outer wall. Once through, they moved quickly into the woods. The snow had started to fall now—heavy, large flakes that began to coat the ground. Esta looked behind them and knew that their tracks would not be visible for long. She kept a close watch on Ivar's emotions, not wanting him to become frightened. Yet it was Ivar who seemed to be the one sending comforting thoughts, telling her that they would be alright, that his father would find them. He reminded her that Mane was watching. Almost as soon as their feet had hit the forest floor, Mane had been close. Esta kept her near enough to feel her presence yet far enough away so that only she and Ivar knew where to find her.

Beor's path seemed well thought out. He moved quickly through the trees, and Esta could read his excitement as they seemed to be getting closer to his destination, even though they seemed lost to her, walking through the nearly ankle-deep snow in a forest of white.

When Ivar began to drag his feet, causing long deep markings in the snow, Beor forced Esta to carry him upon her back. She purposely walked close to low-hanging tree limbs so that Ivar could quickly reach up and break a small twig of a branch, or at least bend it. As the light began to fade, the bottom of Esta's fur-lined cloak was dragging on the freshly fallen snow. It was deeper now than her soaked leather boots, and her feet were becoming numb. If not for the warmth of Ivar upon her back, she would never have made it this far. She continued to check into Beor's emotions. He had no fear of the weather. He did not think he was going to freeze to death. Esta could not help but believe that there must be warmth and shelter coming.

She had been carrying Ivar for a very long time. Her physical exertion was helping to keep her blood flowing, yet Ivar had been upon her back nearly the entire day. The snow that was building up on the ground may have numbed Esta's feet, but Ivar's coat was soaking wet. His teeth were chattering, and he was having trouble holding on. His hands were numb, and he could no longer feel his toes. Esta became afraid that Ivar would not last much longer before he fell asleep and slipped away. She pushed him to stay in contact with her, to hang on.

"Beor, we must stop. Ivar needs warmth. We need a fire." Esta stepped aside as he walked past her on the narrow trail through the woods. She was hit by the feeling of satisfaction and victory and then smug conceit and greed. Beor once again disappeared through the brush. When he appeared again in front of them, he pulled her through the brush and between two massive slabs of rock. A door that looked like a tree growing up between the stone was pushed open, and they were in a small lantern-lit room. A fire blazed in a hearth, and the smell of lamb stew hung in the air. Esta was about to breathe a sigh of relief when Ivar's fear hit her. His grip tightened, and he began to shake. This was not caused by the cold but by a deep-seated fear. She spun, and there, barely lit by the candle light, was the woman from the fortress, the one who had spoken with such contempt about the boy. Esta could feel from her the same feelings toward Ivar she had felt then. She did not like the boy. She walked toward them, anger upon her face as she gestured at them.

"What have ya done? Why are they here?" She spat the words at Beor.

"I had no choice," he hissed back at her through his teeth. "Leave it! I'm near frozen."

He moved toward the hearth and sat in an overstuffed chair that looked just like those in the family solar. Beor removed his boots and wet cloak. He stood and placed several logs on the fire, stoking the flames for more heat.

Esta gently placed Ivar on his feet and walked him to the hearth. She could sense the woman's hatred of him. It was as strong as Ivar's fear of the women. Keeping her own body between them, she opened her mind to Ivar's and thought, *Who is she? Why are you so frightened of her?*

She is Ingwolf, called Inga. She was cousin to my mother.

Esta knew that names carried weight. She found it a bad omen that both Beor's and Ingwolf's names shared the same meaning: wolf.

Ivar agreed. *She is a wolf. She steals things and tells my father I broke them. She is cruel.*

His thoughts were cautious, as if she may hear him and punish him for them. Esta sent the question out, but Ivar scoffed, telling her that the woman's mind was closed to anything not placed before her eyes.

Inga gave Beor a steaming bowl of stew and turned back to the hearth.

"I suppose they will have to be fed." She looked again at Esta with disdain.

"He is cold. Do you have anything to place over him? His cloak is wet." Esta removed the soaked coat and could see that even Ivar's tunic had become wet beneath it.

Inga tossed a blanket at her and pointed at the floor. "Sit."

By the hearth, Esta and Ivar ate their very small bowls of hot stew. Esta took in her surroundings. The cavern was carved out of the large stone, no doubt by years of water runoff. The smooth walls fell away in a nearly perfect circle. The hearth sat in a natural corner, and a shaft had been carved to let the smoke out. The wall behind their backs was warm, and she could not help but feel grateful for it. The floor had rugs, as did two of the walls. There was a door on the opposite side of the room from the entry, and Esta guessed that it held a bed chamber and another fireplace. The room was small, yet it was very comfortable—and very out of place, hidden in a rock bluff and full of stolen goods from Land's End. As Esta scanned the room, she could see tapestries, candle sticks, tables with carved legs. It was almost a replica of the solar in which she had first visited with Ivar. Inga approached to reclaim the empty bowls. As she watched Esta scan the room with a wrinkled brow, she realized that the girl was taking in the stolen items one by one. Her reaction was instant. She raised her arm and swung it hard at Esta's face. The back of Inga's hand landed square on Esta's cheekbone. Her skin split open and immediately began to bleed. Ivar scrambled to her and looked up at Inga with both fear and resentment. Beor sat, seemingly unmoved by the violence. Esta cupped her bleeding face as Ivar pulled a corner of his blanket up to her face to stem the flow of blood. Ivar placed himself close to Esta.

Beor, having sat in the chair before the fire long enough to dry off, eat, and down several mugs of hot mead, stood. He looked hard at them near the hearth. Stepping quickly to a bag, he produced a long piece of cording. Esta knew what it was for. She started to shake her head and tell him that it was not necessary when Ivar placed a hand upon her arm and shook his head. Esta could feel his fear. She could also hear his warning loud and clear. Beor would not hesitate to harm her. He actually wanted to. He could feel it as much as she could. Beor would enjoy hurting her. He was turning over the ways in which he could do so. Esta's hair stood on end, and she could feel her own blood chill with the pure fear within her. Beor went to his haunches before her, grabbing her ankles and bringing them together painfully. He wrapped the cording around them and then brought one end up to her wrists, wrapping them together as well. Standing up would be impossible, let alone remaining on her feet, if she could think of a way to get there. Retrieving another length of cord, Beor then attached Ivar to the same tether. Esta was not sure how he had accomplished it, but it became quite clear that when Ivar moved, the cording around Esta's ankles and wrists became tighter. There needed to be slack between them at all times. Ivar placed himself in Esta's lap and leaned against her. Her heart was beating with the fear that seemed to grow within her by the minute. Ivar too was afraid, yet his fear was not for himself. He also sensed that Esta's fear was not for herself. She feared for Ivar as Ivar feared for her. The two of them looked into each other's eyes and gave a slight smile of recognition, calming at the knowledge that they both cared more for the other than for themselves.

Beor and Inga passed the evening in hushed conversation. Esta caught flashes of anger and fear from both of them. Ivar feel asleep in her lap near the hearth as Esta leaned on the wall, trying to think of a way to get them out. When Beor had tied her feet together and whispered a warning in her ear, she'd believed him. He would kill her, and Ivar would suffer.

At daybreak, Esta's legs were cramping, and her back ached from the strange sleeping position. Ivar had slept with his head in her lap, his hands folded beneath his cheek to keep the slack in the line. But neither of them slept well or for any length of time.

Another day passed with Beor and Inga bickering in hushed tones and Esta and Ivar only being allowed to move about long enough to relieve themselves and eat. Ivar kept Esta informed of their arguments, and Esta kept Ivar abreast of their emotions. She could tell they were angry. They seemed to be waiting for someone or something that would help them get out of the forest. Something that would help them get to the heart of their desire for power.

Fear began to grip her. Why had they not been found? Esta knew that Mane hovered around the hidden dwelling. She was hungry and frightened. The owl had never gone so long without seeing her master or feeding, and Esta was worried about her. Esta had at times felt Mane relax. The owl had moments of fear followed by excitement and then disappointment. Esta was sure that her mood swings were connected to how close people came to the dwelling. Ivar seemed content to wait for his father. Esta, however, felt that the time had come for action, for escape. She needed to communicate with Mane. She could feel her fear and tried to think of a way to get out of the dark, hollow space.

TEN

The Tree Dwellers

Guth had nearly taken the entire village apart looking for his son. Erik and Roan had stayed with Landen until he had regained his senses and told them what had happened. The heavy snow had long since covered any trace of Beor and his captives by the time a search party entered the woods. The hysterical servant girl was unable to give them much information after witnessing the bloody death of the young guard. Both Erik and Roan were not as worried about catching up with Beor as they were of what they might find once they did. The problem was deciding which way to go. Guth and Erik both feared not being on the right path. There were several choices for Beor. He could have gone into the woods on one of several paths or roads, or he could have gone down the coastline for a waiting boat. The latter possibility was the one that troubled Guth the most, for he could not imagine seeing his son taken to some other land, or worse, held for ransom. Roan worried about his ability to control himself if he came face to face with his father. There was no getting around the fact that they would need to split up if they wanted to cover a lot of ground quickly. Guth sent six armed men with Roan and four with Erik. He took three and searched along the wooded path that ran nearest the ocean. Erik headed straight into the heart of the forest and the path that was the main road in and out of Land's End. This left Roan with the longest path through the woods, and Guth believed that both he and Erik could catch up with

Roan once they had searched. The villagers called Roan's path the Old Hollow Road. It was narrow and dark and ran along the steep mountain cliffs. Even in places where the sun shone bright on the cliffside, the path lay in darkness. Heavy moss hung from the trees, and old timbers creaked and moaned from an invisible wind high above them in the canopy.

The men with Roan were seasoned warriors—they had protected Land's End faithfully for years—but the deep woods made them nervous. They had to take the path in single file. With rocky cliffs on one side and moss-laden trees on the other, there were too many places for an enemy to hide. The biggest problem with the path was that the men could not communicate with each other well. So Roan began to ask a few of the better riders to wind and weave their way through the trees, coming in and out of sight of the line of men who searched for a sign on the path.

Esta could not stand to wait any longer. Ivar reminded her that it had only been two days, that the search would take time as they looked in every direction. As much as she tried, Esta could not shake the feeling that something was wrong. A search party should have come close enough for her to feel them, read them. There had been nothing in the woods outside the hidden cottage but Mane, a worried, hungry owl. And there was nothing inside this cottage but pain and anger. Beor had taken his death sentence as a sign that he no longer had anything to lose. Each and every time he thought he had caught Ivar and Esta communicating, he would strike out at the boy, and Esta would place herself between them. It became a game to him, to strike out and see just how many times she would take his punishments. Ivar began to try to push Esta out of the way, staring hard at Beor as if determined to take the blow. Every time, Beor would swing high, coming in contact with Esta's outstretched arms, her shoulder, or her face, and every time she could hear Ivar's scream inside her head begging her to stop. The cords that bound them together had become so tight around Esta's ankles and wrists that the skin had been cut away. The cord was now covered in blood, some of which would dry when they slept and then break open again when she began to move about.

They are waiting. Ivar was tense. *They know something.*

Both Beor and Inga had begun to take their conversations outside or disappear through the door in the dark recesses of the cottage.

They seem to know I can hear them. They are blocking me. Ivar looked wide eyed at her.

Esta was frustrated. *It is no use, Ivar; we must be too well hidden here. We need to get out of here!*

Ivar looked at Esta's bound legs and his mind raced. *You want me to run! Without you?* He was afraid.

Mane will guide you. She will find the closest human.

Ivar chuckled, and Esta could not help but feel that at times he seemed like an old man trapped in a child's body.

Esta, these woods hold more humans than you think. They hide here, live here. And they are not all the helping sort.

There it was again, her conflicted sense of Ivar, his voice so small and young, his wisdom beyond his years. She had to remind herself that he was just a boy. He scowled at her as she had the thought.

The journey through the woods was slow. Roan stopped the men often to check for any sign of movement. The slightest sign that something or someone had crossed the path would cause the men to dismount and look for tracks. The Old Hollow Road was protected in spots where the canopy was thick above them. It had been two days, and the snow had all but melted away from the road, which made finding any tracks or signs even less likely. When at last they stopped for the night, the men built a fire and kept it burning. Roan wondered if Erik or Guth had fared better. Was Esta safe back at Land's End? Had Guth recovered Ivar? There was no way of knowing, so they would continue to search until they knew for certain.

The guardsmen sent with Roan were older. They were men who had seen battle before. They saw Roan as a young, inexperienced pup, put in charge because of his relationship with their lord. Not that any of them would question it. They knew better than to do such a thing. They spoke little to him and avoided any pretense of respect. When the company came to a larger clearing, he ordered that they stop for the night.

The fire cast an eerie glow upon the forest trees and lit the canopy above them. The night brought in a low mist. Fog hovered in the trees and began to dampen their cloaks. Roan and the guards remained close to the fire, turning to warm themselves and unaware of the eyes that were upon them. The loud snap of a tree branch caused the entire group to turn. Roan stepped up beside a large oak and peered into the distance. As if by magic, an arrow appeared, buried deep into the bark just above his head. They spun, all of them, pulling their swords and placing their backs to one another forming a defensive circle. Another arrow smacked a tree well above the head of the guard under it. They were surrounded, yet no one had been hurt. Roan found it hard to believe that they had been missed by accident. He stepped forward between the men and the tree line and began to circle, looking from one mist-filled gap to another. He stopped when directly in front of him, a dark figure began to emerge. A moss-colored cloak hid the figure's face and draped all the way to the forest floor. Roan could not help but notice the fine cloth the cloak was made of, nor the fact that there was no mistaking the figure of a woman beneath it. He turned to face her as she came forward into the clearing. From all sides, cloaked figures stepped out of the tree line. They stood ready to fire their weapons as they watched the woman approach Roan. She walked right past larger, well-armed guardsmen toward him. Reaching up, she slid the hood of her cloak off, and Roan's eyes widened. Her thick black hair was braided in a crown above her brow and then down around her shoulder and over the front of her gown. The deep color of her hair contrasted with the ivory cream of her skin and the deep-blue of her eyes. She stopped a few feet in front of Roan and nodded a greeting.

Roan squared his shoulders and nodded in return. She was like nothing Roan had ever seen, a dark and mysterious beauty who seemed powerful despite her size. She was but a sprite, all of five feet tall, lean and wiry. Amazed, Roan could see no trace of weakness in her.

She looked up into his eyes and tilted her head as if to ask if he were done with his assessment.

"You are lost," she said.

Her voice was deep, and Roan could tell that this was not a question but a statement.

"We seek a lost companion. She was taken from Land's End, along with another. A child." Roan was guarded. His intuition told him he could trust her, but he had no idea who she was or where she had come from—or most of all, why he felt so at ease.

"I am Roan. Of Elvoy." He nodded toward her.

She smiled at him. A smile that suggested that his information was unnecessary.

"I am Ava." She paused as if making a decision and weighing her thoughts. "Come, Roan of Elvoy, let us feed you and your men. Then we can seek your justice."

Roan looked around the little clearing at the cloaked figures. "What do you know of my justice? Do you know of Esta and Ivar?"

He had taken a step closer to her in his haste to find information. All arrows then turned to point in his direction. Ava, undaunted, shook her head and raised her palm toward him.

"We may be able to help you. There is no use in spending the night in the damp and cold, unless you would rather not eat and sleep in warmth." She turned to walk back through the men toward the tree line. "Come."

There was something about this woman that reminded Roan of Esta. It was neither her size nor her shape, nor her coloring. No, it was not a physical similarity. It was the way he felt around her, as if his thoughts were being invaded. It was the way she smiled as if she knew a secret. His secrets. They looked at each other for only a moment before nodding agreement to follow her.

They walked for nearly an hour, snaking between trees and around rocks that seemed to jut up from the ground at odd angles. Roan looked back at his companions, who seemed just as nervous as he was. The men, at first sure it was some kind of trap, only relented when the promise of a hot meal and no harm was given. He looked at his lead man, a tracker who had kept them on the trail through the forest and even found signs that they could be on the right path. He looked around at the trees, the rocks, the path they followed. Roan knew he was taking mental note of their direction, noting landmarks so that they could find their way out if needed.

Suddenly, the man stopped in his tracks. His jaw dropped, and his eyes widened. Roan spun around in fear but saw nothing but the dense trees ahead. He looked again at the man, who had been joined by several others, looking up into the canopy in sheer wonder. Roan followed their gaze.

There in the canopy, well hidden in the thickest part of the trees, were little dwellings. They were beautiful, mystic, and awe inspiring all at the same time. More importantly, they were alive with activity. The mossy green cloak that Ava wore was but one cloak of many. Every shade of green moved among the branches above. It was as if the trees were alive. A rope was lowered near the base of an enormous oak. Roan could hear the faint sounds of people muttering to one another and the clank and whir of mechanical equipment. The rope was not a ladder, much to Roan's relief, but a thick series of small loops. Before he had a chance to speak, Ava slung her bow across her back, walked to the rope, and placed her left foot in a loop. She reached her right hand up just above her head and wound it through a loop as well. She then raised her left arm out away from her body as she began to rise. Her left hand remained free, but she crossed her right leg over her left calf as she flew skyward.

Roan looked around as others ascended. Cloaked figures were also being lowered to help with packs and any cumbersome items. He watched as men and supplies went both to and from the canopy. Seconds later, the rope reappeared, and Roan drew in a sharp breath. He turned to nod at the man who had appeared from nowhere to hold it steady for him.

"I'm Mikel. I will help you aloft." Mikel gestured to the rope, pointing first at Roan's right foot and then to the loop. Roan placed his foot in the loop, wound his hand through another above his head as instructed, and for an instant closed his eyes as he began to fly. He quickly wrapped his free leg around his calf and was amazed at how secure he felt. It seemed only seconds before he was in the canopy looking into Ava's smiling face. A pair of hands pulled him over a platform, and he stepped free of the ropes. Roan turned to watch the process repeated for Guth's men. One by one, they gathered on the platforms to stare in awe at their surroundings.

The ropes worked on a pulley system. A second platform about ten feet above and just to the side of the one where Roan stood held three men and a large net. Rope lay coiled in the net. The rope ran up over a series of pulleys and down to the platform. To the end of the rope was tied a small net containing a heavy rock. This allowed the rope to be tossed through the hole in the platform and reach the ground quickly. Once a person had secured themselves on the loops, the three men would raise them up with a hand-over-hand motion, moving together with a coordination, skill, and speed that Roan had never seen. It reminded him of the larger fishing vessels in Elvoy and the way the men brought in the large nets full of heavy fish.

Looking around, Roan realized just how many dwellings were there. This was a village. A village in the sky. The dwellings were solid and roomy. They were stacked and linked by bridges and ropes. It was no wonder that they could not be seen from the ground easily. Besides the fact that they were so high in the canopy, the appearance of their exteriors was nearly a perfect match with the bark of each tree. They were made of smooth, sanded wood on the inside and rough, natural bark on the outside. Mud and thatch sealed the holes and cracks. The roofs were made to look like the heavy darkened moss hanging off the trees that grew through them.

The men were speechless. Ava led the entire party over one suspension bridge to a house that smelled of roasting meat. Inside were long tables set with breads and meats and mugs filled with mulled wine and ale. Everything seemed unreal, too perfect, too beautiful to be true. Ava smiled at the look on Roan's face.

"We are a peaceful people." She motioned for Roan to sit. Once she had seated herself across from him, she nodded at the men who ate and drank what was placed before them.

"How is this possible? Who did this?" Roan asked. He was not eating. He was not drinking. He was only looking, taking in everything from the narrow peak of the ceiling to the highly polished floor and tables. This hall would have been impressive if it were on the ground; the fact that it was at least thirty feet in the air made it incredible.

Ava smiled. "My grandfather built the first. His home still stands as an example for us all. He met a woman while traveling the trade route. She lived alone in the forest, having run away from an abusive master."

Roan noticed the disdain with which she pronounced the word *master*. He knew that sound. He sounded much the same when he used the word *father*, a deep disdain for the word and its meaning.

Ava went on. "She had built a small, sturdy platform high in a great black oak tree. He woke up there after being robbed and beaten. The thieves had left him for dead. They had not counted on Ingret, my grandmother. She had watched from the safety of the canopy and used a pulley-and-rope system she'd designed to raise his body up to the platform. It took several weeks for my grandfather to heal. Once on his feet, he began to improve the dwelling, first adding walls and a roof and then windows. Before he knew it, he was at home in the canopy."

Roan listened intently before interjecting, "I can understand one dwelling, one family even. But how did one tradesman and a runaway slave turn into this?" He held his hands out wide.

"That tradesman had four sons, who found four wives, and so on." Ava smiled. "There have been others who have found us on their own— people who have left their homes, lost their homes, or had nowhere to go. Those who find the woods a better place for themselves."

"Land's End is but a day's journey from here. Why are you not there? And who is your master—I mean, your lord?" Roan questioned.

Ava smiled again and then stood. "We have elders, much like your island."

He stood and followed her to a window, curious about how she knew of Elvoy. Ava opened the shutter as Roan stepped forward. The opening all but filled with a flurry of white feathers as Mane landed on the sill. She squawked and snapped in excitement at the sight of Roan. His eyes lit up as he moved toward her.

"Mane!"

The owl hopped gracefully onto Roan's forearm, and he stroked her head as she nuzzled his chest.

"Ah, she does know you!"

"Where did you find her? Where is Esta? Ivar?" Roan looked through the window to the forest floor.

"We know where they are and have been watching, but the owl has been waiting for you." Ava nodded at him.

Roan was confused. "Are they alright?"

"I believe so." Ava smiled. "I believe we can help them, but Beor is dangerous, and he has gathered a following that is headed this way. He plans to rule. His sights are set on the castle and Land's End. He will kill anyone who stands in his way."

Roan set Mane upon the sill and turned to Ava. "Are you telling me that there is an army coming?" Roan's hatred for his father deepened.

"I would not perhaps call them an army. They do have the numbers to do great harm, yes, but only if they can take the city by surprise."

Their conversation had caught the ear of the other men, who whispered among themselves. Roan knew he needed to show where his loyalties lay. He quickly divided his men into two groups. He sent one small group back to Land's End to warn Guth and ready the village. The rest remained with him to attempt to stop Beor and retrieve Ivar and Esta. They would all set out at first light.

It would take a day's travel for the men to reach Land's End. Roan hoped that he would be but a day behind them, that he would enter Land's End with Guth's son and Esta in tow. He knew that this would be his final confrontation with his father, for either Beor would meet his end on the morrow or Roan would.

Wanting the men fresh when the first rays of light came in the morning, the decision was made to get some sleep. Ava placed Roan in the landing above her own. It was a small, one-room dwelling with a bed, a table and chairs, a small fireplace, and an overstuffed chair made from carved wood and pillows stuffed with feathers. Mane sat near his head on the sill. Roan was amazed that he found comfort in her presence. His mind drifted back to that day on Elvoy when Mane had spooked his cob and Esta had thought him cruel. That day had been the beginning of the end of life as they knew it. Everything that had happened to them, all of it, could be placed at his father's feet: being forced to take on the watch even though he had just received his cob days before, his mother's death, the deaths of both Erik's and Esta's fathers, the fact that they were even here on the mainland. All of it happened because Guth wanted help with his son, and Beor knew he could exploit Esta's abilities to place himself back at Land's End. Now it seemed that there was a small army headed this way. Roan could not help but wonder who in their right mind would follow a man like his father, cruel and evil as he was. Beor was a warrior. He could wield a sword better than most and kill without hesitation or remorse. Roan knew now that some of that training had come from his father's childhood here at Land's End. He was one of two sons born to the cousin of Lady Eleanor of Aquitaine, who was now queen. His family, his father, had been related to royalty? How could he have been banished with such blood running in his veins? Roan had had little liking for Guth at first, yet long conversations and observations had made it easier for him to understand why he had been so interested in Esta and how he had allowed Beor to once again disappoint him. This disappointment, however, had cost several lives, and Guth was at last finished with Beor.

Could Beor's plans be directed against the first real ruler of Britannia or, more likely, could he be involved with the king to keep his crown? Guth had talked much of the upheaval of court. King Henry seemed unable to rule. Queen Eleanor and her sons believed him mad, and there was much talk of rebellion. Roan's mind spun with questions he knew he may never receive the answers to. Sleep seemed impossible, and apparently Mane also needed attention. She chirped, snapped, and clicked until Roan stood. He pulled on his boots and wrapped a fine, green wool cloak around his shoulders. Stepping out onto the landing,

Roan had to catch his breath. The moon seemed to hang just out of reach through the treetops, beautiful and illuminating. The canopy was ablaze in the silvery light that descended into the complete darkness below. Mane swooped from the landing. Her wings reflecting the moonlight. It looked to Roan almost magical.

Roan waited and watched the treetops for hours, yet Mane did not return. Feeling she had winged her way back to Esta, Roan found his bed and slept.

Esta woke with a start. Mane sat on the rock outcropping just above the entrance to the well-hidden dwelling. She was calm and full. Esta knew at once she had found help. Her mood, which indicated that she had found a safe place to return to if needed, let Esta know that someone was out there. Who it was Esta had no way of knowing.

Ivar stirred, and Esta stroked his brow to comfort his dreams. There would come an end to this captivity, but at what cost? Beor's emotions had been growing darker by the hour. Esta knew that he was angry. He was also excited and full of conceit. Ivar confirmed this by telling Esta that Beor thought of himself as being untouchable. He had not been able to say more. Now Esta could only wait. Mane remained calm and seemed content just to sit and watch over the large stone wall that had a hidden refuge. As long as Esta felt no fear or danger from the bird, she knew it would be best if she slept. Whatever, whoever had encountered Mane would be here soon. She would need all her strength and her wits if she was to get both herself and Ivar out of this unharmed, for she had no doubt that Beor would try to use them to secure his own escape. Adjusting her bound feet as best she could, Esta leaned back against the wall and drifted into a restless sleep.

Roan woke early and gathered the men together in the large one-room hall high above the forest floor. Ava entered as murmurs of shock and disbelief spread through the guard. She wore a dark-green hooded gown of wool and an overcoat; the likes had never been seen before. The hooks came together just below her bust, giving her a very curvy appearance. In the back of the coat, lacing pulled the garment tight for a snug fit. There on her shoulder was a brightly tanned quiver, a shade of green Roan had never before seen on leather, bright like the sun on a spring leaf, like moss on a damp rock. In the quiver were many arrows. Their fletching's stark white left little doubt as to where they had come from. Roan was struck by her image. She looked of the trees, powerful and confident. He was instantly reminded of Esta, who could seem wild and forestlike. He thought of how the village had named her the Night Child because of her wanderings in the near woods at dark, walking with Mane flying above her or landing upon her forearm or shoulder. It was clear that many in the village feared her, others worshiped her from afar, and still others felt her to be a witch, sighted or gifted with some unnatural abilities. These people, these tree dwellers, gave Roan that same odd feeling. They were mysterious. They seemed to carry themselves differently. Speak differently. Know things.

Ava gave a slight nod and turned her attention to those behind her. Three young men carrying woolen cloaks of various green hues entered the room. They began going to each of Guth's men in turn and finding the cloak that best fit him. It did not take but a moment for the guard to realize what was happening. They began to actively seek the perfect fit. These cloaks would camouflage them well. The enemy, whoever that might be, would never see them coming.

Ava cast a satisfied gaze over the men. "They embrace this challenge."

Roan gave the guard a quick glance. "They follow and honor their vow to their lord, Guth. I find a different reason for strength."

Ava tilted her head in question and then smiled as if understanding. "You are from Elvoy. You have only your elders to guide, rule, or punish you, much like us. You find a friend where they seek vengeance."

Roan gave a quick shrug. He also wanted some vengeance.

"Do you know, Roan of Elvoy, who is your king?" Ava asked the question loudly enough to make the guards turn their heads. All eyes were on them.

Roan chose his words carefully. "I know that our king is not a man to be crossed. I know that his sons believe that he has lost his senses. And I know our queen no longer has a seat beside him." Roan shrugged as if he had just failed some sort of test. "As you said, I am from Elvoy, where no ruling lord has lived since the crusade to the Holy Land pulled our last one into battle. Perhaps your question should be directed at my uncle, as he is the one who will decide what is best for the people upon his lands."

The room was dead still. Ava smiled.

"You are right. None of us here question Lord Guth's rule. Today is not the day to discuss such matters. Let us do what we can to save your friend and the boy."

The boy? Roan knew his father well. He knew that as much as Beor might wish Esta ill, he would, if given the chance, lash out at his brother instead. Ivar was in the most danger here. If Beor felt he was left with nothing—no chance to escape, no mercy, nothing but an openly hostile execution—he would kill Ivar for the sole purpose of hurting Guth. And he would want to see it, to know that he had hurt his brother, even if it meant that he would die at the point of Guth's blade.

Roan gave a slight nod in return, and Ava and the men funneled outside to the various platforms from which they would be lowered on the ropes to the forest floor. Roan watched in awe the different shades of green billow and fly from the treetops to the ground like enormous leaves. Once on the ground himself, Roan found Ava, and together they set off through the trees. Ava led them to a well-worn section of the Old Hollow Road. The forest on either side was dark, thick with moss-covered boulders and swags. Along each side of the road there were tree dwellers waiting. They helped the guard from Land's End up into the trees, where small platforms just large enough to stand upon had been constructed overnight. They were each handed a longbow and a full quiver. Some of these men had little experience with a bow, while others were quite skilled. Regardless, this was a well-planned ambush.

Whoever came down this road stood little chance of getting away. Roan saw quickly that his men were spread out, each one between two of the tree dwellers. He now stood on his platform with Ava to his right and a stocky tree dweller named Ham on his left.

As the mist began to lift with the warming of the sun, they heard them. They were out of sight, even from the vantage point of the trees—still on the other side of a slight rise. They were noisy. Roan could hear the clatter of many men and wagons. He watched the man at the head of the archers, who was staring down the path with one arm raised over his head. Ava raised her arm as well, and Roan saw all the tree dwellers load their bows. The guard from Land's End quickly followed suit. They were all watching the lead man, who was sending signals to Ava. He held up three fingers and then spun his hand in a circle. Wagons, Roan thought. There were three wagons. Now the lead man made a fist and then flashed five fingers once, twice, thrice, four times. Twenty men. Roan glanced around the treetops at his eight men, who may or may not be of much help to the ten tree dwellers. They were not so outnumbered as he'd thought they would be, and they had the element of surprise and the advantage of the trees.

The men on the ground drew closer and then suddenly stopped and became dead still, listening. That is when Roan heard them: the clatter of several horses galloping at full speed. The men on the ground scrambled to their wagons and their mounts. They pulled out swords and longbows, crossbows and staffs. Roan's eyes darted from the top of the hill to the men in the road, still out of range. The tree dwellers all looked to the hill as the horses came into view, cresting the hill with a war cry and bearing down on the men in the road. There were more of them than was needed to wipe out the twenty men who had come to sack Land's End, none of whom stood their ground. Seeing that they were outnumbered was only part of their sudden fear. The twenty men also understood that these were hardened fighting men, Guth's elite warriors. His best. The scattering was instantaneous as Erik's charge closed the distance between the two forces at breakneck speed. From horseback, Erik's men wielded their swords with expert precision. Erik, more comfortable on the ground, had slid off his mount with a few others and come face to face with the few that had remained near the wagons. His eyes darted in search of Esta as he cut his way toward an enclosed wagon near the rear of the grouping. He swung the door open to find nothing but a stash of weapons and pieces of armor. Erik turned just in time to see a blade protrude from a man's chest; the man had had his spear raised, ready to take Erik in the back, but a guardsman had saved Erik's life without pause. Erik stood wide eyed, looking down at the man for only a moment before being pulled into a sword fight with another. This time alert and ready, Erik brought the fight to an abrupt end with a lightning-fast reaction, deflecting an overhead swing from his opponent and swinging round with a backhanded thrust. The man's eyes looked down in a moment of disbelief and horror. Then his knees buckled, and he toppled to the dirt road, eyes wide open, seeing nothing.

Roan scrambled for the ground and began to run toward the fray. There were men who recognized him, a fact that most likely saved his life, as he had seemed to appear from nowhere. Many of the men were giving chase to those who had fled at the sight of Erik and the armed men from Land's End. Those who did stand their ground were slain or taken prisoner in mere moments. Ava had followed Roan to the ground and was now walking behind him as he approached the group of men where Erik stood. The men parted as he drew near, Erik looking past him in expectation.

"Where the hell did you come from?" Erik asked.

He was panting, and Roan could see why. Blood dripped from his sword, and a man lay behind him, unmoving.

"We were waiting for them in the trees. Do you have Esta?"

Roan searched the crowd of men for her.

"No, I believed you would have her. The man you sent said you knew where to find her?"

Erik looked past Roan to Ava as she came toward them. His eyes widened as he watched her.

"Erik, this is Ava, a tree dweller. She can help us to find Esta."

Erik gave Ava a slight nod as his eyes took her in from head to toe.

She was much like Esta, he thought—wild looking in a beautiful and confident way.

"Your people have changed what I can do, Roan," she said. "Beor was to meet these men upon the road here. He would have had Esta and young Master Ivar with him. Thanks to the brilliant arrival of our rescuers, I do not think there is a corner of the forest where your arrival could not be heard." She pointed her longbow accusingly at Erik. Then she spun to Roan and shook her head in disappointment. Erik instantly became stiff. He felt the weight of her disapproval upon him and did not like it. Ava was aggravated. Her tone rang of sarcasm. Roan hung his head to hide his smile, for he knew Erik well and knew he would defend his actions.

"Those men were headed for Land's End. We stopped them." He pointed a finger at his own chest to emphasize each word.

Ava nodded. "Yes, well, we had that well in hand. Nonetheless, Esta and Ivar are still with Beor, and after that ruckus, I can't imagine that he will emerge anytime soon."

"Emerge?" Erik asked, sounding both annoyed and commanding. His attention was pulled as a shout from one of the men rang out in alarm. He stiffened and looked around. His men were staring at several archers descending from the treetops just ahead of them on the Old Hollow Road. Shouts rang out in recognition, the men from Land's End making themselves known. Roan could not help but feel that Ava had a valid point. Erik, on the other hand, had had no way of knowing that the tree dwellers were there and willing to place themselves in danger to save both Esta and Ivar.

Again, the sound of horses and men reached the lookouts near the crest of the hill, and again an alarm was raised. Erik signaled his men to form up. Ava, in turn, raised her bow and whistled. This sent her men in every direction into the trees of the forest. Roan looked down at his olive-green cloak and longbow, gave Erik a quick glancing nod, and followed Ava into the trees, ready to fight alongside his new friends.

The horses came over a small rise and saw the band of men and animals before them. They pulled up but did not stop. Erik's muscles relaxed as he instantly recognized Guth astride his large white cob. As Guth approached, Roan and Ava came forward as well. They all seemed to converge on Erik at the same moment.

After brief introductions, the four stood in quiet conversation. The rider Roan had sent had first found Erik, and then Erik had sent a rider to fetch Guth, who had been on his way back through Land's End after searching the coast road. Now here they were, all in one place, but none the closer to their target.

The mist had risen well into the forest canopy now. The men stood talking to each other about who could be behind the small army making its way to Land's End and why. These were not men the crown would consider loyal. They were much like Beor, outlaws and men who had been banished or were not wanted in their own villages. Were they only the first wave? Would this be the men that would gather information to pass on to an actual army at some point behind them? How many men were out there somewhere, near, far? That remained to be seen.

Esta and Ivar had heard the clash of men in battle. Mane had been frightened by the noise and had screeched and snapped loudly in protest. Inside the cave, Guth had become panic stricken. He threw items of clothing into a bladder and pulled on his boots and cloak, his eyes darting from the hostages by the hearth to the well-hidden door. Inga, having packed a small carpetbag, was sent back to Land's End with much protest.

"They know me. I will be found!" she stammered at his insistence.

"Then hide! I must have eyes within the walls!" Beor pushed her toward the entrance. "Stay in the trees until you are well past the fighting. Speak to no one!"

Beor slammed the entrance door behind her and then advanced upon them. Esta could feel the hate, fear, and desperation thick in the air around him. Beor slung the bladder over his shoulder and pulled out his sax knife as he decisively approached Esta at the hearth. Ivar, moving to place himself upon her lap and between them, was roughly knocked out of the way, the ropes that had them tethered together pulling Esta onto her side. She felt the cord bite deeper into her the skin around her wrists. Beor, grabbing the long, loose hair at the nape of her neck, jerked her to her knees, unable to stand her up while Ivar remained attached. He placed the knife at her throat, his face so close to her own that she could feel the heat of his rage. Savagely, he spat his bloodthirsty malevolent hate at her. Esta knew that he meant to kill her. His blade would cut her throat at any moment, and she would meet her end. Suddenly, Beor's eyes widened. He stepped three paces backward and placed his free hand against his temple as if in great pain. His wild gaze landed on Ivar, who had managed to scramble back onto Esta's lap.

Ivar had opened his mind and used his gift to invade Beor's. He screamed as if aloud, *My father will kill you! I will make sure of it! I will kill you! I will scream within your mind until it be mush!*

Beor's eyes flashed from Esta to Ivar and back again, as he could not understand how he was hearing Ivar so clearly, so fiercely in his own head. Again, Ivar sent a screaming rant in his direction. This time, Beor ran. He pulled the hood of his cloak up and over his head as he cried out and bolted for the door. For a moment, they sat, breathing hard and waiting for his return. They stared wide eyed at the open door.

Esta wanted to sob with relief. Ivar too was overwhelmed with emotion. Mane, given an open door and clear path to her master, swooped into the room, momentarily causing them both to jump in fright. The owl flew in a graceful arc to Esta's shoulder and nuzzled her excitedly. Ivar allowed Esta to work at the cording around his wrists until his little hands were free. He then found a knife in the kitchen area and was able to cut Esta free. Her pain was real, her wrists and ankles bleeding in areas where the cord had cut deeply. She smiled at Ivar, who looked at her hands with a furrowed brow.

"It will heal." She touched his cheek and nodded. "Let us leave. Quickly."

A loud whistle pulled Ava's attention away from the conversation. Roan knew as well that the whistle was an alert. He had heard it before.

Ava walked toward the rise in the Old Hollow Road near the hilltop where the tree dwellers had set their trap. It was also where the alarm had come from. Beside her, Roan, Erik and Guth all looked intently at the misty hill. And there they were, walking hand in hand over the rise: Esta holding Ivar's hand with Mane upon her shoulder. The owl suddenly flew toward them, and Ivar smiled up at Esta, letting go of her hand to run toward his father. Esta placed her hand over her mouth to stifle her cry. She could not run; her ankles were cut and swollen from the days of being tightly bound. She limped forward. People began to gather around her. Helping hands nearly had her off the ground as Erik and Roan appeared before her. Erik nearly knocked the breath from her as he pulled her into a frantic hug. Roan also hugged her and began asking questions all at once. It was Ava who knew her pain and her fears. She turned to Guth and Ivar.

"We should go. It is not safe here."

"It is a day's hard ride back to Land's End. I think we should rest. We can post a guard." Guth was still unsure of this so-called tree dweller.

Ivar smiled at Ava, and she heard his words, his voice an echoing whisper in her mind. "He thinks you are outcasts, hermits."

Roan spun, looking first at Ivar and then at Guth.

"What is it?" Guth was alarmed at the sudden concern on Roan's face.

"I thought …" Roan paused and shook his head. "We are closer to Ava's village. It will give us a chance to sit down and try to piece things together."

Esta only knew she was surrounded by good intentions and concern. She looked at Ava, who smiled at her and nodded, and Esta knew she could trust her.

"Follow her," Esta said. "It is the right path."

Erik needed no other convincing. He trusted Esta, as did Roan. They both gave a nod of approval and sheathed their weapons. Guth only knew that she had kept Ivar safe and that he was, now more than ever, sure that Esta was the key to communication with his son.

As they set out behind the tree dwellers, it began to rain. The party moved down the Old Hollow Road, and Ava set the pace, stopping every mile or so to send some of Guth's men or Erik's men off through the trees with a guide. Both men were reluctant to send able-bodied fighters into the woods.

"We should stay together," Erik whispered to Guth as Ava stopped them yet again to send men through the forest. She turned and nodded.

"I understand your concern, but if we plod through this mud in a group this large, we might as well draw a map right to our village. I am not willing to risk that."

Guth looked at her with suspicion. He could not see how a village of any size could exist so near Land's End without his knowledge. He also could not help but feel that Ava smiled at moments that seemed to coincide with his thoughts or mental notes about the landscape.

Esta had been placed atop a sturdy black cob. She could sense the tension between the tree dwellers and the men from Land's End. Curious minds will hold judgment until they have seen what they need to see, know what they need to know. Esta said nothing. She kept her eyes busy scanning the world around her.

Ivar was hoisted aboard his father's shoulders, happy, feeling safe. Esta stayed connected. She was worried that Beor had gathered men and may attack. Ivar felt that Beor knew his moment to flee had come and that he had wasted no time getting out of the area. The moment the horses had shook the ground and the cries of battle had echoed from a distance, Beor had been in a complete panic. One on one, he would face most men with confidence. Knowing, however, that Guth may be out there? Guth he could not defeat. Beor had thought for those few moments to kill his captives, leave them to rot in the hidden dwelling. But Beor was not a stupid man. He'd known that Guth would never give up looking for his son. If it were discovered that Ivar was dead, he would chase Beor to the very depths of hell to rain down his vengeance, and Ivar had made killing Esta unthinkable by giving Beor visions of the same fate if he did. Beor, coward that he was when it came to his brother, had run. He had left Esta and Ivar to find their own way out of the cavern. If they could get themselves unbound. Esta had sensed the moment that Beor had fled. She had also felt Inga's utter panic when the sounds of battle had reached them. The woman had thrown a satchel together and slipped away before the mist could rise, Beor sending her to spy upon the goings on in Land's End. Esta had been able to feel the fear of the men who fought. Their anger, and the desperation of the men who fled. She'd felt even the last moments of acceptance before death.

Once the silence fell, and it was clear that Beor was not coming back, Ivar had untied and cut the ropes. This had been painful for Esta, who winced as she encouraged Ivar to cut her free. He'd helped a stiff and worried Esta to her feet, and they'd cautiously come out of the hidden dwelling. The battle noise had told her that they must be close to the road, yet Esta had wanted to make sure that they stayed clear of Beor. She'd searched her mind for him, searched for anyone, but all she'd been able to sense was Mane's excitement at having her nearby. Once outside, Mane had immediately flown to and fro. After the excitement of the reunion had been over, the happy owl had begun to guide them back to the road. The cavern had not been as far off the road as Esta had thought. It was however, very well hidden. Even Esta was not sure if she could find it again. They'd begun to walk down the Old Hollow Road together, Ivar holding her hand and reminding her that help was just over the rise before them. Very slowly, they had made their way up the hill. It had only taken moments for them to hear and then see those searching for them. Esta had teared up at the sight, and Ivar had looked up at her, Mane on her shoulder nuzzling her with concern and much love. Ivar had mentally sent her the image of his father and waited for a nod from her before breaking into a run.

Now they sat, warm and safe with full bellies. Ivar had not left his father's side since he had launched himself into Guth's arms on the Old Hollow Road. Esta could feel the man's relief and his love for his son. Guth embraced the boy, kissing his head and cheeks repeatedly.

Ava sat near Esta, and for the first time in her life, Esta knew what it felt like to know someone was different, special in some way, and understood the fear that could easily take hold when you did not understand. The difference was that Esta could feel even more from Ava than just her emotions. Her calm, quiet welcome put Esta at ease.

It had taken time to get so many through the forest and up into the trees. Guth left several of his men below, preferring to have a fighting force on the ground should he need them. Both Erik and Guth stared in wide-eyed wonder at the village above them. Roan laughed at the thought of what he himself must have looked like when first he had looked up at that same amazing sight.

Hours of talk had left them all exhausted and with far more questions than answers. Ava took both Guth and Erik on a treetop tour as soon as the sun had lifted the mist from the canopy the next morning. Both men had been impressed by the craftsmanship and sturdy building techniques used in the village. It had taken some time for Guth to understand and accept the village. The fact that nearly one hundred people lived in the trees right there in his own woodlands had at first annoyed him, even more so when he realized that Ivar had walked him directly under some of the houses on the outer edge of the village, fully aware of what and who was above them. He had been confused by the meeting between his son and Ava, alarmed at how they seemed to know one another. There was no way in Guth's mind that a meeting between them had ever taken place.

Ivar had sat next to Guth at a long table in the hall. There was no Dais here, no order of rank. His men and the tree dwellers sat mixed together. There were no servants either. Many of the tree dwellers had helped to prepare the large meal in their own huts and then carried the food to the hall where it was all set out upon a long table against one wall. Wooden trenchers were handed out, and everyone simply helped themselves to what dishes, meats, and breads looked most appetizing. Cheeses, fruits, and mead sat in the center of other tables around the large hall. The same kind of procedure occurred there as well. You simply took what you wanted. It did not escape Guth's notice that only his men filled their plates as if it were their last meal and drained the pitchers of mead into their cups, filling them to the rim. He could not help but wonder at the calm existence these people seemed to enjoy.

It did not take long for Guth to realize that Ivar's attention was often directed at Ava, who was flitting about the hall making sure her guests had everything they needed. When at last she made her way to the table where Guth sat with his son, Esta, Roan, and Erik, Ava sat down across from them with cheese, bread, and a small piece of fish upon her wooden plate. Guth watched closely. She was confident and unlike any woman he had ever known.

"It is a pleasure to meet you at last, little one." She smiled at Ivar, who smiled back, wide eyed.

Guth looked from his son to this woman and back again.

"You know my son?" His tone was not quite accusatory, but it was not friendly either.

"I know that Ivar has been to this part of the forest. I know he is a brave and gentle soul." Ava smiled again.

"How is it that you could be right here and I, as liege lord of these lands, was not aware of your existence?" Guth tilted his head in question.

"Men rarely look up, my lord. My guess is that you will see more than ever before now." She grinned at him. "You have hunted in this part of the woods before. I am afraid that Ivar has looked up when you have not."

"Roan has told me of your beginnings and of your willingness to help find my son. I am grateful." Guth placed a protective hand upon Ivar's head.

"You are most welcome, my lord, although I must wonder at the group of men that your brother had on the Old Hollow Road. These men were not raiders. They carried no banner cloth. I am at a loss to understand how and why Beor would gather such a force." Ava's question was directed at Guth. She made no effort to keep the conversation private, and now many heads had turned to hear the answer.

Guth wasted little time in response. "With many questions about who is rightful king, many seek their own fortune without fear of retribution these days. Queen Eleanor of Aquitaine is exiled to her homelands, but she retains the loyalty of many."

Guth waited. Either the tree dwellers were aligned with Henry, or they waited for Richard the Lionheart to become king. His mother, Eleanor, had raised him well, and she would help guide his hand with the people.

Ava smiled. "Henry may believe that he has won, but all he has done is place the country on a path for Richard. When Richard takes the throne, all will be right with the world again."

Guth smiled. "I believe my cousin would agree with you."

"You are related to the queen?"

Guth raised his brow, and Ava laughed. Guth was happy to see a loyalty between the tree dwellers and the queen. It gave him a sense that they were not who he believed them to be.

ELEVEN

Vengeance is Lost

It took several days of rest and nourishment for Esta to begin feeling like herself again. The tree dwellers' healer put a wonderful-smelling poultice upon her wrists and ankles, wrapping them in a soft cloth. They were healing rapidly, although there would most likely be a scar on her wrists. She was worried about both Erik and Roan, for when they sat with her, she could read a confusion and a sort of anger between them, although they outwardly gave each other much respect.

Guth had found the building of a village in the trees an amazing feat. His long walks to inspect and admire the pulley systems and building skills needed to make the treetop houses had placed him often in Ava's company. Their talks had turned serious many times, as Ava tried to both explain and defend the village. After much talk and time, Guth knew the importance of keeping its existence secret, swearing his guard to silence. Guth asked for and received permission for two of his men to remain. Their task was to learn building and fighting techniques. Roan, Esta, and Erik also remained. At first that was to allow Esta time to rest and heal, but it became clear all too quickly that they were all very comfortable there. Not one of them seemed in a hurry to return to Land's End. Although Erik said often that they should return soon, it seemed to Esta that he wanted to stay.

The fact that Esta was better and that an armed escort was ready to travel with them should have had them back at Land's End by now.

As the weeks passed, Guth began to visit, always bringing Ivar with him. He found that Esta had no desire to return to Land's End. Nor did she want to return to Elvoy. Guth fought against the urge to bring them back by force. Ivar was against it and had asked his father not to demand it of her. Now, armed with the knowledge that his son could and did communicate, Guth had allowed himself to be taught to listen. Both Ava and Esta would spend time with father and son, getting Ivar to send his thoughts to his father more purposefully. Esta had all but forced Ivar's thoughts into his father's head. They'd also begun to work on the spoken word with Ivar. His small voice always seemed in contrast with his wisdom. It was important to Guth that they could now enjoy their conversations without the need for words. This made Guth's need for Esta obsolete. Her relationship with Ivar put her at odds with her feelings about Guth. She still held him responsible for much. Yet he never again mentioned a return to Land's End, except to tell them all that they would always be welcome there. He could now communicate with his son on his own, a far better outcome than he had dreamed. He could not help but feel extremely thankful for both of the women who had taken so much interest in his son. Their visits to the village brought about changes in Ivar as well. He seemed more aware of his thoughts and of who received them. Ivar would work on actual speech with Ava but only if they did so in a place where not another human soul could hear his attempts at verbal communication.

The winter slipped away to spring and then summer. The warm days of summer were spent in trips to the river, games in the meadow, and walks along shady game trails. Then the nights began to cool. The leaves, once so many colors of green, began to change. Bright oranges, yellows, and reds made the canopy into a beautiful kaleidoscope dancing its way across the sky. Soon, it would be winter once again. Travel would become more difficult, and visits to the village would become less frequent. As the leaves began to fall, Esta wondered how the village remained hidden once the cover of the canopy was gone. Ava had smiled at her question and answered with one simple word: "Snow." It was difficult enough to travel the Old Hollow Road when there was not a few feet of snow to barrel through. Leaving the road to traverse through the trees and wild underbrush was unthinkable.

Esta began to flounder. She spent much time alone in the woods walking with Mane through the rocky, moss-laden trails. She had not given much thought to returning to Elvoy and felt much out of place in Land's End. But here in the trees, Esta felt at home. Her mother had arrived on Guth's second visit and had quickly become friends with the man the tree dwellers looked to for their medical needs. He had a good deal of knowledge and had realized right away that Clare had much knowledge herself. Clare's knowledge, however, crossed over to the animals, something the tree dwellers had not had before. She also had a better understanding of those who were to give birth. Yet Clare thought it silly that any man should be bringing children into this world. Together, there was not a living being in the village that could not find help when needed.

As was the custom for anyone who wanted to join the village as a permanent resident, Esta and Clare needed to sit through a series of interviews with the village elders. If and when the elders felt comfortable accepting them, a home would be made available. Whenever a home was emptied due to a death or because the inhabitants built a new or larger flat, it was used to house guests or store things until it was needed again. Now Clare and Esta had been welcomed to the fold. Moreover, they had been presented with a beautiful three-room dwelling high in the branches of an enormous oak that sat near the edge of the village. It had once been the home of Ava's mother. Ava had herself grown up there. She loved giving it to Esta. She felt that somehow she had honored her mother with the gift. Esta could feel some anger and jealousy from several of the tree dwellers when word had spread of this gift, however, for this was the onetime home of an elder. This had been the home of one of the villages most respected members. This was rightfully Ava's home, although she had long since created her own much smaller dwelling above it.

Clare wasted little time setting up the treetop cottage. There was already furniture made of wood but no blankets or padding, as the dwelling had been empty for some time. Guth provided everything else that was needed and then some. Again, Esta felt some anger and jealousy spread through the village. Their dwelling held luxuries that even the richest elder did not have. It looked more like a sitting room in Guth's castle at Land's End than it did a tree dweller's humble cottage. Toward the end of fall, when the first snows were on the horizon, Ivar had insisted that he bring Esta a few gifts. Guth, both unwilling to say no and having no desire to do so, had loaded a wagon with overstuffed chairs, bedding, and tapestries, much to Ivar's delight.

Ava cared little about what others thought. She was happy that both Clare and Esta had decided to remain in the village. Clare gave the women of the village a healer of their own gender, and Esta was yet another wonder of nature, a second healer and even another defender, for Esta had a natural talent with the bow. She had found the talent by accident and developed it through practice. Esta was quite skilled. She could clear her mind and focus on the targets in front of her so well that she at times could outshoot even the seasoned archers of the village. This brought both joyous laughter and jealous anger from some of the men. Roan, however, held nothing but exhilarating joy when Esta would practice. He would have her aim at the smallest of targets, throwing his hands into the air with amazed laughter when she would plant her arrows dead center.

Esta had to admit that the anger and jealousy she'd felt had come from those who were also angry on many levels with many things. These people carried little weight in the village, and their numbers were small in comparison to the total population. Esta felt nothing else but a calm acceptance from the rest of those who lived there. For the most part, they looked on Esta as one of their own.

Roan began to wonder if the village might not be a better place for Hadwin and Landen. While they were very comfortable at Land's End, the fact was that they were the offspring of Beor, and it seemed to Roan that the children were watched closely. Was it that they expected some kind of evil to have been passed from Beor to his children? Roan wished his mother had survived Beor's presence in her life. The people of Land's

End would have seen that it was her love and her strength that kept them all going. She had pulled Roan aside often and told him that his anger was a sign that his father's hate could spread but that he, Roan, was a good man. She'd told him that he needed to believe in himself. Roan had always felt that she worried about him the most. His anger had seemed to grow as fast as he did. In some ways, it was true. He did have anger and hate for many things within him, but Erik and Esta had given him what he needed to begin to change. They had given him friendship and trust. They had given him forgiveness. And thanks to Esta, they had given him understanding that no one else had ever given. He knew that Esta's understanding of his emotions had kept him calm and collected many times. He never wanted her to read the boiling over of anything that would make him seem weak or out of control, not when Erik stood there forever in control of everything and everyone around him.

\The thought of Hadwin and Landin made Roan smile. They seemed to be adjusting well. Hadwin was being smothered by Ivar, who thought her the cutest thing he had ever seen. Her blonde curls bounced as they played together in the garden and ran through the halls. Although Ivar was only a few years older than she was, he had taken on the role of protector, much like a bigger brother. Landin had other goals in mind. He was with members of the guard nearly all day, getting tips and training from anyone who would spare him the time. He was determined to become part of Guth's guard, a valued member of Land's End, a protector in his own right. He felt it imperative that he project an image before those who knew him that was nothing like his father.

Back in the village, Esta stood on her platform gazing at the colors of the setting sun through the remainder of the leaves. It had never occurred to her the number of greens one could see from this vantage point—a color wheel of greens, too many shades to name. Now in late fall, the colors were stunning.

In the gardens of Land's End, the sun had brought its rewards as well. Everything had bloomed for the season. The flowers were starting to fade as the fruit trees began to hang low with their offering. Ivar was growing and talking and was able to use his gift only when he chose to do so. Guth was not visiting the village in the trees as often. Instead, Erik or Roan would bring Ivar for his visits with Ava and Esta. In midsummer, Guth had brought them back to Land's End to train and become members of his guard. Yet they did enjoy the trips to the village, spending time with Esta when they came.

The change in Erik had been gradual but very defined. He was stepping into manhood with confidence and authority. Roan told Esta how close Guth and Erik had become, how Erik no longer spoke of returning to Elvoy, although Roan himself often missed the island. Esta's feelings had been strong when first she found herself away from the island, her anger and grief causing her to declare that she would not see Elvoy again. Now, months later, she had to admit that she thought of Elvoy often. She pictured a home in the forest canopy with Mane coming and going at will. This would be Esta's first home of her own. She imagined it sitting near the edge of the green. Roan listened to her dreams and walked with her in the forest, each visit bringing him more comfort and more anger.

Erik was spending more and more time with Ava and Ivar, and Roan had begun to see the shift in Erik's heart. He began to wonder how or when this change would be obvious even to Esta. Guth and Ivar even began to talk of Ava and Erik in the same breath, always causing a flare of temper in Roan. It was only a matter of time before Roan and Erik would have words on the subject. Roan had long since felt the need to confront Erik about his intentions.

No one expected that it would be Ava who would bring about Erik and Roan's confrontation. After both Roan and Erik had arrived with Ivar, Ava pulled Erik aside. She had no intentions with Erik, and she found it was time that he knew as much.

"It is an awkward situation I am placed in, Erik, for I feel you have much conflict within your heart. You love Esta, as you should. Please do not confuse my feelings of respect and friendship, for your heart is well placed in Esta's hands. But you should know that you are not the only one who loves her."

Erik was both embarrassed and angry. He had been feeling attracted to Ava, but hearing that there was someone else interested in Esta caused him pangs of jealousy and a great deal of guilt. He said nothing but simply turned and walked away. He would search her out, try to explain. His admiration of Ava had taken on a life of its own, and he knew that he had allowed it to grow out of hand. He loved Esta. How had he been so ignorant as to assume she would not be loved by others? He suddenly looked at every tree dweller differently, wondering if they had fallen in love with his woman.

Roan was looking for Erik as Erik looked for Esta. Neither one realized that there were others also searching the woods. Beor had pulled what men he could find back together. These men were joined by another group that Beor had hired with a promise of plunder. They were moving through the woods in a calculated line, searching for the village they knew was there yet could not see. It was just a matter of time, though. A lookout quickly informed the village of the approaching band of mercenaries, and they began to prepare for their defense. Esta arrived back in the village just as the archers were beginning their descent to set up a perimeter. She found Ava on the ground, her leather battle gear strapped on and her quiver full of arrows. She knew instantly that Beor had returned, that battle loomed.

"Can we not send for help?" Esta pleaded.

Ava smiled. "There is no time. We must meet them near the Old Hollow Road. If they make it through our defenses the village will be lost. They would see it destroyed."

"How can I help?"

Esta had learned quite well how to shoot a bow, Ava knew, but her skills would be put to better use if she stayed near the village on the ground, for there would be wounded, and they would need care.

"Help your mother with the wounded," Ava said, catching Esta by the arm before she continued. "If we fail, take her into the woods and try to get back to Land's End."

Ava turned as a whistle rang out. She cast one quick glance back at Esta and ran with the rest of the cloaked figures toward the Old Hollow Road.

Roan came to the village as Esta ran for a lift. He came to her side and helped her ready herself to be pulled into the trees. His eyes held the question, and Esta quickly answered.

"'Tis Beor. He comes on the Hollow. I must help mother." Esta ascended, looking down into Roan's eyes as she shot skyward. She could feel the anger building rapidly in him, the memories of the harm his father had done all hitting his mind at the same time. His brow furrowed deeply as he gathered his control. He turned, pulling his sword, and ran toward the Old Hollow Road to join the battle.

Beor had a mission. For whatever reason, he was determined to find and destroy the village. He seemed just as determined to destroy Esta and now anyone he thought connected with the village. Esta was confused by the feeling of personal anger coming from men she did not know, but the reason soon became clear. The desire to purge the world of some kind of evil seemed to permeate the air. The men with Beor felt they were ridding the world of a cult, a coven of evil—wicked people who had evil ways and evil intentions. These men that followed Beor believed that Esta and the tree dwellers in the village were witches, vessels of the Devil. They would hold no mercy. They would kill without thought or conscience. Beor had convinced them that this was their duty. She would lose friends this day. She quickly wiped away a tear in her eye as she gathered herself for the coming wounded. She looked into her mother's eyes as they prepared blankets and bandages, boiled water, and sterilized small knives and scissors.

The tree dwellers had the advantage on the Hollow. The road was open, and arrow flight paths were clear. On the forest floor among the trees, swords were more effective. The archers only had their camouflage and the ability to hide in their favor. They lined the edge of the Old Hollow Road now, and it was obvious they were expected. Beor's men stayed in the tree line. They fought with both swords and crossbows, giving them the ability to fight both in the woods and on the open road. A crossbow bolt buried itself deep into a tree just inches from Ava's face. She spun away from the tree as another bolt hit, just missing her. A cry rang out as she saw the bowman drop to his knees, Roan behind him, pulling his sword free. Ava watched as Roan scooped up the crossbow and ran for cover. The battle was bloody and close. It did not take the tree dwellers long to figure out that they would need crossbows for the fight, so they quickly began targeting the men who carried them. Soon as many tree dwellers carried the crossbows as Beor's men.

Beor's weapon of choice was his sword, and he wielded it well. He had killed three men and was desperately seeking another when Erik burst through the tree line, sword in hand. Erik had been looking for Esta on a trail near the river, one of her favorite places, when the sound of the battle had reached him. Cursing as he ran, he'd cut through the woods toward the edge of the village and then cut toward the road. Beor spun, and the two came together with anger and a fierce desire kill one another. The fighting was coming to an end. The tree dwellers were more in number, and as they dispatched Beor's men one after another, their advantage grew and grew. Soon there were only a few left of the enemy. Beor, seeing others advance to help Erik, turned and ran. His retreat, however, would not be borne. Erik had seen him escape justice one too many times, and he gave chase. Erik followed Beor down the Old Hollow Road, over the rise, and out of sight of those still fighting. Beor had started with a good lead on Erik, but the distance between them began to shrink, and Beor knew that Erik would soon catch up.

Their feelings flooded Esta as she began to help Clare with the wounded. Erik and Beor were running away from the skirmish. She stood, trying to hone in on them. There were still men fighting their own battles, their emotions thick in the air around her. Although Esta and Clare were far from the fray, they could hear it—men yelling both in triumph and in death, the clash of blades, and the sound of war. Esta hated it. She wished it all away. She wished herself away, suddenly shocked by the knowledge that Erik was in danger. Never before had she been able to feel Erik from such a distance. She could feel not only Erik's exertion and desire to catch Beor but Beor's desire to strike Erik down as well. He was cunning, consumed with finding a way to take yet another life.

Beor began to watch the trail for a place that would give him the advantage in a fight. Erik was tall, agile, and strong. Beor was smaller and quick and relied on other people's mistakes for victory.

Esta could feel Erik's heart begin to pound within her. It was a deep, low rumble with an ache of despair attached to it. Esta looked wildly around for Mane and then ran for the nearest platform. Once on the ground, Esta was on the move. She was nearly at the tree line when she stooped down and picked up a longbow and quiver filled with arrows. Now she ran, sprinting in the direction she felt pulled. There was no explaining it. She was being drawn to Erik, pulled to him as if they were tethered and he drew the line. She knew where he was without knowing how or why, only that she needed to get to his side and quickly.

Beor ducked as he ran under a low, moss-covered limb on the path he had taken off the road. He stopped and spun around; this was what he had been looking for—a place where the world around him could help make up the difference between his own skills and Erik's. Erik came closer, seeing that Beor now stood, broadsword at the ready. Assessing the situation, Erik knew he could not blindly go under the tree. Beor was counting on that. If Erik's eyes fell as he ducked to avoid the limb, Beor would use that split second of distraction to strike. Putting on a burst of speed, Erik leapt toward the trunk of the tree. One foot found its mark, and the other followed, giving Erik a foothold on the trunk he used to thrust himself up and over Beor, who stood waiting to strike at Erik under the tree.

Esta's heart fluttered as she felt Erik's feet leave the ground. She felt his effort and skill as he flew through the air and over the head of his enemy.

Beor was taken by surprise. He had readied himself for Erik to have to bend over and duck the limb, taking his eyes off of his target, not to come flying over the limb and above his head. Beor spun, but Erik was ready. Their swords came together with a great force. Each man had his strength, each his weakness. Both tried to use them to their advantage. Beor lunged, the point of his broadsword extended to catch Erik in the chest. Erik parried and easily deflected the jab, bringing his own sword around in a quick pivot and slicing at Beor's legs. Beor faded, leaping backward and regaining his stance. Erik advanced, not willing to let Beor find stable footing, and again began to slope, moving at a diagonal and purposefully working to injure Beor in the legs. Beor tried an empty fade, leaping backward as if to fade but then immediately coming right back in with an overhead cut. Erik deflected the blow with a front guard, pulling Beor's sword up and off to the side. Erik was taller. He tried to use his height to bring Beor to bear, swinging his broadsword up and over his head and bringing it down upon Beor with all his might. Beor was adept at blocking the blows. He spun and raised his sword up over his head to deflect. His stocky build and massive arms kept Erik's strikes at bay. Beor tried twice to undercut Erik at the knees, but seeing the swings well in advance, Erik would spin or leap above the blade, leaving Beor slicing at thin air. Their skill, though different, was well matched. Back and forth they went, each gaining and then losing the upper hand.

Esta could feel the power of their blows, the pure adrenaline they burned trying to best one another. And there it was, the bend in the path. They were there, just around those trees. Esta's heart lurched as she felt a sudden surge of triumph in Beor. She could feel Erik falling backward, feel the pain and the shock. Over the rise, Esta dropped to one knee while pulling an arrow from the quiver. She pulled and loosed her arrow just as Beor came up to strike the final blow. The arrow found its target: Beor with his broadsword raised above his head, hovering over Erik. The arrow buried deep into his chest. Beor looked up in confused wonder as he stumbled backward, the sword falling from his grasp. He found Esta's eyes as he tried to understand what had just happened. Looking down at the arrow, he felt the warm blood rise up and into his mouth. He coughed and fell to his knees as Esta rushed to Erik's side. Erik lay with a wound to his lower abdomen bleeding through the fingers of his hands, which he held tight to the wound to stay the flow. On her knees, Esta tore at her cloak and pushed the cloth about the wound. Erik looked up. Even without a gift he knew her fear; he could see it in her eyes.

Beor had known that the fight was going Erik's way. He was tired and was quickly running out of ways to avoid Erik's blade. Hearing others approach, Beor had given everything he had in a last-ditch effort to save himself. As Erik had raised his blade, Beor had rushed in, his shoulder making contact with Erik's side. He'd tried to spin out of the way, but as Erik had come around to face him once more, Beor had reversed his blade and thrust it backward, catching Erik by surprise and driving it deep into his stomach. Esta had screamed as Erik stepped back. He'd staggered as he watched an arrow slam into Beor's chest.

Many footfalls came at them. Suddenly Ava was there, as well as Clare, who had followed her daughter into the woods. Esta was pulled away as others bent to help with Erik. She turned to see Roan running toward her, wide eyed and frightened. His focus was on Erik, and Esta could feel his fear. She turned her gaze to where Beor lay facing the sky, eyes wide open and choking upon his own blood. After following her gaze, Roan fixed his eyes upon hers as he pulled out his sword and walked past her to where his father lay, gasping for breath. He looked down into Beor's face, into the eyes he had grown to hate. Roan's eyes burned with tears, and a solid lump seemed to form in his throat. Beor coughed, and the blood splattered back down upon his face. The man's eyes searched the sky above him and suddenly locked onto Roan's. Roan bent over his father, tears streaming from his eyes. The hate ebbed from him just like the color drained from his father's skin.

"Burn in hell, father! You will be forgotten the moment you draw your last."

Roan stood and walked back to Esta, who now followed the men who carried Erik. The group walked away without looking back, leaving Beor where he lay, alone, gasping out his last ragged breaths. Beor's eyes searched the skies, flashing wildly from side to side, seeking help and comfort. He found none. He coughed as his lungs filled with blood, cutting off the last of his air supply, and Beor fell into the darkness that awaited him.

Back in the village men scrambled to get the wounded into the treetops. The dining hall was set aside to tend to those who needed a healer's touch. Some had deep cuts, others arrow wounds. Still others, whom it was beyond the skill of any human to save, simply received love and comfort while they passed from this plane. Erik was taken to

Esta's room, where he was made comfortable. Clare had done everything possible to save him, but there was nothing to be done for it. Erik's wound was deep. The blade had cut his stomach sack and perforated the bowel. He was being poisoned from within, and time was running out. Both Clare and Ava worried about how Esta would take the news.

When they finally saw him, Roan stormed from the room, descended at the first platform, and disappeared into the woods. Esta stood, tears welling in her eyes, turned quietly, and walked to Erik's bedside. He lay sleeping. She pulled forth a wooden stool, sat down, placed her hand upon his beating heart, and lay her head down. She silently wept for hours, refusing to leave his side until at last Clare removed everyone to allow her peace and privacy. She was told that Erik would last two days at most, that he would most likely never regain consciousness. They would allow her these moments, though Ava wondered if it was wise. Esta tried to look into Erik's mind, to perhaps give him peace and remove pain. But there was no pain, and oddly enough, there was no fear.

Esta kept a candle aglow in case Erik awoke. She was glad that she had when, as she watched him sleep, he opened his eyes. Instantly she was there. She smiled at him.

"You scared me."

Erik smiled up at her. Her eyes were swollen, her lips trembling.

"Water." His voice was harsh, dry.

Esta quickly retrieved the waterskin and gave him several long pulls before he signaled enough.

"I'm sorry, Esta," he whispered.

"You have nothing to be sorry for. When you are well, we will travel away from here. Someplace warm." She smiled again, but the smile did not reach her eyes as it had always done before.

"I'm sorry I did not love you better." Erik searched her face. He wanted to remember every line, every freckle, every lash—everything from the curve of her lips to the shape of her apple cheeks.

Esta bent down to kiss his lips, unafraid and uncaring of what others may think. The fact that Erik was awake and able to communicate at all was a miracle, one Esta would long struggle with. Erik had many things he had wanted to say, many things he had wanted to do with his life as well. He talked of the joy he would have at seeing his father again and spoke of seeing the mother he had lost as a child. He talked about the knowing, how he was not afraid but wished things were different. He told Esta again and again how much he loved her, how amazing she was, how he had marveled at her strength and her beauty, both inside and out. He told her that he knew she would be a woman most sought after. He made her close her eyes and picture the life they would have shared. This seemed harsh and unnecessary to Ava and Clare until Ava realized that Erik was trying to give her a lifetime of memories in the only way that he could.

It had been hours since Erik had opened his eyes. His breathing was labored yet still somewhat steady. All knew the time was near. The healers among the tree dwellers had long since departed, speaking in hushed tones with Ava and Clare as if Esta was not aware that his life was ebbing. It was as if she did not have the strength to hold on. She could not grip tight enough to keep him from falling into the darkness.

Erik pulled in a stuttering breath and opened his eyes. Esta was there, holding his hand and looking into his eyes with tears upon her cheeks.

"Do not do that," he whispered.

Esta shook her head, not sure of his meaning.

"Do not cry," he said.

She tried to smile. "I cannot help it." The time for honesty had come. He deserved nothing less. "I do not want to lose you. I love you, Erik."

"A thousand years would not have been enough." Erik smiled but then had a fit of coughing, and there was blood on his lips. "I'm sorry, Esta," he whispered again, tears in his eyes.

Esta closed her eyes and lay her head on his chest. She did not cry out, as much as her heart wished her to. She did not scream in anger, as much as her aching soul longed for it. She wept silent tears and held on to the sound of his beating heart. She felt pure love coming from Erik, the longing for a life he could not give her. And for what? The reasons behind Beor's attacks on Land's End were still a mystery, yet Esta knew it was due to her. Somehow, someway, she was to blame.

Erik slept. Esta never left his side. His energy waned. His life-force weakened. He slipped in and out of consciousness, and Esta lived for those moments of clarity. Each time Erik opened his eyes, he searched for her. He smiled when she placed herself before him. Their eyes would lock, and they would share a moment before he would fade out again. Each time he drifted out, Esta would lay her head once again upon his chest and weep.

"Please don't leave me," she cried. Yet it was inevitable. It would come and soon.

It was late. The moon was full and hung low on the horizon framed in the window where Mane perched. The owl chirped out a mournful cry as it tried to send comfort and love to Esta. Esta, as always sat her vigil next to the bed. She held Erik's hand while she waited for the final goodbye. Erik opened his eyes and turned to find her.

"Hello, my love." He smiled. His voice was weak and breathy.

"I will always love you; you will always have me." Esta kissed his temple softly.

"It is time, I think." He turned to the window and looked at the moon.

"No, no, you are getting stronger. You have to fight." Her eyes filled with tears. She knew the fight was over and yet could not bear to let him go. It was not right to try to hold him here; she knew that. But she did not care.

"I am not afraid. I am not afraid of anything except losing you. I never wanted to lose you." The meaning of that was lost upon Esta, as she had never known that he had started to care for another.

Esta cried and lay her head once again on Erik's chest. His hand found her head, and he stroked her hair.

"I love you," he whispered.

Esta sat up and found his gaze. "I love you, Erik."

His sight faded.

"I love you," she whispered again. "I love you."

Esta held his gaze, repeating her words again and again as Erik slowly drifted away, never taking his eyes from hers, not even when his last breath escaped him and his heart stopped beating. When at last Esta allowed others into the room, Clare softly closed Erik's eyes and kissed his cheek.

Eric was given a hero's shroud embroidered in silks of deep blues and greens. His ascent to the gods would show how much he was honored in this life. Guth had sent a wagon to carry Erik's body back to Land's End. Extra horses had also been sent for those from the village who wanted to attend, and many of them now carried two riders. Once back in Land's End, Erik's body was placed in the great hall so that he could be honored by the people for his loyal service to Lord Guth. Guth, in turn gave one of his own small vessels for the funeral pyre. Erik's body was placed on the pyre, his sword and a few personal belongings around him. Many from the village and Land's End had placed gifts about the pyre and in the ship. Flowers, combs, arrows, cups and platters full of offerings were there. Guth covered Erik with a beautifully tanned hide from a black bear, an honor that escaped no one's notice. The ship was cast off, and many wept as the flaming arrows flew skyward in the setting sun. The blaze erupted, and the oil-soaked ship seemed to carry the fire across the sea and into the sun itself, the two fires becoming one blaze and then vanishing into darkness.

Horses and wagons took the tree dwellers back to their village. Guth and Ivar both tried to persuade Esta and Clare to stay, but they wished to return to the trees. Esta seemed to shut down. She closed herself off from contact, not wanting to talk or share feelings. Ivar, Roan, Ava, Clare, and all who had befriended her tried to get Esta to open herself up to a conversation about Erik and what his loss had meant for her. All agreed that holding such grief and pain inside was not healthy. Esta, however, no longer wanted to feel anything. Her waking hours only seemed to hold tears; her sleep was filled with dreams, memories of those moments spent with Erik that had etched their way into her mind. The pictures were so real as to nearly breathe. Those memories now took her breath away. Esta could hold herself together while surrounded by others. Her new ability to block the feelings of those around her helped, but it was difficult to keep it up for long. So Esta started to avoid the hall and take daily walks at dusk.

The first time she was joined by Roan was awkward. He had wanted to talk of Erik. He had wanted to talk of Beor, whom he refused to call father, and had asked Guth as lord to change his name so he could no longer feel his connection with the man. Guth had reminded Roan of his own self-worth, as well as the fact that Guth himself also shared the name Roan wished to discard. Esta refused to discuss the subject of Erik or Beor. This left Roan to wonder if Esta blamed or held any malice toward him. He had to be constantly reminded that his father's actions were not his own. He was not responsible for Beor or what would happen because of Beor's actions. Roan mourned his friend, even more so because he had been angry with Erik that morning and had purposely walked away from him in the woods. He also mourned for Esta and wondered how they would ever be able to move past the fact that it had been his father who had once again taken a loved one from her.

TWELVE

A Heart in Pieces

ware of Esta's daily walks in the woods, Roan had made a habit of joining her whenever he could. She would wait until that last hour or so before dusk. Most of the tree dwellers made sure they were back by then, and the main hall in the largest tree would be filling for the evening meal. Every time Esta approached the platform, the guard seemed aggravated by her presence. Esta would descend and disappear quickly into the woods.

As she left again tonight, she once again knew that she was not alone. Roan had been watching the platform near Esta's dwelling, waiting to see her descend from the canopy. Mane flew ahead of her, dipping, turning, and twisting her way through the trees. Esta could feel her joy at the freedom and exhilaration of these near-dark flights. On an average adventure, by the time Esta would return to the village, the sentry would be ready to pull up the ropes for the night. He would let her know that she had just made it in time, telling her that one of these days she would end up spending the night in the woods and that it would serve her right for always going out so late. Esta, for her part, would quietly say thank you and nod at his stern warning both when leaving and when returning. She felt no malice from the guard. He even looked forward to his nightly visit from her, although he would never admit it. His feelings of both concern and frustration as Esta neared the platform were strong. It was not hard to be fond of the gruff older man, and Esta hid a slight smile.

Half way down her descent, Roan's feelings came crashing through. She could feel his hesitation to be seen. She could feel the conflict within him. She also knew that he was aware that she could feel him there, lurking.

"You know I can sense you, Roan. Just come out. I feel silly, you stalking me like some giant wolf waiting to pounce."

He stepped out onto the well-worn path just a few feet in front of her, a sideways grin on his face.

"Sorry." He searched his mind for the right words.

"You needn't be." Esta continued forward, moving past him.

Roan turned and began to walk beside her.

"Why are you out here, Roan? You will miss the evening meal." She kept her tone flat. She did not want Roan to believe she was angry with him.

"I asked Ava to save something for me. I wanted to spend some time with you before I left."

Roans visit's to the village were getting further and further apart as Ivar's need to spend time with Ava lessened. Now, walking with Esta in the woods, Roan was filled with a sudden sadness at the thought of being so far away from her. Esta could feel his sadness. It was one of the reasons she went to the woods each night while the others assembled in the hall. She could not stand the flood of pity and sorrow that came at her. As the months had passed, the pity had lessened, but it was replaced by awkward glances and avoidance. Even those who had been there for her when Erik had first passed now seemed to fade from her. Their attention turned back to their daily life in the canopy. Ava was busy communicating with Guth and helping to supply the archers protecting the ports at Land's End. Guth working with the queen's sons to keep Land's End free and open for ships and goods to pass through. The revolt, or uprising, led by Queen Eleanor and three of her sons had seemed to come in waves. The mad king was fighting for a lost cause, for it seemed only a matter of time before the crown would pass to another. Guth had helped with the rebellion, and now as it seemed victory was imminent, he was ready to reap the rewards for his efforts.

Esta was not interested in the politics of the crown or in the fact that Lord Guth was becoming the right hand of the queen. She lived for the small moments of peace she found in the woods and over the months that had passed had come to enjoy the visits when Roan would find her there, walk with her, talk with her. He'd seemed to be gone for so long this time. Esta had realized how much she missed his presence, how much happier she was when Roan walked beside her, when his words and laughter kept her company. She could hardly bear the feeling of sadness she felt coming at her. It tied her stomach in knots.

"You should return to the village, Roan. Your mood is counterproductive to the reasons I walk at night." Esta's voice held a trace of anger, something Roan was not expecting.

"I'm sorry." He stopped and turned to face her. "I'm leaving on the morrow is all. I have no idea when I will return. And you know how hard it can be to travel once winter sets in."

Esta realized that his sadness was much the same as her own. She reached out and took his hand. "You will be missed."

Roan had never before felt such a surge of emotion. It frightened them both. Esta pulled her hand free, and Roan blushed with the knowledge that Esta had felt his love for her, stronger than even Roan had realized at that moment.

They tried to pretend that nothing had changed. Esta talked of Mane and how much she loved the freedom of the tree village. She told him of the platform that had been added to a window in the dwelling just for her. Mane could come and go as she pleased and come in through a small window when she wished to be inside. Roan spoke of Land's End and his sister and brother. Both of them knew that they were avoiding the one thing that occupied their minds: what they were feeling for one another.

It was well past dark when they arrived back at the village. All the ascent ropes were up save one. Roan whistled and gave the rope a tug.

A voice rang out through the darkness, gruff and angry. "Get on, then!"

Esta placed her foot in the loop and wound her arm around Roan, who held her tight as the pulleys flew them skyward. Esta kept her eyes cast down as she stepped onto the platform. The guard grumbled loudly about waiting for her, saying that if he had known she was not alone, he would have pulled up the ropes and gone to bed. Roan quickly apologized and stated that it was his fault, that they had walked further afield than he had thought and that it would not happen again. Esta whispered a quick thank you and disappeared into the darkness, heading for her dwelling, where the dim light from the candles created a soft, warm glow. She walked quickly and kept her focus on just getting to a private space, but upon opening the door and stepping inside, she felt a rush of air as Mane flew past her, and there he was. Roan smiled weakly. They had walked mostly in silence after the chatter about this and that, neither one of them willing to be the one who spoke first, who turned them around and ended this last day they had together.

"I will not go until I have said goodbye to you, Esta."

Roan stepped forward, the candlelight just bright enough to cast dancing shadows as he moved toward her. He was afraid, excited. He felt longing, joy, love. He felt sadness and loneliness. So many emotions were coming at Esta all at once. She lifted her eyes to meet his, something she had been avoiding for weeks now. She had her back to the open door, one hand behind her still clinging to the handle. Roan placed his hands on both sides of her neck. His fingers curled around the back of her head and into her hair. He pushed her entire body up against the door, closing it behind her, and kissed her.

That night held much confusion and emotion for Esta. When Roan first walked away after their kiss, she had felt a surge of joy, a longing for him to stay. She wanted his love. She felt love for him as well. As soon as she'd realized that she was developing real feelings for Roan, she'd become riddled with guilt. Erik had only been gone eight moons. He had passed in the middle of the night. There had been a full moon that night. Now Esta could not see the moon at its peak without remembering those final moments. It had been late fall then; now summer was at its height and the days were long and warm. Esta and Roan both knew that when the frost returned, he would not be coming to the village as often.

Esta's guilt came at her in waves. She could be missing Roan dearly in one moment and weeping for Erik's loss in the next, having feelings of guilt and feelings for Roan at the same time. Her walks in the woods at times seemed to haunt her. She could remember walking with Roan in places they had found together—a meadow filled with wild flowers and strawberries, a waterfall and small pool by a rock bluff where the spring found its way to the river, a place deep in the woods where the moss hung from the branches in giant drapes like green tapestries. Now when she walked alone, she avoided these places, where she saw Roan's face and heard his laughter, his voice echoing in her mind.

Although not gifted in the way that Esta was, Roan could often feel the turmoil within her. She was always happy to see him. She allowed his hello and goodbye kisses. They would often hold hands and hold each other. Yet Esta would often cry when Roan left. He only knew this because she could not hide her emotions or thoughts from Ivar, who in turn would inform Roan how full of conflict Esta was. Ivar could hone in on the struggle within her, the guilt she felt for not saving Erik and for falling in love with Roan. She did love him—Ivar could read her feelings—but she pushed against those feelings, telling herself it was too soon, that it was wrong to love again. Try as she might, Esta knew that her heart now belonged to Roan. Getting her to let go of her guilt and openly express her true feelings was now Roan's sole goal. He loved her. He realized now that he had loved her for some time. She had been a wild, beautiful girl. He had admired her from a distance as a boy, but his anger and harsh childhood had made recognizing feelings of any kind next to impossible then. When he'd had the encounter with her over the cob, his gut reaction had been to hate her. What he'd actually hated was the fact that she was right. As time passed, he had come to respect her and to admire both her and Erik for their goodness and strength. He loved them both as friends—the first true friends that Roan had ever had. For some time now, those feelings had been growing. He'd known that the morning he had gone looking for Erik. He'd been angry because he loved her and felt that Erik had been wrong in giving his attention to Ava. He had kept that encounter to himself, though, and once he had kissed her, Roan knew he was lost. He would give the world to feel that love again, for Esta had kissed him back. Roan also knew that she had not kissed him again the way that she had that first time.

Weeks later, in Land's End, Roan entered his bed chamber. He was met with a loud screech and snap from Mane. Elated, he flew to the windowsill, nearly knocking Mane back out into the night. He searched the courtyard for Esta, but his heart sank as he realized she was not there. Roan allowed Mane to perch upon his shoulder.

"You are far from home. How did she manage that of you, I wonder?" Roan reached up to give Mane a scratch and was immediately drawn to the small satchel tied to her leg and gripped under one of Mane's large talons. He removed it carefully and placed Mane upon the sill before he turned to the light from the hearth to read Esta's letter.

He had been gone too long. He longed for her company and worried that she was lonely, although he truly believed that Esta was happy in the tree village. She was loved and protected there. So, he had not worried about her needing him, not like he needed her. For the first time, he realized that she was feeling the same loss, the same wanting, the same sadness at the distance between them. He placed the letter on his bed and fell backward to lie beside it. He had felt so good when he'd left the woods nearly two fortnights ago. He'd felt that Esta was beginning to let go of her guilt and openly share her love for him. They had fallen into each other's arms after fighting yet again about her pain and guilt at Erik's death. Roan had been unable to keep from finally telling her how very much he loved her. They'd walked hand in hand for hours, reliving and retelling the stories of those moments that had created their love. It was so easy with Esta. They had known each other for so long and had been friends long before they'd discovered deeper feelings for one another.

Mane seemed to understand Esta's longing for contact. The bird remained with Roan, even though the message had been delivered. Esta

would wait. At times the distance between herself and Roan seemed
to span the entire earth. She might as well be at the other side of it. As
long as Roan was in Land's End, he was too far from her. She tried to
reason with her emotions, for even if she could go to Land's End or Roan
could return to the woods, what good would it be. He was the nephew
of a now great and powerful lord, and Esta was now a tree dweller, a
strange and mysterious woman who understood things before they were
spoken and felt things before they were revealed. It could be said that
she had a certain power over the animals around her, both wild and
tame. With the tree dwellers, Esta was loved. She was safe. With Roan
she was loved, she knew that. She felt his desire for her. Yet she feared
a life with him and his temper. His view of the world seemed harsh to
her and hers too soft in his eyes. Esta's thought was always to seek peace
first, understanding first, communication first. Roan was more prone to
acting first and asking questions later. Once he had shaken his head at
her and said, "You see the good in everything, and that is your curse."
She had smiled a sad smile back at him and replied, "And you do not,
and that is yours."

It had been too long without communication. She longed for
the sound of his voice, the way he said her name, the way he smiled
at her. But the distance between them forbade it. Esta sat near the
window with ink and quill in hand. Ava had suggested that she write to
Roan, that perhaps they could remain in some sort of contact through
parchment at the very least. She stared at the blank expanse before
her and wanted to cry. There was nothing, nothing she could say to
Roan on parchment that would carry the weight of her love. At last
she penned a simple request:

My love,

How I long for the sound of your voice, for the touch of
your hand, for the love in your eyes.

She did not sign it. She rolled the tiny letter and placed it in a little
leather pouch. She tied the pouch with a cord to Mane's leg. The owl

had been dancing about on the windowsill but had instantly calmed and stood perfectly still so that Esta could secure the letter. She gave the bird a nuzzle and a pet, and Mane spread her great white wings and flew from the window into the night. Esta placed the image of Roan in her mind, pleading with the owl to find him. She pictured the castle at Land's End and the window of Roan's apartments there. She hoped that Mane would fly straight to Roan. It would not take her long. Esta could hardly sleep knowing that Roan would soon know just how much she missed him.

What would he do? Would he write back? Would he come to her? If he did, what then? Would he pull her into his arms and tell her that he loved her? Or would he keep his heart protected? Esta wondered if he had confided in Guth. And if so, how would Guth react to his choice of a life mate. Is this why he had not returned? Could he not come to her if he wanted to? Or was he perhaps just not able to leave Land's End at this time, just as she was not able to leave the woods? The night seemed to drag on and on. She could not sleep, her mind filled with the thought of Roan and what his reaction would be.

It was very late. Roan had stayed up with Guth and Ivar playing dice games and enjoying Ivar's ability to know what the dice held. He now stood and went to the desk near the hearth for quill and parchment. Roan's skill at letters was not as advanced as Esta's. He could read much better than he could write. He knew, however, that this was not a letter to be written by another, and Esta knew him well enough to forgive any errors he would no doubt make.

My dearest love,

I have left you too long. My heart aches at the thought of your loneliness. If it is even half that of my own, I know your pain. I am coming my love. Look for me on the morrow. I am with you as you are with me, in every beat of my heart, in every breath that I breathe.

Roan took no time to reread what he had penned. He tore the parchment to size, rolled it, and placed it in the little pouch. He tied it around Mane's leg and picked her up to give her a good scratch. He allowed her to nuzzle him and whispered, "Please find her well, Mane, for I do love her so."

With that, mane spread her wings and dived from the window and into the night, and Roan was left to the thought of his letter in Esta's hands. He would pack his few belongings and write some kind of farewell to his uncle, his sister, and Landen, for on the morrow, he would leave Land's End and never look back. His future, his happiness, was waiting for him in the canopy, and he must go. He knew that Guth would wonder at his choice, for it seemed to Guth that Roan should simply bring Esta back to Land's End.

Esta had not slept well. She knew it would have taken most of the night for Mane to make the flight to Land's End. If Esta was lucky, Roan would see Mane right away. If she were very lucky, she might receive a reply this very day. She penned her thoughts before the image failed her.

> I dreamed of you tonight, my love, a wish made while
> sleeping that I was awakened with a kiss, a whisper of
> your voice, a gentle, loving touch. I dared not open my
> eyes, afraid to know the truth. Afraid that the dream
> would fade away and leave me loving and longing alone.

Esta had penned many thoughts about many moments. She had tucked them away in rolls of parchment, tightly bound circles of thoughts stored safely away at the bottom of her quiver, a place she thought safe from other eyes. Who would look into a quiver for letters?

She had overslept and missed the morning meal. It mattered little, for food was the furthest thing from her mind. She wondered if Roan had received her letter, if he had sent a reply, if Mane were winging her way to the village as she sat there waiting. What may Roan have written?

Ava found her on a landing staring off into the distance.

"Why do you punish yourself for feelings you cannot control?"

Esta turned to face her, tears in her eyes. Esta's grief was painful for Ava as well, for she could feel the tides of emotion that Esta struggled with every day. She could feel Esta's love for Roan coming to the surface only to be dashed by her guilt over the loss of Erik. Esta had asked Roan to come, nearly begged him to do so.

"I am continually told that you cannot betray someone who is gone," Esta replied. "I do not believe that is true."

She gave the seat beside her a pat, and Ava sat down, looking at her as she always did, with a wish for Esta to be comforted.

"You can," Esta continued. "You can betray the trust they placed in you to be the keeper of their memory, the connection to them. When that person is still so real to you, still so much a part of you, when you still believe that you are connected, still love …" She pulled in a breath to slow her thoughts. "Sometimes I hear him. I feel his breath on my face. It is like he is still with me. And yet as much as I long for him, I also long for Roan. He is real; he is there, looking at me with eyes that know my pain. He understands my sorrow, my guilt." She stood and walked to the rail as if willing Mane to fly into her arms with news, words from Roan to calm her fears. "And yet he waits for my love. He feels my torment at loving him. He knows I love him so. He knows I love Erik still. Yet Roan pulls me along, and his love builds me up. It fills the hollow places left by Erik's loss, and I cannot help but want to place my lips upon his, to know the warmth of his touch as I have so many times in my dreams, even knowing that the moment I truly give in, Erik may be lost to me forever."

Ava knew some of Esta's pain. She had been very fond of Erik herself. What she found disturbing was how palpable Esta's love was when she spoke of Roan. It was as real as her sorrow for Erik. Her emotions were overpowering. Esta's connection with Roan, the love they shared, made Ava's cheeks burn red with embarrassment and gave her a warm flutter in the pit of her stomach.

"I cannot love Roan so much and mourn Erik at the same time," Esta said, seeming defeated.

"Why can you not?" Ava seemed to be almost angry. "Your love for Erik is not in question, Esta. Neither is the love he felt for you." She pulled Esta to a seat near the railing. "You loved each other with all your hearts. The love shared was special. You had a deep respect for one another, a true lasting bond." Ava took a deep breath. "For whatever reason, Erik was taken from you. He died knowing he was loved. He died looking into your eyes and knowing that you loved him. Do not let others make you feel as if that love is being questioned. You know how real it was, it is. He would not want you to mourn his loss forever. It is because he loved you that he would wish nothing else for you but happiness. If it were possible, he would tell you that himself."

Esta knew it was true. Erik often worried about her happiness.

Ava placed her hand upon Esta's and waited for their eyes to meet. "You must let go of this idea that it is one or the other, Esta. Loving Roan does not mean that you loved Erik any less. It only means that your heart is big enough to love another even after being broken, to love yet again even though love can mean pain. And if you ask me, both you and Roan are very lucky to have found love with one another. You have both suffered enough. You mean the world to him, and he knows you better than anyone else, save your mother."

THIRTEEN

A World on Fire

The day seemed to drag on without end. After talking with Ava, Esta needed space. She needed to go to the one place she could find some peace: the woods. If she left her dwelling, Mane would need to look for her in the woods, or the bird may choose to stay put and rest after the long flights and would be there when Esta returned. Either way, Esta needed air. She descended to the forest floor and disappeared down a path.

The sun was setting. Esta was out here somewhere. Roan knew that when the moon was full and the night was this clear and warm, there would be no keeping her within the walls of her dwelling. She would be with Mane in the near woods. Roan had traveled from Land's End as if on a quest. If she was here, he would find her. He would not leave Esta again without a plan for the future. If things went well, never again would he be without her.

Esta could feel Roan's presence long before she was able to locate him. She was worried when she first realized that he was in the woods. There was something different about him. He was a little angry, as Roan often was. It was, however, the first time since Erik's passing that his anger seemed to be directed at her. Just underneath the anger lay desire—a desire Esta was unsure of. She could not break it down to just one thing. It was layered. Peace, love, physical contact, joy, longing, ownership, release, anger … so many emotions in the desire. But the hunger, she could not or did not realize, all boiled down to her, to him wanting her.

Mane found her first. Esta pulled the rolled parchment from her leg, and the bird released a very loud screech. Roan was there, just through the trees in the meadow. He had heard Mane's cry. He knew Esta was close. Then Mane was there. She came flying out from the darkened woods between two enormous trees. Once Mane was overhead, Roan looked again to see Esta emerge from the shadow and into the light. Her hair was down and loose, slightly blowing in the warm, soft breeze. She wore a simple green, fitted gown with a leather, hooded corset. She carried her bow, and one feathered arrow dangled from her fingertips. She was smiling at him. Roan could not help but think how very beautiful she was in his eyes. He loved her.

Esta's cheeks flushed as she teased him, "Be careful, Roan, you might cause me to fall in love with you, and being the nephew of a great—"

She did not get the chance to finish her thought. Roan grabbed her arm and spun her toward himself. He pushed the hood from her head and wrapped his hands behind her head, running his fingers through her hair. Esta looked up into his eyes, and Roan looked at the full moon reflected in hers. Her face aglow, she did not pull away. She only looked deep into his eyes, as if searching for something. He kissed her. He kissed her once softly and then again and again. Esta kissed him back. She felt herself respond with the same longing, the same desire that she sensed in Roan. Esta's hands let loose the bow and arrow to wrap around Roan's neck and pull him even closer. She needed every ounce of her strength so that there was not even a breath of air between them. Suddenly, Roan pushed her back. He cupped her face in his hands and searched her eyes for the answer to his unspoken question. She could feel the hot tears welling in her eyes and knew that Roan could see them. His eyes too held tears, but of joy. Esta could no longer contain the flood of emotions. She tried to speak.

"It is not right ..."

Roan would not release her. He held her gaze as she tried to cast her eyes downward.

"I have never in my life felt so sure of anything as I do right now," he said as he forced Esta to look at him, willing her, wanting her, to probe the truth in his heart.

It was true. Esta could feel his love and peace at finally knowing she loved him in return. He pulled her into a warm embrace and kissed the top of her head while she wept. He did not move. He barely dared to breath. He held her close and stroked her hair, laying his cheek upon her head. She was letting go. Finally, she was letting go. When Esta at last looked up, she had at last given in. Roan wiped the tears from her eyes and kissed her lips. His thumbs ran down her cheeks as his fingers found the base of her neck. They kissed as if they may never see one another again, as if this moment meant everything.

They began to walk through the woods together, and Roan began to work out how to make things permanent. He was more than willing to live here in the trees with her, but he admitted that he wanted more for both of them than a life in the canopy could give them. Esta was not sure any more about remaining in the village. She was, however, sure that she did not want to live in Land's End. Roan understood this. Everything that had happened was the result of Beor convincing Guth that Esta was the key to unlocking Ivar's communication and connecting Guth with his son. Beor had known that this was his brother's one and only deep desire and had used it against him. Esta had always felt that Roan was yet another victim of his father, but Guth should have known better. Guth, she felt, was not a victim. He'd known who and what his brother was, and he turned that man loose on the village of Elvoy. He'd banished Beor there and by doing so had ensured that many would never see their loved ones again. Beor's wife had often felt the back of his hand. His children as well. Roan, being the oldest, had often taken the brunt of it, doing what he could to save his younger brother and sister from Beor's anger.

Elvoy had been on Esta's mind a lot of late. She missed the island she'd vowed she would never return to. Her home, no doubt, would belong to someone else by now, but there was always the woods, and there were the little shelters. One in particular she could build upon. Would Roan return to Elvoy? What would he do to keep them together?

How much would he give up? How much would she give up to hold on to Roan? Esta's realization that she loved Roan came at a price. It came with such a mixture of joy, fear, pain, guilt, and confusion. At times, she wondered if she would ever be able to enjoy Roan's company without the guilt that always followed the pain when he left her. Esta began to think about the treehouse she had grown to love so much. The village would always remain very small, living off of the land and doing a small amount of trade. She was not busy enough, not like she had been on Elvoy. She smiled as she watched Roan ascend to the platform. He waited for her there with the pully-man, giving her a kiss on the cheek as he headed off to find Ava, who had a gift she wished to send to Ivar.

The wars between the king and his sons had spilled into villages and the countryside, the castles and manor houses across the land. There was much loss of life, and both sides were nearing their limit of resources. This conflict would end soon, and choices would need to be made. King Henry was making his last push, and it was working. He knew that if he could cut off the supply lines for Richard and Geoffrey, then he could put the uprising to an end. One of those supply lines ran directly from Land's End, both by sea and by the Old Hollow Road.

The warnings came in cries, not whistles. There was no need for stealth. The village was under attack. Doors flung open, and men and women poured onto the decking and were immediately under fire from arrows, both tipped and flaming.

Esta dropped to the floor of her cabin. Her dwelling sat high and off to the side of the main dwellings. She cursed herself for not feeling the approach of so many battle-weary men. Their thoughts, their emotions, were very clear to her now: Destroy the village. Kill, if needed, and then return. This was a simple mission. Rid the woods of this village and its strange occupants, and then the Old Hollow Road will be clear for an attack on Land's End. Esta could tell that the tree dwellers were now fighting back, for fear came from both those on the ground and those in the canopy. Fire! The fear was overpowering. It was the fear of burning. They were setting the village aflame. Oil-soaked flaming arrows landed on the dwellings, on the suspension bridges and the decking. Some were trapped, and Esta could feel their panic as she scrambled for the door. The dwelling shook as the door burst open. Roan filled the frame, looking wildly around before locking eyes with Esta, who was on all fours. He said nothing but ran past her to her furthest window. He dumped the rope ladder over the sill and nearly pushed Esta over the edge.

"They are trapped!" Esta screamed, knowing Roan would not allow her to remain in the canopy but knowing that he himself would.

"Go! Head toward Land's End. Move quickly away from here! Go, Esta, please! I will find you."

Roan watched as Esta began her descent, and when he was sure she would reach the ground safely, he turned and ran back toward the main part of the village. Much was ablaze at this point. Several archers had managed to make it to the forest floor and now provided cover for those able to get to a descent platform. Roan, grabbing arrows at each platform, pulled his bow from his back. Scanning through the smoke, Roan released arrow after arrow, and each found its mark. He watched those pathways open up for retreat. Moving along the bridges that burned, Roan knew that he could not stay in the trees much longer. Screams could be heard over the roaring of the fire that was now igniting the neighboring trees. The forest was on fire. Even the enemy began to understand the danger and now ran from the blaze they had created.

Esta could feel the enemy's shock and fear upon realizing that they had miscalculated what the fire would do. She helped those who could run into the woods and pointed them in the right direction.

"Stay together. Follow the Old Hollow Road to Land's End, but stay in the trees!"

The tree dwellers knew better than to travel the road in the open. They sprinted into the woods in small groups and wove a trail of their own in the general direction of the sea.

There were still people on the platforms above when the first dwelling came crashing down in a ball of flame. It was time to go or risk being trapped by the fire on the ground. Suddenly Roan was there above her.

"Get out of here! Go, Esta! Go! Now!"

He pointed at one of the only paths into the woods left open, and Esta ran. Tears clouded her vision as she dashed into the thick undergrowth. She heard and felt the others as they ran, some before her, some behind. Only once did Esta feel the presence of the enemy. An arrow streaked over her head and clattered against the trunk of a tree. She quickly changed directions and could feel the man's disappointment at having missed her. She disappeared through the woods, leaving cries of anger, pain, and victory behind her. Esta concentrated hard on the sound of her own feet, the soft padding of quick strides. She concentrated on her breathing and scanned the woods around her.

Roan and several of the guard had managed to get most of the villagers to the ground. Some did not fare well once they got there, and a few were shot down with arrows from the platform. Once the fire had reached several buildings and connection bridges, the enemy on the ground began to pull back. The fire was reaching out to the tops of the other trees, and the men had to pull back to stay out of harm's way.

Roan was one of the last to descend. Within moments of touching down, the platform ropes and railings above him were ablaze. He looked up at the treetop village. It was gone. The canopy, the dwellings, the beautifully carved doorways, the twisting rails of the platforms, the woven vines, and the well-hidden suspension bridges—it was all gone.

The trees went up now like torches being dipped in kerosene. Sudden and violent bursts took the canopy away in flashes of fury, one tree at a time. There was nothing left to do but run. Looking wildly around for the safest way out, Roan and those last few men who remained had to follow the enemy retreat. To some, this may have looked as if they were giving chase, for they continued to rapidly fire their arrows at the backs of their enemy. The simple truth was that the woods were on fire, and there seemed only one way out for everyone. The men who had set the blaze were in just as much danger as those from the village, only now there were two enemies to avoid.

Esta crossed the river where the current was slow and the water shallow. She had often used this pool as a place to bathe. It was quiet and well-hidden by a huge rock out cropping. On the far side of the pool was a small slab that sat back under the large rock overhang. She would wait there for the fires to burn themselves out. It was safe. No one could see her from the rock cliffs or the far side of the river unless they crossed to the exact spot where she now sat. She was breathing hard and did her best to stifle her coughing. The smoke had burned in her throat. Her clothes, her hair, everything smelled of woodsmoke. It was a smell she usually loved, a smell that always triggered her best memories of times spent hovering around a fire with her parents, with Erik, and now with Roan. Those had been times for relaxation and conversation, times to hold each other and keep each other warm, to watch the light flicker and reflect in Roan's bright hazel eyes and watch the shadows dance across his face. She loved the smell of woodsmoke that lingered on Roan's tunic, in his shorn hair, and on his skin. It had always given her the urge to take a deep breath, to drink it in. She pushed herself as far back in the low crevice of the overhang of rock as was possible while still being somewhat comfortable. She laid her bow and quiver down, keeping her dirk beside her, and wrapped the extra folds of her overdress around her legs. She was not cold, but the rock was cool in the shade. She wished she could move into the sun, lay upon the heated surface, and wake to find this all had been a dream.

The Old Hollow Road was nearly impassable. Because of the fire, some trees had fallen across it, and the enemy soldiers that still lurked behind the parts of the woods that had not burned made it a dangerous place to be. Yet off the road was not much better. Many downed trees still smoldering cast off enough heat to burn anything that came too close. Roan had to hide several times from enemy soldiers, burning his left hand and even some of his clothing.

After catching her breath, Esta again looked for survivors. The sight of the trees burning gave her such pain. Falling again to her knees, she screamed her pain, which quickly became anger. As she wiped her tears with the back of her hand, Esta's anger grew. Her anger was fueled by the knowledge that the forest home was no longer a choice, by the understanding that nothing would ever be the same again for those who had made their home there. Another feeling of loss and sadness. She was sick of feeling loss, sick of feeling pain. She wanted no more of it. She worried for Mane, having sent the bird off at the first moments of the fire. She knew the bird would find a safe path but did not know where she might be or how to find her.

As the day turned to night, Esta slept. Morning brought the smell of smoke, but try as she might, Esta could not find another living soul. She waited out a large portion of the day in the safety of the rocks on the riverbank. When dusk approached, it was time again to move. Somewhere in the forest, Roan was running as well. Suddenly, she knew that Mane was with him, and Esta felt some comfort in that.

Once she moved away from the river, Esta could at times both see and feel other tree dwellers. She caught fleeting glimpses of green dashing through the woods, jumping over downed trees, and dodging around obstacles. Esta could feel their fear, grief, and complete sadness at the loss of the village. Their hearts were hurting. They had hidden and waited just as she had in the few untouched places of the forest, in the large rock outcroppings or meadows that offered more safety from the fire. Now they ran, and with every step they took, their distance from her grew, and Esta could feel herself losing each one of them. They would never be together as they had been. The village was gone, lost to her just as Elvoy had been after her father. Suddenly, Esta was not alone. She stopped and turned, watching the river path behind her intently. Then they were there. Ava, Clare, and a giant wolf came over a ridge and joined her on the path. There was not a single word exchanged, only a glance of acceptance. They followed the wolf, trusting his instincts to guide them away from both the remaining fire and any possible threat.

Esta's mother was in excellent condition for her age, but she was not nearly as fast or as agile as Ava or her daughter. She began to fall behind. When Esta slowed to wait for her, Clare threw her hand forward, gesturing for them to keep running. Esta shook her head. She would not lose her mother. Ava was there, and the wolf beside her panted but did not seem frightened or panicked in any way.

"We are clear, for the moment." Esta glanced at the plume of smoke that could be seen far above the canopy of the forest. "We will need to reach the other side of the river. This fire will burn everything in its path."

The fire still raged out of control in many areas, and the fire seemed to find new fuel in several places in the midday sun. They would continue to follow the wolf and find a place to cross the river once more.

It was nearly dark when they reached the falls of the river. The only safe places to cross were well above the cascading waterfalls that increased in size and ferocity. Once they were on the banks, there were signs that other villagers had also made their way here. Both Esta and Ava knew that everyone who could not get across the river would be in danger, both from the fire that had driven them out of the village and from those who had set it. There was only one other way across the river from this point: a bridge on the Old Hollow Road near Land's End. If villagers had managed to stay ahead of the blaze until it began to burn itself out, they would head down the Old Hollow Road in the woods. The bridge was the only way over the river to finish the journey to Land's End above the falls.

Esta stood near the water's edge and looked downstream. From her vantage point near the top of the falls, she had a clear view of the river for miles, a view that had once included the rich, green canopy of the forest that had hidden the village. Now only patches of green remained. It looked like most of the fire had stopped spreading. Hot spots remained, and there were still a few areas where she could see visible flames. It was nice to be above most of the lingering smoke. The air at the top of the falls was clear, and all of them were pulling in deep breaths. The climb to the hilltop was steep, yet the sparce shrubbery there had not burned. Clare was doing her best, but Esta knew that this escape was taking every ounce of her mother's strength. Esta could not shake the feeling that the woods now looked haunted with the smoke and the knowledge that some had not been able to escape the flames. Ava turned to her, knowing what she was thinking.

"Esta, you have no idea where to look."

Clare kneeled to get a drink from the cool stream and then said, "It matters not. I cannot continue at this pace. Ava and I can get to Land's End now. We can help others who show up here to cross. I need to rest."

Esta had been scanning the woods for others for quite a while, but she had not sensed another living soul. Neither had they seen the enemy. The wolf that had been running with them had stopped at the bottom of the rise to the falls. He'd watched them pass as he sat. Esta shared a thankful moment with the animal, who then simply walked away. She had encountered animals before in the woods. They had always been curious about her but had let her be. She had shared moments with rabbits and young fawns. She had even had other birds allow her touch. The wolf was much larger and more dangerous than anything she had encountered before. It was a strange feeling to be running behind the animal knowing it was there to help them find safe passage and not chasing prey.

Clare hugged her daughter, held Esta's face between her hands, and kissed her cheeks. "Be well, and return to me."

Esta watched as both her mother and Ava waded into the shallow water and crossed the river. They would wait on the other side for a while. Esta trusted that Ava would know when it was time to finish the journey to Land's End. She trusted that Ava would keep her mother safe.

Esta made her way back down the rocky ledges, descending the falls and staying well back from the tree line. There was ash drifting, at times heavy, and embers floated to the ground. One touched upon a pile of dry scrub brush, and within seconds, the bush was aflame. Those flames quickly jumped from bush to bush, the undergrowth roaring into a new blaze. Esta could hear the dull roar. The flames whipped in the wind, consuming the ground cover and exploding the treetops as if they were massive torches. Near the bottom of the falls, the river became rapid and wide. The falling water had carved many pathways over time, and several smaller falls and pools had developed.

Another person's presence made its way into her mind. More than one. She slipped behind one of the smaller falls and pressed her back against the rock, moving toward the center of the river. All at once, the wall fell away behind her, and she stood in the deep shadow of an alcove behind the tumbling waters. There were men on the bank, and they were searching. They were looking for someone who had caused them loss. They were angry. They wanted vengeance. As they moved upriver, Esta feared for Ava and her mother. There could be others looking along the riverbank for tree dwellers. She had to believe that Ava would protect them. She would keep them well away from harm. They would both be waiting in Land's End when she returned, hopefully with Roan by her side.

Although the alcove sat behind the falls, the rock near the base of the alcove was somewhat dry. Esta slid down onto her bottom, lay her bow across her pulled-up knees, and leaned her head back to rest. She could sleep here with little danger of being found. The path to the falls was steep and slippery, and she doubted that anyone would take the time to check it, as it was a visible path to the falls. Getting soaked was a given if you did not know there was an overhang and trail behind the cascading water. She was tired. Knowing that she would need her strength when morning came, Esta slept.

As it happened, the falls acted as a sort of filter, cleaning the air and allowing Esta to breathe freely. When she emerged from behind the glassy sheet of water in the predawn light, she nearly choked on the amount of ash and smoke in the air. Esta had cut a piece of cloth from the bottom of her cloak, and she now wrapped it around her head to cover her mouth and nose. The pool of water before her had grey silt floating on the surface. The sun's rays cut through in sections like light shining through a black cloth that had holes poked through it, except the holes seemed to shift with the smoke, causing the rays of light to come and go.

There was a surreal beauty in it. The colors of the rainbow would dance through her vision, and then the beam of light would simply illuminate the particles within: dust, ash, and even the light drifts of smoke. If it weren't for the smell of the burnt wood and grasses, it would nearly look like fog being raised away for a beautiful day.

But there would be no rising. This smoke would permeate these woods for weeks. Hot spots and flare-ups would keep the area in a haze. Esta knelt down to the water's edge. She pushed at the ashy silt to get to the clean water below and brought it to her lips. Roan would have stayed near the village and fought until he was certain that everyone had gotten away, even if it meant that he would not. She would make her way back toward the village in circles, her path narrowing in like a swirling target. She would find him. The forest floor was hard to navigate. There were smoldering logs and stumps. Esta made her way through the thick fog of smoke, going from one patch of remaining greenery to another. She constantly scanned for movement, staying well in touch with her senses.

It was nearing sunset when she found Roan in a burned-out section of the woods. A small fire burned on a stump, and there next to it lay Roan. He lay back against a large rock. He was there; she could feel him. He was injured. He was in pain. His eyes were closed. His right hand was wrapped in a torn piece of his cloak. His fingertips were blistered. Esta could see that the burn went well up his arm. There were burn marks on his shirt, his tunic nowhere in sight. There were holes seared into his leather boots and his breeches. A red-hot blister lay along his hairline above his brow, and he was nearly black from the amount of soot and ash on his face. Esta knew that some of that ash had been blazing hot when it had come into contact with his skin.

Esta slowly lay her bow upon the ground and reached out to touch his cheek.

"It took you long enough."

Esta smiled through her tears. "I'm sorry. I will try to be quicker in the future."

Roan opened his eyes and looked at her. "It will heal, Esta. I will be well."

The tears were cascading now, even though she tried to smile at him. "I need to gather herbs, ease your pain." She brushed her hand across his cheek, angry that she had slept behind the falls while Roan lay in pain, alone.

Roan looked at her and gave a weak smile. "Stay with me. I just need to rest a bit."

Esta moved to make Roan more comfortable. She pulled her cloak off and laid it over Roan's legs. Standing, Esta scanned the area. This was a rather large burned-out area of the forest. She could see small patches of green here and there but nothing close, nothing that looked like it would offer shelter. She closed her eyes and searched for the nearest human. Nothing. Only emptiness. She needed to find a place to take care of Roan's wounds and burns and find clean water and herbs.

"Where is Mane?" Esta asked. There was a small amount of fear in the question, although Esta believed she would have known if Mane were no more. She would have felt it.

"I sent her off. They knew of her; they were aiming for her." Roan looked to the sky. "It will be dark soon. Perhaps she will find us then?"

Esta scanned the ground near Roan. She began to clear away the burnt topsoil and debris with a branch that had somehow escaped destruction. It blackened her hands with soot, but it served its purpose. She was able to clear everything away from the slow-burning stump in a wide circle. Next, she removed Roan's tunic and shirt. She took the quickest path to the river, where she cleaned both, and then used the tip of an arrow to help cut the green tunic into strips. Roan's shirt had holes in it, their edges singed where hot embers had found their way in. Some had reached his skin, where bright-red spots appeared. She gathered up the cut cloth and soaked the shirt once more before returning to the clearing. Roan was happy to drink the water Esta had carried back with her quiver, thankful that the tree dwellers had learned long ago to make the leather quivers water tight. She used the damp shirt to clean Roan's face, hands, and burns as best she could. She used the clean strips from his tunic to bind the worst burns. Those upon his hands, arms, and shoulder were far worse than the ember burns upon his chest, back, legs, and face. She untied and removed his boots, using his boot cords to secure the bindings. Back to the river once more, Esta cleaned the now blackened shirt and refilled both her quiver and Roan's with fresh water. She navigated the last hundred yards back to the clearing by the glow from the stump, trying to keep her feet beneath her.

With a cool, clean shirt, bound burns, and water, Roan began to regain his strength. They remained close to the smoldering tree trunk that night and well into the next morning.

"Do you know where we are?" Roan asked, turning full circle.

Esta stood, swinging her bow over her head to rest upon her back. "I believe it is the meadow." She sighed. "What now? Where do we go from here?"

She sounded saddened. Roan saw only one purpose at the time.

"Esta, we must try to get back to Land's End. They most likely have been sacked, but we must try."

Land's' End frightened her. She could not say why, only that something about being there—being near Guth—was dangerous. She had no fear of him and nothing but love for Ivar, yet the place itself seemed to push her away. Her mother was waiting there. She knew they must go. She wanted nothing more than to see Roan safe and well healed. Nodding, Esta turned and began walking, determined to put the burned-out forest behind her.

FOURTEEN

No Place to Hide

They traveled on the Old Hollow Road most of the day, Esta keeping up a constant search for emotions of anyone who would do them harm. They passed only frightened animals making their way back to the woods. As they approached Land's End, they could see columns of smoke rising above a few of the courtyard houses. Roan asked Esta to purposely seek Ivar. Ivar's thoughts, or rather words, would tell them what they needed to know. As Ivar's thoughts came through, Esta sat back with a smile. He was overjoyed to know that Roan and Esta were safe. He beckoned them to the great hall. This was a clear sign that all was well. Then there was the loud shriek that Esta had been longing to hear. Mane. She had returned to Land's End, knowing that Esta would make her way back. Now the bird swooped down upon them, receiving affection and a few happy tears from her keeper.

As the giant doors to the great hall swung open, both Esta and Roan were greeted by those they loved. Landen, Hadwig, and Ivar ran forward with arms open wide. Behind them in the doorway stood Guth, Ava, and Clare, all smiling. After making sure both Roan and Esta were well, they all retired to the great hall, where Roan's wounds were tended by Clare, who placed a cool, soothing poultice on the burns. Instantly, Roan could feel the burning sensation lessen and the tightness of the edges of the burns relax. They were fed a much-needed meal of roasted boar, seasoned vegetables, mulled wine, and a beautiful spice cake that was followed up with even more of the mulled wine.

Roan was having a semiprivate conversation with Guth while Esta spoke with Ava and her mother. It seemed that most of the tree dwellers had returned to the woods. Some had made the choice to remain in Land's End, and others had not yet said where they would go. Guth gave most of them the supplies they needed for whatever their journey would hold, even sending some of his own men along with those who intended to find another grove of the giant oaks in which to rebuild their treetop homes.

The army that had marched on the village had been that of King Henry. Luckily for Land's End, Richard, Geoffrey, and John had heard news of their father's bid to sack Land's End and moved to cut off the revolt from behind. They had sent many men by ship to defend the village. Henry's small army was quickly dispatched after pouring into the village expecting little defense. Now it seemed that one of Queen Eleanor's sons would soon visit Guth to praise him for his loyalty.

Esta cared not for would-be kings or the fact that this war had managed to once again cause such loss. Beor had made the village known. Even from beyond the grave, he seemed to continue to hurt people. His information had caused Henry's army to burn the tree dwellers out on their way to Guth. They'd known the tree dwellers would defend Land's End. Afraid that they would come up behind the invading forces, they'd decided to simply remove them. Many were burned badly, and many had died trying to get out of the forest. The men had been killed, and the women had left to find their way to Land's End alone. The destruction of the treetop village was cruel and unforgivable. Guth vowed to both help with the reconstruction and with a reckoning for the lives lost.

Roan found little time to comfort Esta before they were spirited away for the night. He would find her in the morning, when they would make a plan for their future. He would follow Esta back to the trees, back to Elvoy, or anywhere else she wished to go.

Esta found herself once again in a guest solar with her mother. She opened the window and allowed Mane to perch upon the bedpost. The bird was anxious and did not want to leave her. Exhausted, Esta slept deeply and dreamed of a life without such constant turmoil. Dawn brought on a confusing chain of events. She woke to find Clare placing a beautiful gown across the small table. They stared at it and ran their fingers over the thick brocades and the silks of the under garments. This gown, Esta was sure, had once belonged to a queen, or perhaps Lord Guth's late wife. She could not bring herself to understand why it was there.

She closed her eyes, trying to get a feeling as to where she might find Roan, yet she could not find Roan's presence. Although she at first felt that the size of the castle may be to blame, it was not, for a small knock upon her door told her that Ivar was on the other side and that he was nervous and sad. She felt that he held something for her, something from Roan. Esta cast a worried glance at her mother and walked to the door. She smiled down at Ivar's worried expression and reached for the parchment.

"He has been sent away, hasn't he?" Esta sighed. "It is not your fault, Ivar. You need not worry so much."

Ivar placed the folded letter in her hand. "He will return within a fortnight, and with the queen!" Esta tried to smile. That explained the gown. She could not meet the royals of Britannia in a burnt and stained tree-dweller's leather bodice. After a hug goodbye to Ivar, Esta turned back to the small room and closed the door. Her mother's fear hit her hard. It was unexpected, and Esta looked about the room for its source.

"What is it?" She quickly approached her mother and took her hands in her own.

"Why would Guth introduce a lowly midwife's daughter to the queen of Britannia?" Clare sat, holding her daughter's hands and forcing her to look into her eyes. "Why would the mother of the future king of all of England want to meet you, Esta?"

Esta's mind began to race. Would Guth really hand her over to the crown like some piece of property, some trinket? She stood.

"No, he would never do such a thing. No," she said. But even as she voiced the rebuttal, she wondered. "Stay here mother."

It was a flat command. Esta spun and headed out the door and down the hall. She only wore the dingy green tree-dweller's gown. Her feet were bare and her hair down and unkept. She had not had time to change or bathe and cared little to do so at the moment. She opened her mind, trying to find Guth. He was with Ivar in the family solar. She quickly asked Ivar mentally to allow her to speak with Guth without him being forewarned of her coming. He did not like it but excused himself and left his father alone to face her questions.

Esta did not knock. She opened the door quickly and stood in the frame, staring at Guth as if he had been caught red handed at some kind of crime.

"Esta, what is it?" He came toward the door, thinking that the village was once again under siege, for she was disheveled and bare footed.

"Do you intend to hand me over to the crown?" Esta's tone was flat. She did not wait for a response. "I will not be owned; I will never be owned!"

Guth could see now the anger, the accusation. He shook his head and beckoned her to enter the room with an outstretched hand.

"I know not where this idea came from, Esta, but I assure you, that is not my intention."

Esta probed his thoughts. She could find no hint of a lie. She could find no deception. "Why then the gown?" She was still cautious.

"The gown?" Guth did not understand why gifting Esta and her mother clothing after they had lost all—both in leaving Elvoy and in the fire at the treetop village—would need explanation.

"The gown?" Esta said again.

"Please sit. You must explain your anger, Esta, for I meant no offence." Guth sat at the small table and again gestured for Esta to sit.

She moved to the table slowly, keeping a close read on his emotions. He did indeed seem confused. Esta sat. She placed her hands in her lap and tried to draw a calming breath.

"It is very fine, the gown. And far too splendid for someone of my station."

Guth leaned back in his chair. He tilted his head to the side as if to take a closer look at her. He nearly chuckled at her appearance at the moment, for he knew her to be a handsome woman but she looked like a wild river cat ready to spring.

"You feel unworthy." It was a statement.

"I am a young woman learning her mother's trade. I hope to become a healer, not a noble."

Guth chuckled. "I do not believe that you will ever be a mere healer, Esta, although I understand your words." He paused. "You must remember that you are also favored by my nephew. Roan may not become liege lord of Land's End, but he has earned my favor."

Esta looked up into Guth's eyes. He was proud of Roan. He wanted things for him. Her mind began to race with what things could be waiting for Roan with a woman like her at his side. She only wished for a simple, small life of peace. However, as much as she loved Roan, she could not, would not, live in Land's End.

Esta stood, and Guth followed suit. "I beg pardon, sire. I was mistaken."

Guth tried to read the expression upon her face. He tried to give her a comforting nod, yet Esta left the solar without another word.

Several dresses were delivered to Esta and her mother over the next few days, all of them beautiful in their own way. Clare pushed Esta to wear the gowns when out of their private quarters. It was expected. She knew that Esta was struggling. Esta waited for Roan to return for one reason only, and that was to tell him goodbye. Esta had discovered that many of the tree dwellers had found a home upon Elvoy, and still others had gone to one of the other small islands that dotted the coastline. There were many to choose from between the Shetlands and Orkneys alone. Guth had promised supplies and trade in exchange for a loyalty oath, and most if not all had given it, pledging to heed a call to Guth if he were to give it.

Esta did not like the idea of young people from the islands fighting in future wars. She also knew that wars would always come. Men were greedy. Power and wealth ruled all. Some ruled well; others did not.

Roan was due to return at any moment. Esta looked forward to and dreaded the first moments they would have alone together. She had no doubt that Roan would want to talk about their future together, and Esta simply saw no future for herself if she were to remain in Land's End. Yet Land's End held Roan's future as a noble. Here he would be wealthy and well respected.

FIFTEEN

An Evil Presence

Esta had spent the last fortnight exploring the city. She walked in the garden daily and then would venture out beyond its wall. She would often exit through the secret door, slipping away from the castle and those who kept an eye on her. This included Ivar, who reminded her every time he saw her that he did not want her to leave. Guth rarely allowed Ivar outside the wall walk. Esta found that she needed time away from the feelings he pushed on her. Nearly every side street had now been explored. She found walking the narrow cobblestone roads relaxing. Most paid her no mind, busy with the routines of their day. Others gave her a dip of a knee and a nod if they made eye contact. The truth was that very few of them even knew who she was. She could easily blend in when she did not wear the clothing Guth had offered. She had asked for and received a few dresses that better befit her station, telling Guth that she could not walk about the village in a garment so grand. She did, however, promise to wear the better dresses when the royals arrived. Esta liked the fact that she could move about without fear of discovery. If only she could trade the stone for the forest. As it was, the sheer number of people with thoughts and emotions made the city uncomfortable. Esta longed for the quiet of the woods. Mane missed the trees as well. She would remain in the garden when Esta walked, scanning the rich grasses for voles or mice and waiting for Esta to return to her.

Esta remained closer to the castle this day wearing a fine gown. She had walked for hours, making her way around one of the outer walls of the castle to where large iron gates extended to a low, narrow stone surface on the ground. Her first thought was that it was some sort of root cellar. The top of the building only reached her knees. Just inside the gate, Esta recognized the colors of a tunic. This was one of Guth's men, a soldier, a guard of some sort. He was at one end of the low structure standing as if at attention. Esta looked past the man to the inner wall of the castle and saw a large door. She guessed that it would lead her into a hallway just outside of the great hall, perhaps around the back side of it. She could find her way back to her chambers if she entered here. She wondered if Roan had returned while she was out or if he was still somewhere at sea bringing the queen or future king to Land's End. She tried for a moment to sense Roan and pulled back. She felt pain, hunger. She looked around her, searching for the source. Pushing the gate open and stepping through, she was immediately confronted by the guard.

"This is not an area for a lady. Please go around to the portcullis, my lady."

He was not being rude; he just wondered why she was there. Again, Esta could feel hunger and pain, now with a longing. A longing for freedom. A longing for justice. Again, Esta looked around her and then at the guard. These strong emotions were not coming from him. They were coming from behind him. They were coming from the low stairs that disappeared into the earth under the stones.

"What is down there?" Esta pointed past the man, who now seemed concerned about her presence.

"'Tis the prison, my lady. Please go round the other side." Again, he waved her back through the gate.

"There is something wrong," Esta said as she swept past the man and down the stairs. She could feel his astonishment and anger.

"Hold!"

It was too late. Esta burst through the door at the base of the stairs and was hit by the smell of rotting flesh, human waste, foul body odor, and stale air. This caused her to throw her hand up over her mouth and wrinkled nose as she made a sound that showed her distaste. Two men sitting at a barrel jumped to their feet. They were eating a hunk of roasted meat and drinking mead. Esta could see their lack of manners. Both men had spilled mead and grease upon their dirty tunics.

Esta turned to see a small square cell next to her. Deep in its recesses sat a woman, curled up in the corner like a frightened child. The cell next to that held an elderly man, who stood at the barred door, face framed in the bars he held in his hands. She continued her scan, walking the perimeter of the small room and gazing into each cell, only one of which stood empty. The other six all held a prisoner, five of them men. They were all excessively dirty, all in pain, and all extremely hungry. One of the guards stepped before her.

"You cannot be in here, my lady. You must go." He was in charge. His voice held authority, and his thoughts were arrogant. He believed he would be obeyed without hesitation. Instantly Esta knew that he would be very disappointed.

"What have they done to deserve such vile treatment?" She could feel his anger mount.

"'Tis none of your business what they've done. They're all scum, criminals." He came toward her, looking her up and down.

"Who are you? What gives you the right to come in here?"

Esta turned to face the man. He was foul. His face held a permanent wrinkle of distaste as if the repulsive smell of this place had etched its way into his features. He looked at her with this disgusted ire.

"Ya need to get out. Ya have no business here!"

The elderly man at the bars of his cell spoke out.

"Do not listen to him, my lady. They eat our food, they …"

He had no chance to finish, as the guard rushed the door of the cell and slammed it several times with a thick wooden stick. The level of fear coming from the other prisoners increased instantly, and Esta knew the stick was meant to cause both fear and pain.

"Get back and shut yer mouth!" The guard rapped the door a few more times to keep the man away from the light.

Esta could not find malice or evil within those behind the bars. The only cruel-spirited person in the room seemed to be the guard in charge of holding them here. She looked past the table at the other guard. He was younger and looked at her differently. Tuning in, Esta realized that he knew who she was and was afraid of her. She focused her gaze upon his, and he visibly quivered. The young man took several quick jerky steps to the captain and whispered into his ear.

"'Tis the woman they brought back from that island, Captain Eegon. The one they say has second sight."

The man's eyes widened, and he gripped the stick more firmly, bringing it up in front of himself as if he needed protection. His hand opened and closed around the club one finger at a time as if to increase the strength of his grip. Esta could feel his fear of her. Yet there was also a thrill, a desire to strike her down. She was viewed as evil by this man, and he wanted her to pay for it.

Taking a step back, Esta felt the need to remove herself from the cells. She also was being overwhelmed with a sense of hope from the prisoners, who had all found their feet and were at the doors of their cells staring out at her. The woman's hope was the strongest. It was as if she were begging to be saved. Something else was there as well—fear for Esta. She feared Esta could suffer the same fate. The girl was afraid for her. Esta felt she needed protection, and she stepped back toward the guard, not wanting him to believe she was frightened.

"Is Lord Guth aware of what happens here?"

She directed her gaze at the captain, and he knew what the young man had whispered in his ear was correct. This woman, this girl, was a witch. Esta could feel his conflict. If he put his hands on a noble, he would suffer. Yet she was a witch; she was evil. She turned on her heels and marched back to the stairs. The guard outside all but jumped out of her way to allow her to leave. She headed straight for the doors in front of her. Those doors would either open directly into the great hall or into a connecting room or hallway. She could feel the captain emerge from the cells. He was behind her. He was determined. He was gaining. Esta pulled the door open and stepped into the outer walk, almost directly across from the hall. She could hear voices and feel the presence of both

Guth and Roan. He was there, just inside the double doors. She turned the corner to see two guard on both sides of the enormous wooden doors. They turned to face her as she made her way straight to them. Behind her, a door slammed shut, and she knew the foul-smelling captain was fast upon her heels. She went to enter the hall and both men threw their staffs across the entry to block her.

"I must speak with Lord Guth. 'Tis urgent." She looked from one man to the other.

The door behind them opened, and a young man nearly ran into one of the staffs as he stepped out. Esta seized on a moment of distraction and ducked beneath the staff and around a few noblemen as they spilled into the hall. She looked behind her to see the cell captain's face disappearing as Guth's men closed the door behind her.

"Esta!" Roan came to her with a smile and a quick hug. He pulled back and looked at her in her fine gown. She was beautiful.

"I must speak with your uncle."

Roan knew this look; he knew the sound of her voice when she was frightened. The smile faded quickly and was replaced with a look of concern.

"What is it?" He looked past her to the closed door. "Esta?"

Guth had noticed Esta's entry into the hall. He had hoped that introductions would never be necessary, that Esta would be just one of many ladies at the tables or in the hall. He had given her the gowns to cause her to blend in, not stand out. Now there she was, and all eyes were upon her. The hall was more crowded than Esta had expected. There were many people dressed very finely. Even Roan was wearing a very fine doublet.

Esta looked about and was suddenly embarrassed. "Get me out of here," she whispered quickly. It was a desperate whisper.

Roan glanced behind him and noticed the worried look on his uncle's face. He quickly turned Esta about and headed for the door. She knew who was out there, yet she was with Roan. He would put the man in his place quickly. She was shocked to find the hall empty of all except the guard. She let out an audible breath as Roan turned them toward her chambers.

In the great hall, Guth sat with the princes, one of whom was the future king of England. It mattered little to him whether that would be Geoffrey or Richard, although he found Richard more likable. They spoke of the uprising. They had come so close, yet at this moment they needed to pull back, regroup, and come up with a plan. They needed to find a path that would remove Henry without tearing the entire country apart. The king sat reveling in his victory. Geoffrey, Richard, and the queen would do their best to reason with him. They had hope that he would listen, for no other reason than that another uprising could destroy everything.

After entering her chambers, Esta began to calm. Roan held her. He waited, knowing she would tell him what had happened when ready.

"Did you know that there is a dungeon prison just outside the inner wall near the back of the great hall?"

She was no longer so upset. Roan could tell that she was afraid and angry.

"I'm not sure. I guess I've seen it. I never paid much attention to it." He was not sure what to say.

"I felt them," she said, looking up at him, eyes full of pain. "I was walking by, and I felt them."

Roan thought he understood. "It is a prison, Esta. I'm sure you felt much despair."

She shook her head. "I did, but not in the way you mean. They were in pain and hungry, and there was a woman among them who had been ... tortured."

Roan caught the pause. He tilted his head in question. "A woman?"

"There are things happening to those people, Roan. Things that should not happen."

Roan nodded. "Esta, I understand your concern, and you may even have a point, but these people are there for a reason. Reasons we do not know."

"I do not care what the reasons are. The captain, a man named

Eegon, he is vile. He is cruel. He eats their food. He hurts them for his own enjoyment." She looked hard at Roan, daring him to defend the abuse—abuse she knew he had suffered himself at the hands of his father.

The words stung, as Roan knew that they were meant to. "You know this is nothing to do with me, Esta. You can speak with Guth about it when the royals take their leave. I'm sure he will take your concerns seriously. If the guard needs to be replaced, I see no reason to believe he will not do so."

His voice had taken on a flat tone. Esta knew she had hurt him, but she had not told him everything.

"He means to see me dead."

Roan had started toward the door but now stopped and spun round to face her. "Who?" He did not know and did not care; he would kill them regardless. "Why? Why would anyone wish you dead, Esta?"

"Captain Eegon. He believes me to be evil. He believes I am a witch and wants to see me pay for my evil." She came to Roan and took his hands in her own. "He followed me to the great hall. He had a sort of sick satisfaction when he was behind me. That is why I went to the hall. I did not know you had returned. His vile desire to destroy me blocked out everything else, even you."

Roan's mind raced. They could not have an unpleasant scene while the royals were here. Guth had made it clear that he wanted no trouble. He hoped to keep the visit short and return his lands to their normal state of being as soon as was possible.

"I will pull my uncle aside and tell him that we must speak with him quickly. Come with me. I want you to wait in the family solar. You can keep company with Ivar until I come back."

Esta nodded in agreement. The family solar was reserved for a very few. There would be no chance of seeing the captain of the guard there, and her time would be well spent with Ivar and Hadwin. She enjoyed their good-natured play, and she could remove them to the garden to check on Mane.

Captain Eegon of the cell guard was not a stupid man. He knew that Esta's tongue would be wagging the moment she entered the hall. He needed to make sure he would not pay the price. He went first to his quarters and demanded fresh water, enough to bathe. He would clean himself up and put on a fresh set of clothing. Next, he would go straight to the priest at the abbey. He would claim that his post, his ability as captain had been assaulted. He would tell the priest that this "witch" had forced her way into the dungeons and caused the prisoners to stand at their cell windows shouting lies and making false claims. He would beg the priest to intervene on Lord Guth's behalf and save him from this evil. This woman from Elvoy, who had somehow calmed the mind of Guth's son and made the boy who had never uttered a word able to speak as if he were an older, more mature young man, threatened men on the open waters with drowning and had an unnatural connection with a creature of the night.

The priest was a pompous, solemn man with ideas of his own importance. He took the captain's accusations about a witch in Land's End seriously. Knowing that the royals were present only seemed to heighten his sense of duty. He would make an example of this woman with the hope that it would place him in a noteworthy position.

Esta had spent the afternoon with Ivar and Hadwig. They had played in the garden and walked on the beach. In both of those places, they had been surrounded by other servants and Lombard. Mane had soared along the breaking waves, catching air currents with great satisfaction. The children had run laughing in the surf, collecting shells, rocks, and small pieces of driftwood, and Esta had turned her long, loose dress sleeve into a makeshift basket for their treasures. Now back at the keep, they were at this moment sitting in the family solar, making things from the beautiful shells and rocks they had found.

Sensing it at the same time, both Esta and Ivar looked up at each other in shock and horror. Ivar ran for the door to bolt it as Esta stood, clutching the cod shell in her hands. The door was kicked open, narrowly missing Ivar, who jumped back to avoid being struck. He stepped into the frame and looked up at the priest and several guards.

"How dare you!" His words were strong for one so young, especially since he had just found his voice not so long ago.

The priest shot a glance at the captain as if in horror. The boy had spoken, just as the captain had said. He looked to Ivar and then past him at Esta.

"You." He motioned to one of his guards. "Take the young ones to the garden."

The young man walked forward, and Ivar sidestepped out of his reach. Hadwig was suddenly behind Esta and very frightened. Even at her tender age, she could feel the danger, the malice coming from the priest. The guard advanced once again at Ivar, who once again escaped his grasp.

"Fine!" The priest looked at Ivar with a weak smile. "Bring her." He turned and headed back down the hall. All four of the guards, including the captain, who did not look like the captain at all, stepped into the room to retrieve her. Ivar went to step between them, defiantly.

"No, Ivar, get your father. Hurry!" Esta said urgently.

Hadwin screamed as they took hold of each of Esta's arms and led her from the room. Her cries were nearly drowned out with the closing of the door, becoming a distant wailing of fear. Ivar ran before them, dashing around the corner of the hallway and nearly knocking the priest out of his way as he headed for the great hall. Knowing that the boy was on his way to Guth should have given them pause. Esta thought they would surely wait for council from their lord. But their pace only quickened, and the hold on her arms only tightened.

Esta was taken down a hallway she had never been in before. It spilled into a covered walk that bridged the distance between the castle and the small church. She had seen the church on her walks, even crossed the stone path that she now walked upon. She had passed its beautiful windows and arches. She had not, however, ever entered the church, preferring to spend her days of worship in the near woods or walking on the beach with Roan or the children. There was not a church per se on Elvoy. The elders would simply give advice on keeping one's soul free from that which would stain it. As they approached it now, she was frightened. There was something about it that caused her to feel fear. This was the feeling she had experienced in the woods, the reason she had not wanted to return to Land's End. She had the overwhelming sense that it would be her end. She had not been able to name it before, had not understood from where it came or why. Now she knew that this man, this priest, would find a reason to find her unnatural. She was different; she had always known that. Now this difference would be used against her.

Once inside the chapel, the priest approached the altar and turned to face her. He pointed to the floor before him.

"On your knees."

Esta would not. She would not bow to this man. This man that would condemn her. A sudden impact with her stomach had her bending over. Captain Eegon had used the pommel of his sword and brought it around to slam into her abdomen. The two men on either side of her forced her to her knees as the air escaped her.

"You stand accused of witchcraft, most unholy acts of the mind! I see before me a child of the devil! Do you deny it?"

Esta shook her head, her eyes wide with fear as she searched for someone to save her.

"If she will not speak," Captain Eegon screamed, "then we should burn her!"

Esta's heart lurched. At that moment, she caught a glimpse of fear from the priest. He feared fire. He feared it greatly. Esta scrambled to find a way to use that knowledge, and without thinking of how it would only confirm the priest's thoughts, she bellowed, "You, even you, fear the flames. Please, please release me!"

The clergyman's eyes grew wide with fear. He stepped backward as if to put distance between them. Coming to his senses with a shake of his head, he set his lips in a tight line. His eyes narrowed into a gaze of pure disgust.

"Bind her, and the lord will see this evil banished."

⚘

Ivar burst through the side door to the great hall. He stood looking wildly about for his father, who stepped aside as if to excuse himself and found Ivar's eyes. Guth's head was being bombarded by Ivar's words.

They took her. They have her. They are going to kill her.

All of these words came at him quickly, jumbled, mixed, as if Ivar were yelling them all at once. Guth placed his hand to his temple and shook his head. Ivar ran. He crossed the hall in seconds and began shouting, this time using his voice—a voice that still came as a shock to Guth, who had been overjoyed when he had first heard it.

All eyes turned to the shouting youth as Roan's hair stood up on the back of his neck. He too ran to Guth, crossing the hall in a panic.

"He'll kill her!" Ivar was shouting.

Roan came skidding to a stop next to Guth, who looked confused and unsure of what was happening.

"Who took her, Ivar? Where?"

Roan pulled Ivar's attention from his father's worried gaze.

"The cell captain took her. He believes she is a witch."

This word alone brought a collective gasp from those in the hall. Worse, Geoffrey and Richard gave one another a curious glance, stood, and came forward.

Roan turned for the doors, and with Guth beside him, they very quickly left the hall out the side door nearest the abbey. Guth's mind raced. How could he explain Esta's gift? How could he allow any harm to come to her when Ivar had similar gifts of his own? His son. What would they do if they knew? Hiding his son from harm was all he had done since he was born.

Roan threw open the abbey doors. Nothing. They were not there. He turned to Guth, wild eyed and seeking guidance. Ivar closed his eyes tight, listening to his inner thoughts.

"They are at the moorings. They mean to drown her!" His voice broke, high pitched with fear.

The two men raced down the cobbled street toward the docks. Guth could see the crowd that had gathered on the wooden docks. There were more people moving toward the scene. The priest was reading loudly from the holy book in his hands. Both Roan and Guth were yelling, but the crowd roared and chattered loudly. Their voices were lost. As Guth pushed his way through, the onlookers stepped aside and quieted, seeing their lord's angry advance. He was mere feet from where Esta stood, hands and feet tied together. Her eyes were full of tears, searching the crowd for rescue. The captain of the cell guard pushed her off the dock. Esta fell backward a good ten feet before hitting the cold, angry waves.

Roan did not stop. He dropped his blade as he ran, pulled his tunic over his head as he hit the edge of the dock, and dived, flying out over the water to the place where Esta had gone under. The cold water engulfed her. She had held her breath as she hit the water, but it was all that she could do not to gasp at the icy temperatures and draw the freezing water into her lungs. Her eyes closed tight, she struggled against the ropes that bound her. Hands grabbed at her now, clinging to the dress and her arms, pulling her upward.

Guth found himself at the edge of the dock, searching, waiting. Slowly from the crowd emerged Geoffrey and Richard. Soon after Ivar and Clare appeared. Esta's mother screamed as she realized that Esta was in the water. Roan's head broke the surface of the water, and he pulled Esta up with him. They gasped for air. Roan flipped her to her back, talking softly in her ear.

"I've got you. Relax, Esta. Let me get us ashore. Relax, I have you. I have you."

Clare ran toward the shoreline where Roan was headed. Guth turned, finding the priest's angry face before him.

"Thou shalt not suffer a witch to live!"

The man held his holy book up over his head as he shouted his proclamation. Several of the onlookers cheered as if in agreement. Guth's face became red with rage.

"She is no witch, you ignorant fool!"

"She has been accused by your own captain! I have questioned her and found her to be unnatural."

Ivar was there, his son. His only thought was to protect him. Ivar's thoughts invaded Guth's mind. He wanted his father to get rid of all the people, to get Esta back to the safety of the castle. Guth spun to face the many onlookers, who could see without a doubt how angry he was.

"Go back to your business! Your homes, now!"

Hearing this shouted command caused several men to start pushing people back and away from the docks. A few guards that protected Geoffrey and Richard also began to thin the crowd, shouting, "You heard him. Move!"

By the time Roan was helped from the water to dry land, only a few remained. Esta shivered uncontrollably. Her shaking was as much from fear as from the cold. Roan untied her hands and feet, and Esta threw her arms around his neck. She cried. He gently pulled her arms away, and Esta could see his hate. She could feel it. Deep hate and anger. Roan stood and turned toward the priest and Captain Eegon as if he would kill them with his bare hands. Seeing Roan charge up the bank, the priest once again pleaded his case with Guth.

"I swear, my lord, I only meant to rid the village of an evil presence." He backed up and allowed Guth to place himself between him and Roan. Guth placed his hand on Roan's chest to still him and turned back to face the priest.

"You are wrong! The only evil here today is your attempt to murder my nephew's bride! She is more worthy of the gods' love and mercy than you will ever be!"

Guth paused as a look of utter terror crossed the man's face. He turned to see both Geoffrey and Richard on the rocky beach helping Esta to her feet. Richard removed his cloak and placed it about her shoulders as they began to walk together toward the castle. Clare held Esta tight to her side, nodding at the royal prince as if to thank him for his help. They moved quickly up the bank, where Roan turned, scooped Esta up into his arms, and headed for the keep.

Guth stood for a moment and watched them quickly head for the warmth and safety of the castle. He turned again to the wide-eyed priest, who now stared at the royals in awe.

Ivar sent his father a quiet message. *He is going to try to impress them.* And Guth could see the priest's envy and need to curry favor with two royals before him. It took several minutes for the priest to inform Guth that the captain from the cells had reported Esta to him. He told Guth that Esta had found herself in the cells and that the captain had claimed that the prisoners had been brought to a wild state of hurling accusations by her presence there. The priest told Guth that he would have to deal with this, and quickly. Several of the guards looked on in fear, while others looked at the priest as if he were mad. Turning to his own personal guard, Guth gave several orders in quick succession.

Guth ordered that all those involved be summoned to the great hall. He meant to get to the bottom of the matter. He commanded them to have Roan and Esta report to the great hall as soon as dry clothes were upon them. He then summoned the priest and made sure those who were held in the cells were brought to the hall as well, including the prisoners and the other guards. This action brought a cry of protest from Captain Eegon, whom Guth silenced with a mere look of fury.

Geoffrey and Richard put their heads together in whispered conversation many times yet offered no council and directed no action. Guth wondered how long their silence would hold and why they said nothing in the midst of this kind of accusation.

Ivar invaded his thoughts once more. *They seek information about Esta. They have heard things. They have heard rumors about a person being able to understand things before they happen before. It has something to do with their mother.*

The queen? Guth wondered how on earth the queen would have a connection with anyone on Elvoy. Of course, he had had no idea that the tree dwellers lived right under his nose in his own woods—woods he had hunted in, surveyed, and built a road through.

"Over," Ivar said aloud, flashing him a smile. "Over your nose, father."

Guth smiled. The sound of his son's voice was still new to him. It was a sound he much preferred to hear out loud, as the mind-speak still caused him unease. Ivar needed to be protected at all cost. If these men could find Esta unworthy of life, what on earth would they do to his son?

SIXTEEN

No Man's Pawn

he hall was set up as it was when Guth held council or court, the only difference being that Geoffrey and Richard also had seats at the dais next to Guth. The members of council where all there, most of them having heard and seen much already. Guth worried that minds had been made up. Ivar seemed to think that most were just curious about her and the rumors they had heard. People had died when the city was attacked, yet not nearly as many as would have perished if they had not received the warning. Ava, Clare, and many others from the tree village had appeared to both forewarn and help defend Land's End. When the ship arrived with reinforcements of several hundred men, armed and ready for combat, they were able to push the smaller company that had been sent to sack Land's End and destroy the tree village back into the woods. The enemy dispersed and withdrew in desperation and defeat. That ship, which had carried the royals' forward guard, had arrived by chance and had not been foreseen by the king's mercenaries. They had literally saved the village.

Guth wished that Ava were present. Her presence seemed to calm the minds of those who did not understand. Esta could only read people's feelings, and often when hate or anger came at her, she would wear the hurt upon her face. Ava, on the other hand, always kept a calming lid on uncomfortable conversations. Ivar could communicate information to people's minds, but Guth had forbade him to speak this way or give away his ability. Ava's calm wisdom would have served them well. Guth would try to channel that.

In her chambers, Esta fell into her mother's arms and wept. Roan sent Landen to fetch dry clothes and boots. He then tried to warm himself by the hearth, as his body still shook, though this was largely because he was more afraid at this moment than he had ever been. Not in the whole of his life, even when Beor's anger had rained down upon him, had he been so afraid. This time his fear was for another, for Esta. He loved her. He loved her, and he refused to lose her.

Esta slowly pulled herself together. Clare combed out her wet hair, dried it as much as she could with a strip of cloth, and braided it beautifully around her head and down her back. Esta refused to wear one of the gowns sent to her by Guth. Instead, she donned the gown she had been wearing the day Guth and Beor had attacked her people upon the pebbled beach of Elvoy. Efforts had been made to clean the gown of the blood stains, yet some remained. The white gown now had subtle shades of pink. The red cloak was as stunning as ever. Roan's reaction when she entered the room was a mixture of shock, fear, and amazement. He shook his head and was about to protest, to beg her to change. He looked into her eyes searching for an answer. Esta reached up and gently placed a finger to his lips.

"No, Roan. It is time. I will not run. I will not hide who I am. I never asked to be here. I never asked for any of this! I want to go home."

It was the first time Esta had mentioned the word *home* out loud in a very long time. Home. As much pain as that island had brought, it was home. Roan nodded and reached out for her hand. They walked together down the long, wide hallways made of white stone. They walked in silence. Esta had a foreboding feeling that this would either be their last day upon this earth or their last day in Land's End. Either way, Esta was done being afraid. She was finished with taking on the feelings of others only to find that they misunderstood, distrusted, or even hated her. It was time to put herself first for a change, even if it may come at a price, even if it was too late.

Roan walked beside her. He would leave this place if it meant that they could be together. He would turn his back upon this white wonder and never look back if Esta could walk beside him. He would do whatever was necessary to keep her safe. That he knew. Even if it cost him his own life, he would find a way to save her.

There were audible gasps as Esta and Roan approached the dais. Esta could feel Guth's disappointment and fear. She blocked it out. She blocked it all out. Every feeling in the enormous room—blocked. She had never been capable of such a thing before. It emboldened her, and she raised her chin just enough for Roan to realize she was determined to fight. He gave her hand a slight squeeze. Guth motioned for the pair to take their seats. He waited for a moment for the hall to quiet and then began.

"I have been informed that Esta of Elvoy entered the dungeons and that this is where this trouble began. I will hear from all who wish to speak and then render a decision. That decision will not be questioned!"

Guth made this statement with slight hesitation, given that the future king was sitting in one of two seats right beside him. While waiting for the hall to be set up, Guth had asked the princes if they meant to take command of the situation. They had declined, stating that this was his keep, that he was lord here, and that they would simply watch at this point. Those words echoed in Guth's mind—*at this point*. He glanced behind him, where Geoffrey and Richard sat stoically. They kept their faces and body language well under control, a habit most royalty had well in hand. It made governing a bit easier.

Esta had thought that Captain Eegon or the priest would speak first. However, Guth had used information gained by Ivar when the prisoners had been brought in to decide that those held in the cells should speak first. It had the desired effect. The priest and the captain were angered by it. This reaction did not go unnoticed by those on the council. Of course, that was the intention.

The first person brought forward was the old man who had spoken to Esta from his cell. Esta could not help but think that Guth was getting guidance from Ivar. She remained closed off. Ivar had looked at her several times trying to send her his thoughts, yet Esta's wall held. Guth asked only one question.

"What, if anything, can you tell me of the events that have led us here today?"

The old man tilted his head to the side as if he did not quite understand the question. "About the girl, sire? The one who came into the dungeons?"

Guth simply nodded, and the old man looked over at Esta. His head snapped back to the dais, wide eyed for only a moment before seeming to calm. Esta looked at Ivar who sat near the dais with an angelic look upon his face staring at the old man.

"Well?" Guth said, making a motion with his hand for the man to get on with it.

"The girl came into the dungeons. I think she must've heard the wailing." He gave his head a jerk toward the female prisoner behind him. She stood in filthy rags between two guard with her eyes cast down, shoulders hunched in fear.

"Wailing?" Guth fished for more, knowing full well that Ivar was coaching the man.

"The captain had been in the fishwife's cell, my lord. He enjoys making her scream."

At this, the captain was on his feet. He came forward several steps, seething with anger. "You filthy ole—"

"Enough!" Guth's shout brought him to a frozen silence. "You will have your say! Sit!" He pointed at the bench, and the captain quickly regained his seat next to the priest.

"Continue," Guth barked, "and stick to the facts."

"Sire"—the old man looked at the floor—"as I said, the wailing had been going on for a while, and then the girl was there, askin' why the other one was in so much pain." He paused as if expecting Guth to speak. For a moment the silence seemed to swell, and then he quickly rambled on. "Captain Eegon was angered. He tried to force the lady to leave. He became even more angered when she started to speak to us, all of us, askin' us questions about how we been treated. He forced her out." He paused. "That is all I know, sire. He followed her out, though. I did see that. He followed her out."

Esta was confused a bit. Again, she had the feeling that Ivar was coaching the man, trying to put the correct picture before the court. She found it both disturbing and enlightening that the captain's given name would mean "to inspire fright." She also found it interesting that the two royals seemed a bit amused. She thought for a moment to reach out and check in on their emotions but then thought better of it. She did not wish to open her mind to others. The old man stood, waiting for what came next. Guth, glancing quickly at Ivar, asked a new question. He asked as if he knew the man's answer would not be well received.

"Tell me why it is that you are serving time in my cells? What was your crime?"

The old man looked up at Guth, a brief flash of a smile crossed his face. "I am accused of not paying my taxes, sire." He put a little too much emphasis on the word *accused*.

Guth pounced on it. "Accused? How is this just an accusation? Either you pay the taxes owed, or you do not."

"I work at the docks mending nets and spears and creating anchors, oars, and whatever other items I can for those who lack the time, the skill, or the energy to do it themselves. My way is made by trade, sire. Food or needed materials in exchange for my services."

Guth shrugged his shoulders.

"I do not deal in a great deal of coin, sire, so I had none to give. Yet my small home requires a tax be paid. So, I spend my time in your dungeons from time to time to pay my debt."

Guth seemed to be in deep thought for a moment. He looked over at the members of his council, some of whom sat with wrinkled brows.

"This has little to do with the matter at hand, but I do not recall asking that my tax collectors place such a burden upon my people. I will be looking into this matter in depth, my good man, and can assure you that your time will be forgiven if this statement bares out. I release you to return to your home."

The old man nodded his head and gave a slight bow. "Thank you, sire." He turned to leave and then stopped. He looked longingly at the doors as he turned back to the dais, searching for the words he needed. "My lord, may I ... I feel I must speak but fear the words may cause yet more discomfort. I am torn between my desire to leave this hall as fast as my feet would carry me and my desire to speak and perhaps suffer the anger my words would bring."

Esta could take it no longer. There was a conversation happening here beyond her understanding. She opened her mind, questioning.

Guth stood. "Land's End is not without its faults. I will not allow corruption within these walls. It is a man's deeds that define him, not his words."

The old man nodded timidly and began, "Your bailiff—"

He had no chance to finish. The captain was on his feet, advancing quickly on the old man with his staff raised to strike. "You shut yer cake hole, you mangy, stinking ..."

He meant to strike. He intended to silence the old man permanently. Ivar, it seemed, had managed to discover just how cruel and corrupt the captain had been and had passed the information to Guth, who had merely poked the bear, waiting for the captain's true colors to shine through. Guth and Roan sprang forward. Guth pivoted, swinging his sword round his head and bringing it across in a wide arc before him. At the same time Roan grasped the captain's staff from behind Eegon's head and spun the bailiff away from the old man, who had thrown his arms up over his head and cowered at the advancing club. Several shrieks were heard from the women in the hall as Guth's sword cut the captain. He had come around 180 degrees with his swing just as Roan had turned the man toward him. The wide arc of his blade had come across in front of him, slicing at the captain's midsection like a hot knife through butter. The bailiff brought his empty hands down to his stomach, where blood instantly spilled from between his fingers. His eyes grew wide with fear as he stumbled back and then forward, watching the blood quickly spread upon the stone floor. He sunk to his knees for one brief moment and then fell at Guth's feet.

Esta's hands flew up to cover her mouth as she stifled a scream.

Roan stood stock-still, staff in hand, looking to Guth for some kind of guidance. Esta, having opened herself to the emotions in the room, was faced with an onslaught of them—everything from anger and concern to pity and indignation at the injustice to confusion. She glanced up at Geoffrey and Richard. They were both on their feet, although they remained behind the dais. Their emotions also ran the same gamut of anger and confusion.

Guth spun, He faced the people in the room with a confidence that seemed entirely out of place. "This man who lay before you deserved no mercy!" He held up his hand for silence. "I have learned from many that his crimes reach depths I could not have imagined. He has willingly harmed those in his care. He has taken that which did not belong to him, causing others to suffer. Know this! I will be looking into the inner workings of Land's End. Very carefully. If I find that any among you has harmed, has robbed, has injured the people of Land's End for your own gain, you will suffer the like!"

Guth turned his gaze toward Esta in anger. For one brief moment, she was frightened. Then she realized that he was looking past her into the crowd of onlookers, who had come to see if a witch was among them.

Her mind now open, Esta knew that Ingwolf was there. Ivar had discovered her presence in the hall and had pointed her out to his father. Hidden in the sea of cloaks and hoods, she waited for revenge. Information came at them so quickly they could scarcely keep up. Ivar's words were rushed and chopped.

She told him. She told him Esta was a witch. She helped Beor. She hoped Esta would burn. She is scared. Beor is dead, and she has nothing and nowhere to turn. She has been spreading the lies. It is her fault! She's going to run!

Guth allowed the flow of Ivar's words to fill his head. He then walked slowly toward the bench seat where Esta sat. Clare clutched Esta's arm, frightened of Guth's advance. Ingwolf began to make her way out. She had stepped back, acting as if the scene before her were just too much. She made her way toward the doors, ducking behind larger men and moving slowly.

"You!" Guth pointed through the crowd with his blade, the sword dripping blood upon the white stone at Esta's feet.

Every head turned to see whom Guth was pointing at. The onlookers seemed to peel back on either side of her, leaving her alone, frozen with terror. She had turned for the door but now stood exposed.

Guth said it again, this time more quietly yet sounding even more angry, if that were possible, than when he had shouted it. "You."

Ingwolf slowly turned, her breath rapid, her hands visibly trembling.

"You helped Beor try to remove my son from this house. You helped him hide my boy from me! You continually harmed my son. You aided in his capture, along with the capture of Lady Esta. If this were not enough, you returned to this place to do nothing but wag your tongue, spreading lies and deceit about Lady Esta to any and all who would listen to you."

Guth looked now at the priest who sat wide eyed, staring at the man on the floor. His eyes darted from Guth to Ingwolf and back again. He suddenly realized that he had an opportunity to save face, to save himself. The priest stood and turned to look at Ingwolf, who was shaking her head yet was unable to speak.

"This woman came forward with the captain as witness against the accused, my lord." He paused. "Do you deny it?" he barked at her.

Ingwolf shook her head. It was not an admission or a refusal. It looked as if she had loud voices coming at her from all sides. Her eyes were darting wildly about the room, looking for who was screaming accusations within her head.

Esta tuned in. Ivar was assaulting her verbally, silently torturing her from within. Her hands shot up to cover her ears.

She screamed, "He is unnatural! The devil is upon him! And that one there!" She pointed wildly at Esta.

Guth allowed the priest to confront her. "You planned this! You hoped you would cause an innocent person to lose their life? All this for your own amusement?"

Again, Ingwolf was shaking her head. She walked backward in a stuttered, searching gait, looking for an escape.

Guth threw his hand at her in a wave of dismissal. "Take her.

Remove this woman from my sight!" He turned his back on her and walked back to the dais. He tossed his sword upon the long table as her screams echoed. The guard dragged her out of the great hall.

Guth stood, his hand over his eyes, gripping the bridge of his nose as if he now had an enormous headache.

Esta looked around the room, but all she could feel was that everyone was confused by what they had seen. Even the royals were confused, yet they also seemed curious.

"I am ashamed, my lords." Guth spoke directly to them now. He bowed before them and stood shaking his head. "My people here are not usually so gullible. The past several months has brought much change. Beor's deceit cost the lives of several innocent people on Elvoy. Now the tree village that had long protected our back door is gone. Our villagers had not even known of its existence. I had seen to that," he lied. "There was no need for them to have this knowledge. Much of the forest lay in ashes now, and so might Land's End if it had not been for the warnings they gave us. My people mourn the loss of loved ones without an understanding of why. The king would see Land's End in a heap of ruble, and my people follow rumor, hate, and fear to the edge of the water to persecute what does not exist. A witch?" He said the last word as if it had a foul taste. "Call her a dragon, for it is just as believable."

He turned back to the room filled with the village council, and Esta could feel their shame. It had begun to build within them as he spoke.

"Return to your homes. Return to your shops. Return to your lives, and think about your freedoms here, how swiftly they could be taken from you." Guth turned to his personal guard. "Clear the hall."

For a moment the guards just looked at one another. Then one quickly moved forward and started to funnel people toward the double doors. The doors were held wide open as the crowd made their way out into the hallway. They whispered and huddled together in small groups, talking about how disappointed their lord was with his people, about what would happen to Ingwolf, and about how naive they had been to believe that Esta was a witch.

Ivar sat with a satisfied grin on his face. He had gotten some revenge upon the woman who had caused him such pain. He looked over at Esta, who had not moved. Roan helped Clare to her feet and motioned for Esta to stand. He would escort them from the hall. Esta, however, seemed rooted. She looked up into Roan's eyes, sadness, disbelief, and even fear upon her face. The bailiff's body still lay in the middle of the floor, his eyes wide open, his mouth agape. She had not asked that this man, this man she knew to be evil, be killed. She had not known that Ingwolf was in the hall. Once she had cut herself off from Ivar's words and the emotions of those in the hall, Esta had experienced the events of Captain Eegon's death just as everyone else had. The result was not what one would expect. She had been both shocked and horrified by Guth's execution of the man. There was no other way to put it. He had planned it from the moment he had brought the old man forward. She knew it.

Esta was so lost in her thoughts that she did not see Guth lean in to whisper in Roan's ear. She did not see the guard come forward and escort her mother from the hall. And she did not notice Ivar's approach, not until he placed his small hands upon her cheeks. Wherever she had been, lost in such shock, Ivar's touch brought her back. Her eyes began to fill with tears, this time of anger born of her grief.

"You murdered that man." Her words were clear and strong. They did not match the tears or the frightened look upon her face.

Guth looked confused. "I had no choice. He meant to kill the old man. What would you have me do?"

"I ... I do not know. I came here ready to be accepted or shunned for who I am, not to see more blood spilled in the name of my protection." Esta tried to keep her voice low.

Roan understood the action, even though it had caught him by surprise. "Esta, he needed to find a way to protect you."

Esta stood. "And who, may I ask, will protect them!" She pointed at the doors of the great hall, to those who were beyond them. "Who keeps them safe? Who decides their fate?"

Esta turned. Guth looked hurt, his gaze asking her to stop. Esta had shut them out. She needed strength.

Roan stepped to her. He reached out to her, shaking his head. "Esta."

"No, the man was vile, I know that." She shook her head. "I do not wish to be responsible for this! I do not ask that people be punished so that I may live. Why must people die?"

She looked into Roan's worried gaze. The royals had lingered near the dais, watching the exchange. Guth, seeing the look on Roan's face, turned. The princes were now descending the dais to the floor and were heading straight for them. Guth looked back at Esta, pleading with his eyes for her to leave it be.

Geoffrey looked down at them as he approached. "What happens here, Lord Guth? Who exactly is this woman?" He did not sound amused but rather annoyed. There was more to this story than a young girl being pulled from the lee.

Guth sighed. It sounded like the breath of defeat. "'Tis Esta of Elvoy, Your Grace. She saved the life of my son. I'm afraid the death of the bailiff has upset her. She is sensitive to the feelings of others."

Richard raised a brow. "Sensitive? Given that they had just tried to drown her, I cannot imagine why."

He came forward. Richard was a rather imposing man. Esta felt small and insignificant. Even Guth seemed a lesser man in Richard's shadow.

"Are you telling us, Lord Guth, that there is truth in the accusations against this girl?"

Ivar clamored to place himself between Richard and Esta. "Esta is good!" He looked fiercely up at the future king. Guth seemed to bristle a bit. "She is no danger, Your Grace."

This only caused Richard to look at Esta with intense interest. He seemed to be making up his mind about her, assessing her.

"Tell me, Esta of Elvoy, why are you angered by the events here today? Events that pulled you from the bay and placed you safely here in the protection of this hall?"

Esta had remained closed off. Now she questioned herself. Should she open up so that she could read this man's emotions, so that she could take her testimony in a direction that would please him and that he would believe. She looked at Roan, whose eyes showed fear, and,

Ivar who she knew was desperately trying to communicate with her. She pushed them all back. She would not use her gift ever again for the purpose of lies, deceit, or manipulation.

"I left my room early to take a walk," she began. "I hoped that Roan would return this day. I walked for a long while. I felt pain and suffering coming from a place I did not know."

Guth's head snapped up. He knew Esta meant to tell all. He wondered if she would expose Ivar.

"I found myself in the cells. There were people being ... mistreated. The bailiff, or captain, was dishonest and cruel. I left to find Lord Guth and speak with him about my findings. Men came to his lordship's solar and took me by force to the priest. The captain then convinced him that I was a witch." She paused. "They bound my hands and took me to the docks." Esta spread her hands as if to say, *And here I am*. "The rest, you have witnessed for yourself."

She turned and sat back down, continuing to keep herself free from the emotions in the room. Guth looked intently at the royals. He could have sworn that he saw a slight smile cross Richard's face. Geoffrey, however, raised his eyebrows and made a smirking facial expression. Guth could not tell if he was annoyed, bored, or completely disinterested. He hoped for the latter, since the war with his father was weighing heavy upon them all. Guth prayed that he could spin this all as a petty grievance upon his lands and nothing more. He was about to say as much when the wooden doors swung open again. Two guardsmen appeared in the hall, approached the bailiff's body with a plank, and placed it on the floor next to him. Gathering him up like a mule deer off the forest floor, they placed him across the board to remove him from the hall.

Esta could not take her eyes away. The enormous amount of blood that had spilled upon the floor around the body was now disturbed by footprints and smears. The bloody prints continued toward the massive double doors and then disappeared. The white stone was now as damaged as her gown. She wondered if there would be shadows of pink on the pristine whiteness of this hall. Would there always be a stain upon this place?

Richard spoke, and all eyes were drawn once again to her. "You said you felt pain and suffering. What did you mean by that?" Richard now looked as though he was concerned, a deep wrinkle upon his brow.

Ivar, Guth, Roan, all were begging her silently to just say she heard their cries, anything. Anything other than try to explain the unexplainable.

"I felt it," Esta said matter-of-factly. As if on cue, Guth and Roan both let out a breath and closed their eyes. Ivar looked hard at the would-be king as if daring him to condemn her.

"The fear and pain. The sadness and despair. The overpowering sorrow coming from those I could not see."

There was an audible sigh from Roan. Richard looked at Guth questioningly, and Geoffrey moved in closer. Roan felt that they did not understand and tried to explain.

"Esta is very in tune with the feelings of others. She carries a great deal of concern for those who are wronged. She is true and just, my lords."

Geoffrey tilted his head to one side as he repeated Roan's words. "In tune? And that means?"

Esta began to feel that same uneasy fear she had experienced when being questioned by the priest, as if she were unnatural, unwanted.

Guth moved forward. He held up his hand to Ivar as if asking him to stop. He shook his head, tossing out the barrage of words coming at him from his son. Esta could see that Ivar was frightened.

"Your Grace." Guth paused. He turned to Richard. "Your Grace," he said again, making sure he addressed both royal princes. "Esta has a gift. A gift that remained a hidden asset to the people of Elvoy until such time as my brother discovered it. Beor foolishly believed that Esta could read the minds of men. He believed that he could use Esta to regain a foothold here in Land's End. His greed, his true nature, came to bear upon many innocent people in Elvoy. Esta lost her father. The village lost its peace keeper and a cherished elder. Beor even managed to get word to the king, who threw a weak and unprepared attack at our door to capture Land's End, and by doing so, Esta. I assure you that Esta can no more read the minds of men than you or I can. Her understanding of what a person may be feeling comes from years of study at her mother's side, her mother being Elvoy's healer. Esta from a very young age has seen people at moments of pain and loss. It is no small wonder that she can now recognize those feelings without need of words."

Guth's speech was not urgent. It was not impassioned. It carried with it no plea. He simply spoke as if her gift were nothing unworldly or special. He spoke as if it just ... was. Esta was not sure what to think. Part of what Guth had said was true if understated, and yet other aspects were complete falsehoods, said for no other reason than to mislead.

Roan placed a protective hand in hers. He smiled at her, begging her to let it go. The royals were curious. Esta could now feel that. What she could not feel was fear or dislike. She was not sure why they seemed more open minded.

Richard spoke. "Do you remember our mother, Lord Guth?"

"I was young when my mother passed, yet I do remember that she spoke often of her cousin, who then was Queen of France." Guth was not sure where this was going.

"She is a woman often whispered about." Richard inclined his head in Esta's direction. "Intelligence in a female is rare. Our mother has a gift for language. She can speak in nearly every foreign tongue. Read it. Write it even. Weak minds think it impossible for her to carry such knowledge." Richard waved a hand in the air as he said this, indicating that he placed those in the village in the same category of ignorance. He waved a hand of indifference.

Esta could feel that these men were not so worried about the events that had happened here as she thought. They seemed more intrigued by her than anything else, amusedly wondering about how bright she may be.

The doors to the hall opened once again, and their heads turned to watch a royal guardsman approach. He came to the royals and dipped a knee toward both Geoffrey and Richard.

"Your Grace, I am sent to say that a messenger has arrived, sent by the queen. He waits just outside, Your Grace." The young man dipped the knee again and then held himself there, waiting for instruction.

Both Geoffrey and Richard stepped toward him in earnest.

"Send him in, immediately," Richard said. He waved the boy off in a hurry. The royals crossed the hall toward the great oak doors and met the messenger almost the very moment he stepped into the room. The man gave a quick bow and pulled a large scroll of parchment from under his bright-blue cloak. As the royals looked over the document, Guth nodded to Roan with a quick jerk of his head toward a side door of the hall. He looked down at Ivar and nodded again. Quietly and quickly, Roan took both Esta and Ivar from the hall. The door behind the dais led to a staging room for meals being served in the great hall. Now it stood empty, and Roan moved them through to the hallway and straight to Guth's family solar. Once inside, Roan turned to Esta and pulled her into his arms.

"Either you are the bravest woman I have ever met"—he smiled down at her—"or you have a wish for death that I cannot understand."

She allowed herself to feel his emotions of love and relief. Ivar smiled to see Esta open her mind but did not intrude. He walked to the hearth and warmed himself.

Lombard bustled into the room. "Beg pardon, sire." He nodded to the little round table, and the two servants who had entered the solar fast upon his heels set trays and pitchers of warm mead upon it. As the servants dashed out, Lombard gave Roan a quick nod and backed through the door. Ivar thrilled to see the treats and mead, chirped out in happy gratitude.

"Lombard, you are a marvel," Ivar said. He smiled wide at Esta. "I think he is even more gifted than you are, Esta. He can hear my stomach growl from the other side of the keep." He laughed.

Roan lead Esta by the hand to the fur-covered seat at the table. "Eat. I will return for you soon. I want to know what happens in the hall with the royals."

Esta looked up at him. "I will be waiting for you." She tried to smile, though it did not reach her eyes.

Ivar had. a large chunk of venison in one hand and a round of warm bread in the other, alternating now between hands for the eighth or ninth time: one bite of meat followed quickly by one bite of bread, then again to the meat, and then the bread.

Esta watched him and grinned. "You were hungry."

Ivar nodded. His mouth full, he communicated in his own way. *Yes, I was. I am.*

He paused, and Esta felt his enjoyment. The food was good. With the bread near his mouth, Ivar's eyes snapped up to hers. He froze and then slowly lowered both hands to deposit his rotating meal back upon the tray.

"You are leaving," Ivar said, looking into her eyes. He was sad to see her go.

Esta was sad to know she had caused his sorrow. "I cannot stay here, little one. I need to go home."

The word surprised him. Elvoy was home. It was time to return. In what way, Esta did not know. Would her mother wish to return? Would Roan? How could she ask Roan to return at all? He would be giving up so very much. There was Hadwig and Landen to consider as well. How would they feel about being torn away from such a beautiful place? Here, they had everything a child could want or need.

"Roan loves you, Esta." Ivar was trying to understand the complex emotions Esta was feeling.

She smiled again, that soft knowing smile. It was a smile that held heartbreak within it. "I know he does. And I love him as well. That is why I cannot tear his world apart. I cannot ask him to choose."

The tears wanted to come. Esta could feel the lump in her throat. She swallowed and closed her eyes. She was not going to cry. She would be strong.

Ivar shook his head. "There is no choice more important than the one that is taken away from us. You know that all too well."

Esta could not help but chuckle. "If I did not know better, I would swear you were an elder hiding in the body of a child."

"I do not think I like that image," Ivar said, wrinkling his nose a little. "Most elders I know are all old and wrinkly." He shuttered at the thought.

The evening wore on. Fires were kept burning, meals were served, and Ivar was taken to his bed chamber after he fell asleep by the hearth. Esta sat and stared at the flames, feeling she should return to her own chambers soon. She wondered why it was taking so long for either Guth or Roan to return.

SEVENTEEN

Home

The door opened slowly, and Guth poked his head in to scan the room. Esta, alone and awake, watched him enter and quietly close the door behind him. "You're awake. I was afraid I would find you sleeping."

Esta knew not what to say. Although she did not view Guth as evil, she did hold him responsible for much of what had happened. He was a ruler. Esta had discovered that the rule of one person alone was not the way to find peace and justice, because only that person's ideas of right or wrong and opinions about how, where, or why something should be done ruled. A place ruled according to one person's perspective, one person's lust, greed, or need for power or revenge? This was not a place she wished to be. She felt that the elders on Elvoy knew this, that the wisdom of many could find answers that did not make those involved feel belittled, persecuted. Although Esta had been angered by the elders actions on Elvoy, she understood now why they had made the choices they had made. They had the weight of so many lives upon their shoulders.

Guth, waiting for some kind of response, was not sure what to do.

Esta waited a moment, thinking Roan would appear behind him. When he did not, she asked. "Where is Roan?"

Guth moved toward the hearth. He knew Esta would be upset that Roan once again had been sent away.

"He is with Richard. The royals are being hunted down by King

Henry. Queen Eleanor sent word to them to return to her as soon as was possible. It was decided that they should take two ships, well-armed with men in case they were discovered. The two ships would carry the royals separately, each taking a slightly different route. They hope the ships will arrive at their destination at nearly the same time. The queen is surrounded by her own supporters, well away and safely out of the king's reach."

So, Roan was on his way to France. Without so much as a farewell. Guth could read the hurt upon her face.

"He could not have known he would be leaving the moment he returned to the hall, Esta. Decisions were made quickly, and one does not delay or question the future king."

The decision to send Roan on the journey had come in a moment of haste. Richard had asked that Guth accompany him but then quickly made a statement about the need for him to remain and put his own house in order. It was at that moment that Geoffrey had inclined his head toward Roan and suggested that he represent the men from Land's End upon Richard's ship while one of Guth's other trusted guards did the same upon his. Guth had had little time to select the soldiers that would travel. He'd kept his small ships and their fighting crews here to protect the village from the sea. When he'd nodded his agreement and turned to face Roan, he'd been able to see the look of shock in his eyes. Now he could see it in Esta's. He had once again taken someone from her without thought, and he was ashamed.

Esta nodded. "Of course." She headed for the door, but as she placed her hand upon the carved wooden handle, she paused. Her mind raced to find the right words to convey her wishes in a way that Guth could not or would not refuse.

Guth knew that things would never be the same. Ivar had tried to reach Esta in his attempt to control the events unfolding in the hall. Time after time, Ivar had conveyed that Esta was blocking him out, shutting her mind off to him. Guth watched her now slowly turn to face him.

"I wish to return to Elvoy. I know not if my mother wishes this as well, but I do. I am asking that a boat return me to Elvoy as soon as is possible."

Guth had not expected this. He wished Ivar were there to help him understand. "Should you not wait for Roan's return?"

Esta was not willing to hear anything except an acceptance of her request. "No, I am asking that the one responsible for removing me from the island return me to my home. If you cannot see your way to do this, I will simply leave this place and try to find my own way back."

She was making a demand of him. Guth was not sure he liked it. Or perhaps what angered him was the fact that she was speaking the truth and that he knew she had every right to say it. His forced removal of Esta from Elvoy had initiated a series of events that seemed to have no end. He could not place blame on others. Even if Beor's actions were to blame for much, he was lord here. He'd placed Beor on Elvoy.

"Esta …"

She did not let him finish. "Am I prisoner here?"

Guth's head snapped up. "You know you are not."

"Then return me home." She looked him in the eye, almost daring him to deny her.

Guth had no choice. He sighed. "I will have a boat made ready for you. You may say your goodbyes and plan to depart at the next tide, if you wish." He turned back to the hearth.

Esta could feel his hurt and anger. He really did not want to lose her, but he had Ivar. The knowledge that Guth took solace in the fact that his son was even more gifted than she was enraged her. She left the door as it was and quickly made her way down the dimly lit hallway. The candles fluttered as she passed.

Back in her chambers Esta shared with her mother the events of the evening after she had been removed from the hall. Esta was hurt by the fact that Roan had allowed himself to be taken away, that he had not insisted upon seeing her before he left. She broke down, shoving the chair that she sat in back suddenly and tipping it over to clatter upon the floor. She grasped then threw a candle holder at the wall while a harsh scream escaped her. She stood at the small wooden table, breathing hard as if she had just run through the woods. Two sharp screeches brought her eyes to the windowsill. Mane sat, fluttering her wings, chirping, and snapping her beak in worry for her keeper. Esta knew that the bird had come to her, waiting for the nightly trip to the gardens. She knew the bird was concerned. She closed her eyes and tried to slow her breathing, calm her thoughts. She opened her eyes and walked toward Mane. The bird ruffled her feathers, puffing up like a soft collection of clouds, white, golden brown, and grey.

"I'm sorry Mane. 'Tis not your fault, is it? I'm sure you would like to go home, wouldn't you?" She brushed the feathers beneath Mane's chin and between her ear tuffs with her fingers.

Clare sat silently at the table, allowing her daughter to process her feelings of loss. She nodded at Esta as she left the room, knowing that it would be useless to try to stop her. Esta needed air and solitude, and Clare allowed her that space.

Mane's calm happiness helped to relax Esta. She roamed the garden path in circles, unwilling to return to her room until she could do so without displaying the hurt she felt to her mother. She would not put her mother in an uncomfortable situation after the loss she herself had suffered. She would wait for morning to speak again with her, letting her know of her plans when they would not seem born of emotion. Then she would find Landen and bid him farewell. She would miss him and his young determination to be a good man. She had no doubt that he would become a valued member of Guth's guard, perhaps a knight in his own right.

Ivar and Hadwig would be easy to find. They spent a bit of time each day in the courtyard gardens. Esta knew that they would be saddened by her leaving. She also knew that they were young and would heal rather quickly with the company of each other.

After Esta had spent much time grooming and petting Mane, the bird flew off to hunt. Esta waited for a moment on the bench beside the door, willing herself to find some peace and be able to sleep when she found her bed. The door opened, and for one brief moment she thought that Guth had come to find her. It was Lombard. He held a steaming cup of mead in his hands and proffered it to her with a slight smile of encouragement. She took it with a nod of gratitude. Lombard would normally disappear after that service. This time, he did not. He looked at her as if to speak yet afraid to intrude upon her quiet.

"May I tell you a story, Miss?" Lombard softly closed the door behind him. He looked at the bench seat beside her as if seeking permission to sit.

"You have been very good to me, Lombard. I would hear your tale." Esta patted the seat, and Lombard lowered his immaculately clean, shoeless frame upon it.

"I was once a slave in the fields near Genua. I was much younger then, my body used to the hard work in the sun near the sea. I was on a roadside, bringing in wheat for my master, when I first met Lord Guth. I will not trouble you with the events that led up to our first conversation other than to say that at the moment of our first meeting, I was tied to a tree and being whipped like an animal. He stilled the hand of my tormentor. I had been accused of a crime I had not committed. That was not the reason he stopped the beating, of course. He stopped it because he is a good man. I know this is hard for you to accept, even more so after seeing the events in the great hall this day. I only ask that you try to look at this world from his viewpoint, knowing that the protection of his son is placed above all else, as it should be."

Lombard patted her thigh as if she were a child and stood. He took the half-empty mug from her hands and gave her a slight nod. Then he simply left her there to ponder his strange tale.

Esta returned to her room only to find it empty. Her mother had found an empty apartment to spend the night in in order to give Esta peace. Esta prepared herself a glass of warm mead and tried, at last, to get a few hours of sleep before the sun came up.

Although tired, Esta could not seem to calm her mind. The image of the bailiff and the words that had been spoken haunted her. From the moment Lord Guth had stepped foot on Elvoy to this very moment in time, Esta had known that what was believed about her was the cause of every evil that had been committed. Beor had spread rumors. She asked herself why he'd believed that Esta had powers beyond what she actually did in the first place. What she found was the knowledge that she had been taught from a young age to hide her gift and that because of this, those who had known there was something unusual or different about her had only been able to guess at what it was. There was fear attached to it. Her nature and her love of her parents encouraged the rumors, for she'd told them things that had made everyone around them aware that her parents had access to feelings or thoughts that were private, hidden, or at the very least only known to the person who was having them. Elvoy had, for the most part, accepted her. That, she knew, was due to her mother's skills as the village healer and midwife. It was also due to the elders. Esta had come to know them all well. Each one had at some point taken a special interest in getting to know her, teaching her. Esta had been one of very few children who were taught by the elders. She'd learned to read and write. She'd learned her figures and sums. She'd been able to tell the difference between plants and animal families and understood how the human body was put together and how it worked. Looking back, Esta realized that she had been groomed from a young age to be an asset to the village. She was to have become a healer and she would have married Erik, who was to have become the village protector. Her insight would have helped him perform his job very well. She knew that her insights had helped her mother in the role of healer many times over. Esta now wondered if she had ever been in charge of her own fate, ever made a decision that had not already been planned out for her.

Esta rose early. She gathered up what little she had left to her and packed her belongings into the same satchel she had arrived with. She had been given much since her arrival at Land's End, but she had lost much as well. Leaving behind the fine dresses that were far above her station, Esta packed most of the clothing and leather gear she had received from the tree dwellers. She needed and was given an extra satchel for them. She packed the green cloak, tanned quiver, and hooded vest, thankful that she had been wearing them when the village had been taken. They would remind her of a world that was now lost to her.

Clare was torn, wanting to remain with her daughter but not wanting to return to Elvoy. She had also formed an attachment with the tree dwellers' healer. She did not want to leave him. Esta could feel her conflict. She understood that returning to Elvoy would be difficult. Their home would by now belong to another. The crops grown there were too valuable for the land to be neglected. The elders would grant the farm to a worthy farmer, most likely one who had an older son ready to take on a farm of his own. The father would move on to a larger, more important piece of land, and the son would remain, taking over the father's plot. Esta wondered who she would find in her childhood home. She had not given a moment's thought to where she would live when she returned. Now thinking about it, she knew where she would go; the little hut where she, Erik, and Roan had hidden out would be the perfect place to start. Mane would be right at home there. Esta could perhaps slowly add to the hut. Regardless, she would be dry and warm.

Clare stood in the alcove overlooking the small ships anchored in the lee. Her heart was aching, and Esta knew she needed to comfort her.

"I will miss you, but I am sure Lord Guth will help you visit if you ever wish to," Clare said, turning to Esta with tears in her eyes.

Esta smiled. "You are not remaining in Land's End, are you?" She went to her mother with open arms.

Clare cried as they embraced. "The tree dwellers are rebuilding. It will take time, but a good area for new homes has been found. I will join them there."

Esta pulled back and smiled again. She took her mother's hands in her own and looked into her teary gaze. "I am happy for you. Truly I am."

Clare hugged her again. "Where will you go?"

Esta turned away and busied herself with the packing. "I will stay in the mentor's hut. I will ask the elders for the small dwelling. It is not needed by anyone else, and it will be all I need for now. The worst of winter is over. There will soon be good weather and a lot of time to make improvements."

Guth had contemplated not allowing Esta to leave. He feared Roan would blame him for her absence when he returned, although that would be nothing in comparison to his anger should he treat her as a captive. And he had no doubt that Esta would use every tactic available to her to leave Land's End. He might as well see her safely returned to Elvoy. It was an island. Roan could find her at will.

Ivar eased his father's pain. Allowing Esta to return to Elvoy was the right thing to do. He begged his father not only to make her return agreeable but also to help her should she need it once she was there, much like he had at the village in the canopy. Ivar did intend to visit her, and he knew that he would want to see her well suited and happy. He also knew that he could convince his father to do as he wished.

Esta made her departure in the early morning hours, going out with the tide. The boat was laden with gifts from Ivar, though Esta would not become aware of that fact until they arrived on Elvoy. She stood near the rear of the boat as the men began to row and waved at those who had come to the bay to wave their farewell. Ivar, Landen, and Hadwig all ran along the wooden dock, waving their arms and calling out to her. Guth stood near the end of the docks, one hand in the air, feeling both saddened and worried for her, although he had made sure that Esta would receive anything and everything she needed over the next few days. He would not allow her to find herself wanting when she reached home. He also wanted to make sure that she was well received and respected.

Esta had to admit to herself that she had been rather hard on Guth the last few days. She also knew that the feeling would pass quickly, for she would always hold resentment about the way she had been thrust into a world of war and hate.

The journey across the vast open waters to Elvoy was relatively calm. There were moments when Esta thought she may retch from the motion of the boat up and down and side to side as it drifted over the swells. She could not help but wonder why she had not been so ill when they left Elvoy. The answer came to her quickly: fear. She had been gripped by it. Fear and loss. The events that had placed her upon the sea had been so very different than what they were at this moment.

The elders welcomed Esta home with open arms, even offering her a small home in the heart of the village. She refused it. Her only wish was to take over the small stone hut in the near woods. But that, it seemed, was also not to be, for Esta learned that several tree dwellers who had lost everything had now made their homes on Elvoy. They had been given money and goods from Land's End to make a new start. They had built their homes in the trees of the near woods. Esta was beside herself with excitement. She would join them and live in a small home in the trees, where Mane could come and go at will, where peace and quiet comfort would guide her back to some kind of a life. Although the elders did not like it, they knew that Esta was no longer a compliant child. If they wanted both her skills with healing others and her skill of understanding others, they would need to be supportive. So, they did the only thing they could; they sent several people to help make sure Esta had a dry, well-equipped dwelling very quickly.

The pulley systems that carried the tree dwellers up to the platforms took some time to forge. They were smaller than those of the old treetop village and made for each individual dwelling, a big difference between this new home and the one she'd had in the woods near Land's End. Each home was separate. Hers stood a little lower in the trees and had its own platform. There were not bridges between the dwellings, nor did there seem to be a plan to make them. This meant that Esta had to learn how to hoist herself to the front platform of her home. Empty hands were a necessity, so Esta found herself making a basket that she could fasten to her back and waist with leather strapping. A few of the villagers were so impressed with the function and quality of the basket that they requested baskets for themselves. Esta was able to trade for the first time on her own. As soon as the dwelling was finished, she received several gifts.

Two days after the dwelling was finished, Esta stepped through the door and marveled at what she saw. The walls still smelled of fresh-hewn wood, and the floor was smooth, even to her bare feet. The windows were open, allowing a spring breeze to cross the room. There was a small, round table with two bench seats, and a lovely low wooden chair with an overstuffed cushion sat near the hearth. In a separate room, a bed sat under a high window that looked up through the branches to the night sky. This opening could be shuttered during bad weather, keeping the room warm and dry. Esta was happy save for one thing: she missed Roan. Word was that many of those whom Lord Guth had sent to accompany

Geoffrey and Richard to the queen were still fighting somewhere, as the sons of Eleanor of Aquitaine continued to try to remove her husband, the mad king, from power. Roan had not returned to Land's End; he would not know that Esta had returned to Elvoy.

Weeks passed, and then months. Esta was living comfortably in her little treetop cottage. Mane had a few large branches that cut across the corner of the home. She could perch on her own limbs and then fly out of the adjacent window when she needed or wanted to. Esta kept the window closed when the night air chilled. Mane was happy with her interior branches but also loved the outdoor box that had been built just outside the window—a large box, watertight and facing away from the prevailing winds. The small opening for entering the box kept the inside dry and free of draft.

The trees on the island had stood long against the wind and rain. The few pockets of forest that were left held trees of immense size and strength. The small houses among the branches had been built to cause as little impact as was possible, yet the inside of Esta's home was amazing. Not enough of the tree dwellers had come to Elvoy to warrant a large meeting hall or cookhouse, so each small dwelling was equipped with its own stone fire place. These were very carefully constructed so that the heat from the flames would warm the inner stones and the dwelling but not harm the tree. The dwellings were amazingly beautiful, inside and out.

As the weeks passed, Esta put her healing skills to work. She helped an elder in need of stitches, a young man who had fallen from his running cob and broken his arm. With these, along with the occasional person who found themselves sick and the few women in the village who were with child, Esta could fill her days. She also started tending to some of the village livestock. This was a delight to her, for she truly loved animals. The humans who owned them often felt that Esta's connection with their animals was a bit odd, for she no longer hid this connection. She would speak with the animals as if they could speak back, often calming an injured cob, birthing cattle, or healing a sick goat. The animals would give Esta their undivided attention and nuzzle her as if they had great affection for her. Many birds would sit in her tree, often putting Mane in a mood, for her sleeping during the daylight hours would be interrupted by their chatter. A tree squirrel made its home under the fireplace in the trunk of the tree. It found warmth and a friendly protector in Esta. When Mane would leave the cottage to hunt or sit within her box, the little creature would often appear on the windowsill, waiting for Esta to open it and invite her in. Esta would giggle at the squirrel darting and dashing about. She named her Whiskers and allowed her to nuzzle and chitter in her ear.

Word had reached Elvoy of the wars between those who would rule. Guth had been called away many times to give aid. Each month that passed gave Esta the feeling that Roan had made his choice. He remained far from the island, far from her, yet he was always on her mind, in her heart. Ivar had visited a few times, coming with the trading boats that traveled back and forth from Land's End. He assured her that Roan was still alive and that his father had seen him a time or two when he had been called to help. Ivar also mentioned that Guth had not told Roan that she was back at Elvoy. It would do no good to do so, he had said, as it would only upset Roan, and he needed to believe that everything was well, not be distracted by the news. Esta, though, did not consider her moving back to Elvoy to be bad news. She was at home now, and as much as she missed Roan, she knew she would not return to Land's End. Her last visit with Ivar had been a happy one. He loved the new home in the near woods and had fallen in love with Whiskers, who in turn had found a willing hand full of treats whenever she'd appeared. He'd stayed only a day, returning with the boats to Land's End with a promise to return soon. After waving at him when he departed, Esta could feel the need for companionship and made her way to visit a few new friends she had made upon her return to the island. Her days, filled with routine, slipped by—summer became fall, fall became winter, and now winter became spring.

Esta had wintered well upon the island. There had been a lot of favorable trades made. Esta had offered her healing touch in exchange for fur boots, warm cloaks, and plenty of fresh meat and vegetables. The spring was bringing many changes, including the appearance. of a large male owl that refused to enter her dwelling, leaving Mane to tend five eggs and pop in and out to accept the small rodents, fish, and rabbits he brought to her. Esta realized that Mane had made the choice to lay her eggs on the small corner ledge near her perches instead of in the box outside in order to keep her young safe. Each day, the promise of summer grew. Esta kept track of the passing days since Mane had laid the first egg. Another egg came two days later, another a day after that, and so on until there were five eggs resting on the flat bottom of Mane's perching ledge. Soon, the eggs would begin to hatch in the order that they had been laid and the owlets would arrive. All the animals around Elvoy were giving birth, including Whiskers, whom Esta had not seen in a while.

The crops were breaking through the topsoil. This was the rainy season, not that it did not rain often on Elvoy. This time of year brought the warmer days and the breaks of sunshine that pulled the crops forward. As the days grew longer, Esta found herself walking the near woods often. As each warm day's sun was setting, a cool breeze would find its way through the trees, and she could often smell the new growth and sense the contentment of the animals. She found that she was also content, though at times she did feel lonely, especially now that Mane rarely joined her, preferring to stay put upon the eggs. Esta had named Mane's mate Viss, which meant "wise." She gave him this name because the wild owl was smart enough to choose such a wonderful partner and wise enough to know that Mane had a desirable connection with the humans, that their children would be looked after, well fed and strong. His line would grow. Viss did not care to let Esta touch him at first, but on the occasions when he sat upon the eggs to give Mane a chance to spread her wings, he did not nip or screech at her when she gave the feathers under his chin a tickle. The bird's nesting was always very short and sweet. He preferred to sit upon a nearby branch just outside the window rather than come inside.

A beautiful warm day was passing. It had rained late in the afternoon, a quick burst of showers that had soaked the ground and puddled up, the earth not able to absorb the rain quickly enough. As the low clouds were blown away, the sun returned. Steam rose from the ferns and moss, as the temperature change was quick and extreme. Esta could hear the birds chirping and dancing about the puddles on the two-track road to the village. Walking the dirt road would be a muddy excursion if she made the trek to the green today.

Esta sat in her fur-lined chair, snuggling down into the warm, soft sheep's wool that covered it. An egg had begun to crack; the first of Manes owlets would arrive today, thirty-two days after it had been laid. A cup of hot tea in her hands, Esta looked out of her window at the lush, green lands of Elvoy. Somewhere out there, somewhere far away, men fought for power. Roan was among them. No one had told her that Roan had died, but no one had told her that he still lived either. Esta knew he was alive. She could not feel his emotions, but she knew he lived. As her thoughts turned to Roan she sighed. It had been more than a turn of the seasons since she had seen his face. She had not seen Ava, Guth, or Ivar in half as long. She wondered if maybe she could go to Land's End to visit during these months of warmer weather and calmer seas. Yet there was still much unrest and war in Britannia. Guth may not even be at Land's End at this moment. Ivar would be with Ava wherever they would be safe. Since the attack on the tree dwellers and then Land's End, there had not been anymore attempts at sacking the city. The battles between the mad king and his many sons had remained closer to the large cities of Britannia.

Esta's tea steamed between her hands as she sipped at it, content and waiting for the first little owlet. She had been thinking of Roan so dreamily that it took several moments before she realized that his emotions were actually there with her. She sat up abruptly, spilling some of the hot tea over her fingers. Setting the mug down quickly and wiping her hand upon her overdress, Esta closed her eyes and opened her mind. Tears welled up in her eyes, and Esta could feel her heart pounding, surging blood through her veins. Roan was there! He was close. He was racked with guilt for having been gone so long. He was also afraid. More afraid than he had been in any battle. He was in awe and proud. Why? Why did he feel pride in Esta? Because he was looking upon the tree house with joy and admiration. He was looking upon the tree house. He was looking upon the tree house!

Esta flew to the window, leaning so far out that her feet left the floor and dangled below the sill. There he was. Roan stopped dead in his tracks. He was weighed down by a large broadsword, a leather satchel, and a large woven bag that held everything he owned. He dropped the bag and satchel and then pulled the strap of his sheath up and over his head. He lay the broadsword upon the woven bag and stood.

Esta made her way to her platform and lowered herself so quickly that the rope burned one of her hands. She did not feel it. She stood now just breathing, trying to slow her heart, trying to believe her own eyes.

Roan took the first tentative steps toward her. She could see the look of hope upon his face, feel the fear that she may no longer desire him. But Esta could think of nothing else except to wrap him in her arms. She burst forward, covering the ground between them in a heartbeat. She leapt at him, wrapping her arms around his neck and her legs around his waist, and Roan let loose a bark of joy. He threw his arms around her and spun around as he pulled her closer and closer. She leaned back to gaze into his eyes, and Roan gently placed her back upon her feet. He cupped her face in his hands.

"I have missed this face more than you can know," he said with a smile.

Esta could still feel small amounts of fear coming from him. He was nervous. She reached out and took his hand. Roan allowed her to lead him to the base of the tree. The area had been cleared for the staging of things to be lifted to the platform. There were six other tree houses, all circled around a small, round stone hut. It had been improved upon and was no longer hidden just off the wooded path. Roan could tell that the little hut was used often. It was now a smokehouse. Just outside of the hut, there was a young man securing fish to racks, ready to place them inside. He stared wide eyed at the reunion, smiling at the joy in Esta's embrace. Roan turned in a circle, admiring the landscape. It was a miniature village much like the one he had once admired and loved on Land's End. Yet this one was different. There were clearly some new, amazing improvements, as Roan could see the smoke coming from the chimneys of each tree cottage. They were beautiful.

Once in the tree, Roan turned in a circle in compete awe. Esta had made a home here, and it was hers. Everywhere he looked, he could see her. Fully formed nests, beautifully dried flowers, shells, and unique rocks lined a few shelves. Charcoal drawings of Mane, the treehouse, and other forest animals hung upon the walls. It was amazing. There was a working cookstove—in a tree! It had windows that could be swung open or shuttered closed. Roan could see that Guth had been generous as well. The furniture was well carved and sturdy. Beautifully tanned hides and soft rugs lay upon the floor. Esta's chair near the hearth was lined with sheep's wool. Roan walked from one marvel to another, touching things, picking them up, and turning to her with a wide-eyed smile.

Esta laughed, seeing Roan gape at the dwelling. He shook his head and walked to her.

"You are amazing, you know that?"

Esta smiled, "It was not only me. I did very little, actually, between the innovations of the tree dwellers, the workers the elders sent, and Guth's builders who arrived out of the blue. It is a wonder, is it not?"

There was a long moment of silence as they looked at each other. Esta was trying to decide if she should give Roan the privacy of his own thoughts or not. But the time for waiting was over. They had spent more than a year apart, and it had not diminished the love they had for one another. Esta reached out for his hands, pulling him around to face her. She looked into his watery eyes, and he looked into hers.

"Welcome home."

She kissed him, and she knew. She kissed him, and he knew. Their life together was just beginning. In the warmth of the tree, as life began again, an owlet screeched for the first time. Esta was reminded of that day in the glen when an owl had placed its child in her hands, believing she would cherish it, believing she would protect it. Now Roan stood before her, his heart in her hands and her heart in his, a wall of love around them. She would protect it. She would cherish it. Always.

THE END

Printed in the United States
by Baker & Taylor Publisher Services